bait

INTERNATIONAL BESTSELLING AUTHOR

JADE WEST

Cover design by Letitia Hasser of RBA Designs | www.designs.romanticbookaffairs.com
Book design by Inkstain Design Studio | www.inkstaindesignstudio.com
Cover image by Wander Aguiar | www.wanderbookclub.com
Edited by John Hudspith | www.johnhudspith.co.uk
Cover model – Jonny James
All enquiries to jadewestauthor@gmail.com

First published 2017

To Scandinavian pine kitchens, 42-inch plasma screen TVs, grey Ford Fusions, and the idiot who placed them above the life growing inside me.

This one's for you, asshole.

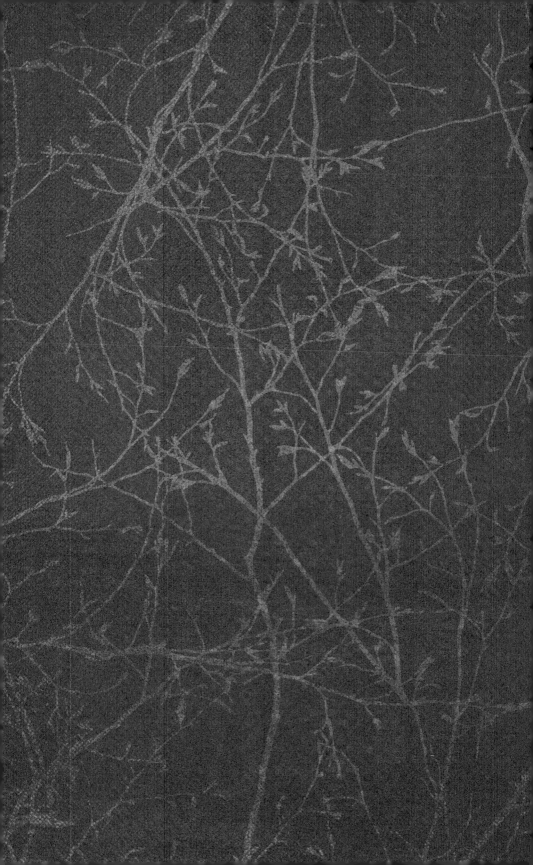

bait

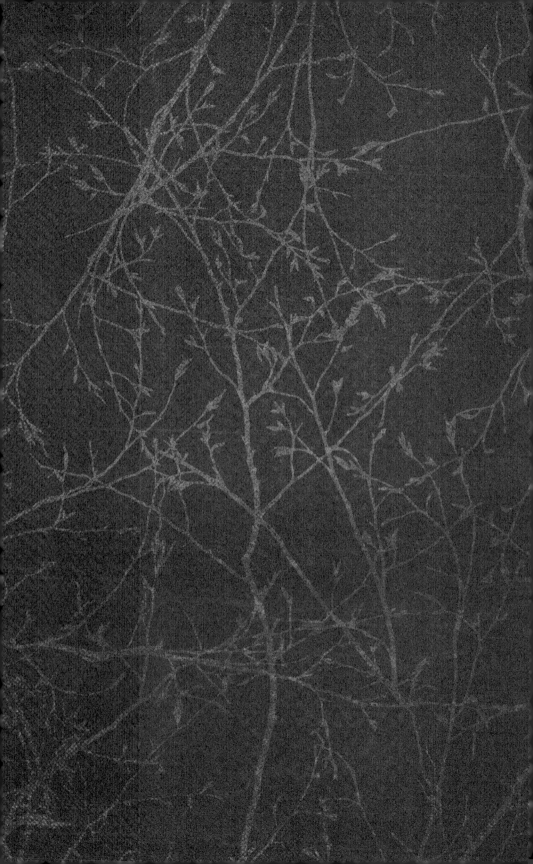

one

*I want to keep my dreams, even the bad ones,
because without them, I might have nothing all night long.*

—JOSEPH HELLER

abigail

I can't tell you the exact moment the night terrors started. There was no traumatic childhood experience that set them off. No defining moment that marked the beginning of the screams at night. No significant event that led a happy five-year-old girl to wake up sweating and wailing in the darkness.

My parents put it down to TV I shouldn't have been watching. Scary stories from older kids in the playground. An overactive imagination.

It doesn't matter where they came from. Not really.

They arrived without invitation and took up residence. Permanently. *That's* what really matters.

Every night without fail the monster would chase me through the undergrowth. Every night I'd feel his hot breath on my neck as I ran for my life.

Every night the beast got a little bit closer. A little bit bigger. A little bit more terrifying.

1

bait

I may not be able to tell you when and why the monster started hunting me in the first place, but I can tell you when I stopped screaming.

I can tell you when the nightmares stopped being terrors and the monster became a man.

I can even tell you when I started wanting them. Wanting the chase. Wanting *him*.

And I can tell you when, finally, one day the nightmares came to life.

My name is Abigail Rachel Summers, and tonight I am bait.

two weeks earlier

Jack Dobson is a guy you could call conventionally attractive. He has a symmetrical face, high cheekbones, and just the right amount of gel in his salon-messy hair.

He's a member of the pink shirt brigade at the office, and he's wearing one now, looking thoroughly out of place in the spit and sawdust joint I picked out for dinner this evening.

Jack's a guy my parents would approve of. The kind they could make small talk with over a Sunday roast. Maybe even engage in a friendly debate on the current political landscape.

I have no interest whatsoever in this going further. I don't want to see what he's packing under his pink shirt, and I have no inclination to let him see what's under mine, either.

By all rights that means I shouldn't be here, but the steak is good and I was coerced by the admin girls at the copy machine this morning.

I didn't have the heart to tell them that Jack Dobson is a nice guy. Too nice for me.

He laughs as he recounts another story about a colleague I haven't met. I smile politely as I finish up my mushrooms.

"You haven't met the Worcester guys yet, right?" he asks, again. I nod, again. "Don't worry," he says. "Once you hit the six-month mark you'll be like part of the furniture. Summer barbeque coming up. After that you'll know *everyone*."

I don't want to hit the six-month mark and I don't want to know everyone. I don't care about my job at Office Express, and I don't care that maybe someone like Jack could be good for someone like me.

Maybe in another place and time, but not here and definitely not now.

I'm rootless here. Three months into a life I never wanted to be living. Three months into the paper-thin existence I figured was my best chance at a fresh start.

I'm here with Jack because I'm death-gripping the hope that one day I'll wake up without the soul-destroying pang of loss in my gut. That I won't be clutching my belly and crying into my pillow as I realise all over again that this is my world now.

I'm a pragmatist. Or I am these days.

If I'm ever going to wake up and realise this new life isn't all that bad, it needs to actually be a semblance of one.

So, I force another smile. Fake another laugh. Order another drink. I try to be interested in Jack and his kind eyes and his pink shirt. I try to pretend I'm a normal girl living a normal life without a shit ton of baggage trailing from the noose around my neck.

I think he believes me. After three glasses of white I'm even beginning to believe myself.

Until I see *him*. The guy at the bar.

He's wearing too much denim. Dirty denim tucked into big muddy boots. He has a moustache and greasy hair to his shoulders, and eyes that aren't kind at all, not even close.

And he's looking at me.

I suddenly know for certain that I'll never find out what's under Jack's pink shirt. My breath hitches and my nerves coil in my belly, my heart already thumping at the thought that this may really be it.

Maybe denim guy will be the one to chase me.

Maybe he'll be my monster.

"Earth to Abigail." Jack's laugh is so blissfully unaware. I smile as I jolt back to him.

"Sorry," I say. "I must be tired. Long day."

"Thursdays will do that to you. Delivery day, right?"

I nod. "Still learning the ropes. Product codes coming out of my ears."

"You'll get there," he says kindly. "It's a lot to take in."

It's not, but I smile anyway.

I haven't even registered I've put my cutlery across my plate until he suggests we get the bill. The panic is instant and intense, my heart in my throat as I grab the dessert menu from the stand between us.

"Maybe some chocolate will wake me up," I suggest, and he rests a hand on his stomach.

"Not for me. I couldn't eat another thing." He pauses. "You have one, though. Maybe it'll pep you up enough to hit a club. It's disco night down at Divas. Thursday night special, some of the sales guys are already out."

I watch denim guy down a whisky at the bar then order another. He smooths his moustache with his mouth wide open, staring right at me as Jack calls the waitress to take my order.

Denim guy wants me. I can see it in his eyes.

The sly smile on his lips tells me he knows I want him too.

My dirty soul must be a beacon to other dirty souls out for a good time. It's always like this.

They must smell it on me. Taste it on the air. Hone into the fucked-up frequencies of freaks like me.

Luckily regular people, like sweet Jack here, have it roll over their heads without a clue.

I don't want to feel the tingle between my legs as I think of denim guy's dirty hands on me. I don't want to clench my thighs under the table as I think about his filthy cock inside me.

I don't want to want him, but I do.

This place is on the outskirts of the city centre. I already know that the river path runs along the back of the car park.

I know it'll be dark and quiet on a Thursday evening with barely a soul around.

I'm trying not to look at him when my gateaux arrives. I ask Jack questions about his ten-year history at the office, shamelessly deflecting him from asking any questions about me.

Denim guy's had two more shots by the time my plate is clear. He licks his lips and smirks as he flashes me the shocker. My pussy throbs at the sight of his extended fingers.

Two in the pink, one in the stink.

He really is disgusting.

I really don't want to want this.

I feel as disgusting as he is as I meet his eyes and give him the gentlest nod. Jack doesn't even notice, he's too busy raising his hand for the bill.

Denim guy finishes up his drink and heads for the rear entrance. He brushes close enough on his way past that I smell the diesel on him. I wonder if his cock smells like that too.

Jack pays the bill before I can protest, all smiles as he grabs his suit jacket and shrugs it on.

"Let's go hit the dance floor," he says, and I feel like a bitch when he registers my copout expression.

"I'm still really tired," I lie. "I should get back home, long day tomorrow."

He nods. Shrugs. And then he shows he really is a decent guy, unlike the piece of shit waiting for me outside. "Sure, of course. Some other time. I'll walk you home."

"No need," I say. "I'll call a cab." I hold up my phone.

"Then I'll wait for it to arrive," he offers, but I shake my head.

"Seriously, there's no need. Head on down to Divas with the guys. You'll get a decent dance in if you're quick."

He looks uncertain until I gather my things. I don't look at him, pretending I'm keying in the cab number as he dawdles awkwardly. I press the fake call to my ear and tell him I'll see him in the morning.

I'm still holding the handset when he says his goodbyes and heads reluctantly for the front exit.

I wait twenty seconds before I head for the back.

It's dark out here, just like I knew it would be. The spotlights cast the kind of ominous orange glow that gives me shivers. The car park is empty enough that it's easy to see denim guy propped up against a battered old truck. He's smoking as he waits, barely straightening up as my heels clack across the tarmac in his direction.

I hold up a hand when he tries to speak, flattening my body to his as I land my lips straight onto his filthy mouth. He tastes of smoke and whisky. His moustache tickles my top lip and it makes me shudder.

He flicks his cigarette away and slips his dirty fingers inside my jacket.

My clit tingles at the memory of his hand gesture. *Two in the pink*. I part my legs as his filthy hand slides up under my skirt.

My knickers are already wet through. I whimper into his open mouth as he rubs me through the lace.

He's rough. Unskilled. His fingers press so hard it aches.

"Dirty bitch for such a pretty little thing," he grunts.

"Fuck me," I hiss. "I like it rough."

He yanks my head back by my hair. "Is that right?"

The darkness is inside me already, adrenaline pumping at the thought of taking his filthy cock.

He's lean but muscular. Tall and wiry. And fast.

I'm sure he'll be fast.

I palm his dick through his jeans and loosen his belt, sucking his tongue into my mouth for one more kiss before I push myself well clear of him.

He stares at me with dark eyes as I back away a few paces.

"What's the fucking deal?" he grunts, but I keep on walking.

My skin prickles as he follows. His footsteps are heavy. Hard.

Fast.

"Hey, bitch. What's the fucking deal here?"

I shoot him a look over my shoulder but keep on going.

I quicken up as he closes the distance, breaking into a jog as I reach the entrance to the river path.

And then he grabs me. His hand closes around my arm and hauls me back to him, his breath hot in my face as we stare at each other.

I moan as he squeezes my tit through my blouse. It feels good enough that I hitch myself against his thigh and grind my pussy through my knickers.

"Gonna fuck all your holes, you filthy bitch," he rasps.

For a second I contemplate if I should let him.

I wonder if the adrenaline in my veins really is worth all this.

If feeling *alive* is worth all this.

But feeling alive is all I have left. Passing moments are the only things that keep me going.

bait

He grunts in anger as I push myself off him for the second time. I barely make it ten paces before he's back on me and my heart is thumping in my temples.

Monster.

His breath on my neck.

His hands on me.

But no.

It isn't him.

It never is.

"Do you want to fuck or not, you crazy bitch, huh?!" I'm glad I can't see his eyes in the darkness. "Make up your fucking mind!"

And I have.

"No," I tell him. "I don't."

I stare into the darkness of the river path, adrenaline subsiding as he curses under his breath and heads back the way he came.

"You're fucking tapped!" he yells before he reaches his truck and bleeps the alarm.

I hear the truck pull away and I'm glad I didn't end up trussed up in his trunk. He's too drunk to be driving anywhere.

I might be fucked up, but even I have sensibilities.

I stare at the glow of the city across the meadows, listening to the hiss of the river as I picture my tiny little apartment in the distance. The lights will be off. The room sparse and cold, decorated with only the handful of trinkets I brought along from my old life.

My tears of shame are quiet. The numb ones are always the most pitiful.

But it's not the grubby finger marks on my knickers, or the taste of whisky on my lips that make me cry tonight.

These aren't the tears of someone who is ashamed of wanting a monster in the darkness. Of wanting to be taken without mercy. Of wanting the promise of relief that comes through being on the edge of something truly petrifying.

They're the tears of someone who's grieving her lost life.

Her old friends. Her old job. Her old apartment with the green hallway and the dreamcatcher in the living room window.

The baby they stole before he even took a breath.

And the man who put him inside her.

The man who destroyed me.

two

Monsters are real, and ghosts are real too.
They live inside us, and sometimes, they win.

—STEPHEN KING

phoenix

There's something about pounding the hillside with misty breath and my pulse in my ears that lends the illusion I'm getting somewhere. Sometimes I feel that if I could just run fast enough I'd outrun all my mistakes.

Dawn is breaking over the ridge as I power on up toward the beacon at the top of the Malvern Hills, lights twinkling below as people begin their Friday morning. It's bittersweet to think of the early risers down there crammed around the breakfast table. Chatter and laughter and arguments. Songs on the radio. Music in the car.

That Friday feeling.

Family.

Once upon a time I thought that would be me.

If Mariana was still here, she'd laugh. Sometimes when I close my eyes I still feel her ahead of me, as though she's still running and I'm still chasing. Sometimes I'd swear I hear the ghost of her breath along with mine. Sometimes her memory feels close enough to touch – her breaths ragged as I caught her, her mouth hot and hungry. Her nails on my back.

Her wildness as she fought me.

The darkness in her eyes.

The way she loved me.

And then I remember her tears as she ran for the last time. The pain in my gut as I held myself back and watched her leave.

I allow myself a moment when I get to the top, doubling over to catch my breath as I stare at the land below. The view is spectacular up here. I'd stay to admire the way the world falls away if I wasn't so damn afraid of staying still.

I'll never outrun my mistakes, but I'll keep trying.

The run down is always an anti-climax. My heart is always in my throat as I head around the back of the house and let myself in through the porch. I've made my daily routine close enough to clockwork to cruise through on autopilot. I'd be happily on autopilot right now if not for the text message burning silently in my pocket.

They're willing to negotiate.

It's such a shame I'm not.

I only allow myself five minutes in the shower. I towel off in a rush as I pull a fresh shirt from the closet.

Cameron's footsteps are on the landing before I've fastened my tie. He's in spaceman PJs this morning – his favourites.

His sleepy eyes meet mine as he shunts my bedroom door open. My boy's hair is a dark tangle straight from bed. He looks so much like his mother it takes my breath. Every morning the same.

"Hey, little guy," I greet, hoisting him onto my hip as I grab my jacket from the hanger. I check he's not wet himself before we head downstairs. "Cornflakes?"

He shakes his head as we reach the kitchen.

"Krispies?"

Another head shake.

"Shooting Stars?"

He has Mariana's dimples when he smiles.

"Alright then, Stars it is."

He still has his special high chair, even though he'll be four this coming summer. He still has his favourite blue bowl and spoon, even though he's big enough for big boy cutlery now.

The speech therapist says he'll speak in his own time. The psychologist says he'll stop wetting the bed in his own time too.

Everything in its own time. Always in its own time. Time is the great healer and all that crap.

Time changes nothing, not for me and not for him either seemingly.

I'd give anything to change things for him. I'll never stop trying, but for now it's always tiny steps. Such tiny steps.

Every tiny step is enough to keep me going. A smile. A laugh. A new expression.

"Shooting Stars for little Cammy!"

Cam turns his head to smile at my sister as she props herself in the kitchen doorway. I feel her eyes on me as I grab myself a coffee.

"Well?" she asks.

"The answer's still no, Serena. No."

"No?"

"No."

"You're really going to turn them down? Jeez…"

I hear the hiss of her breath as her words trail off into nothing. I know she's fighting back expletives to spare Cameron's ears.

"This isn't healthy," she tells me, and the cutting edge of her voice bristles above her self-restraint. "Not for *any* of us. You have to move on, Leo. We *all* have to move on."

All. I know exactly who she's referring to, but my considerations are in this room only. Me and Cam. Fuck everyone else.

Fuck *him*.

My voice is low and calm, at odds with the twist in my gut. "Their offer was an insult."

"They said they'd negotiate…"

"And I said no," I tell her again, even though I haven't. Not yet.

"You have to speak to Jake, Leo. He's got to have a say in this too."

"My name is *Phoenix*," I tell her for the thousandth time. "And *he* lost his say a long time ago."

I flick on the worktop TV and turn the channel to Cameron's favourite as he digs into his breakfast. If he's bothered by our exchange he doesn't show it. I almost wish he would.

Serena joins me at the counter, and when she speaks again her mouth is close enough to my ear that the little guy won't hear her.

"Jake is still my brother. Yours too. He's still blood. And you're still Leo, *Leo*."

My eyes burn hers, so close. So similar. All three of us, so fucking similar.

"He's no brother of mine, and I'm not still Leo," I hiss. "He's not Jake anymore either, he makes that clear enough."

She shrugs. "I give up. You're both as bad as each other."

I wish she really would give it up, but Hell will freeze over first. Another family resemblance.

I down my coffee, then plant a kiss on my boy's head before I grab my wallet and keys. I ruffle his messy hair on my way out, even though he barely looks away from the cartoons.

"I'll be back later, champ. Be good for Serena."

She pulls her dressing gown tight as she watches me up the path to the truck. I see her shake her head before I pull away. Her brows are heavy, like mine, her dark hair piled up in a messy bun so stark against her pale skin. She's still fighting the obvious, still holding on to hope that Jake and I have long given up on.

She should really just give up too. Let go of the notion that one day we'll all be bright and breezy again. That one day we'll play happily families like our whole life didn't burn down and Mariana didn't burn with it. That maybe one day I'll be able to look my brother in the eye and see anything other than hate staring back at me.

His hate is redundant. I despise myself easily enough for the both of us.

The early shift workers are piling into the warehouse as I pull into my parking space. Jake's space is empty beside mine, just as it's been every day for the past six months we've been trading from this location.

Scott Brothers Logistics the sign on the frontage reads, but now it's just a name. I watch my tattoos flex as my fingers grip the steering wheel.

The office lights are still off, waiting for me to jolt the place to life for another day of the same old shit.

Goods to pack and dispatch, customers to invoice, money to be made. Fifty percent still goes to big-brother-Scott, even though he hasn't stepped foot inside this business since the day my Mariana passed away. *My* Mariana. Fuck what he has to say about it.

I pull out my phone and bring up the text message.

They're willing to negotiate.

My fingers are shaking as I key in my reply.

It's not for sale. Not now, not ever.

A tick flashes up on my handset as the message disappears. Job done.

I have plans of my own for that place. I don't know what they are yet, but I'll be damned if they involve selling off our old premises to the cloud of vultures circling overhead.

They'd pick at my bones if I let them. Hers too.

The scars on my back itch. Flames prickling across my skin. *Under* my skin.

I climb out of the truck and slam the door behind me.

And then I run, again. Only this time I'm walking.

This time it's all in my head.

abigail

"Abigail Summers! What the hell happened to you?"

I register the question with bated breath.

My skeleton melts and sags. My secrets ready to tumble from my unhinged jaw in a river of pure relief.

It's the question I've been waiting for. The question I figured inevitable from the moment I stepped foot in this building on my first day here.

Lauren Billings is staring right at me when my mouth drops open. It's only ten minutes past nine when I'm finally ready to blurt my sorry life story to the virtual stranger in front of me. But then she speaks again.

"Last night, I mean. I thought you were heading to Divas with Jack. We were all out. We could've hit the dance floor."

My jaw clamps shut, my skeleton toughening to marble as I shove my heart back in its cage. It pains in protest.

"Last night?" I bluster. "Oh, I was tired. Long week, my dancing shoes weren't up to much."

"And I thought you'd be part of the cool gang." She laughs as she rolls her eyes at me. "Jack thinks you blew him out. You didn't, right? I mean, you're still interested?"

It's sad that she thinks I ever was. I feel like a leaf blowing on the wind, curling at the edges.

"I told Jack we'd do it another time," I tell her, and she smiles as she takes her papers from the photocopier.

"I should think so. He's a great catch." She tips her head. "I think you'd make a good couple. You'd look good together. Well suited."

I look down at myself. My boring blouse, my knee-length pencil skirt. My semblance of normality.

Well suited.

"He's really not a dick, you know," she continues. "He wants to get serious. I mean, he goofs around, but he's not a jerk. He'd take care of you."

The bile rises in a heartbeat. *Take care of me.* The world swims around me as I try to focus on her voice.

"I know some guys around here act like they're so cool, but he's not one of them. He really likes you."

My hands are shaky as I shove my purchase order into the copier. I wish I could turn to jelly in front of her and sob my heart out onto the dull beige antistatic carpet.

But I don't.

It seems paper walls are tougher than I thought. They get tougher every day.

And still every night they burn.

I hold my breath until my copy comes out the other side, and then I wave it in her general direction, armed with generic excuses about work piling up on my desk. It's a lie, of course. I have nothing piled up on my desk. I had to dumb down my resume to get this position, downplaying everything I'd been doing for the past six years previous.

Just your average girl called Abigail. Nothing special. Nothing to note.

A nobody.

I retreat to the safety of my desk among the other desks, scrolling through my purchase software as though I'm pondering something important. There's nothing important. Nothing I have responsibility for. I key in and send out, nothing more. A constant blur of the same old product codes I'd learned by heart by the end of week one. A blur of days and faces and coffee breaks and pay checks.

It's not enough.

My fingernails pinch my thighs under my scratchy skirt. I'm itchy, like a flurry of tiny beetles are scurrying across my skin. *Under* my skin.

So I run, even though I'm only walking. My expression is empty as I pace through the sea of desks, back past the copier in the hallway, and past the kitchen and the stationery cupboard to the bathroom out the back.

I sit. Tug my starchy skirt up and scratch my naked skin until it turns pink.

I think of denim guy, and the darkness of the car park last night, and how much I wanted to feel alive.

Needed to feel alive.

I think of the relief in the middle of the night, when I dream of the man chasing me and not of the man who cast me aside like I meant nothing to him. Like our baby meant nothing to him.

And then I make a choice, right here and now. I make a choice between breakdown and breakthrough, even though I'm not sure where the two meet anymore.

If I'm going to stay standing I need to keep running.

I need something real. Something more than the unrealised fantasy I've been clinging on to through long nights these past few months.

I need to meet the monster.

And this time, for once, maybe even finally, he needs to catch me.

three

It is only by risking our persons from one hour to another that we live at all.

—WILLIAM JAMES

abigail

Part of me regrets turning down the girls from work when they asked me out with them this evening. Part of me wishes I could find solace in the drink and chatter of a regular Friday night out with colleagues.

Once upon a time I loved weekend drinks with people from work. With *him*.

I stare at the words on my laptop screen, my heart pounding with a strange mix of horror and excitement.

I shouldn't click the OK button. There's no way I should post this online, and definitely not with one of those arty obscured pictures of myself with the contrast raised up high and my hair covering half of my face.

I'm standing on the edge of a precipice, staring into the unknown, and it's so stupid to flirt with disaster by inching that bit closer to the darkness, but behind me is just more of the same. More days at my desk, more evenings trying to convince myself life is good here. More fake smiles and self-help books as I try to get through everything that went so horribly wrong back home.

I used to browse profiles on this website when I was younger, plucking up the courage to explore some of my darker fantasies. I never did. I was never brave-slash-reckless enough to risk it, not back then when life felt right.

But now it feels like a different story.

I send a text off to my parents with the usual *things are good* message I've been sending them every week since I arrived here. I reply to the photo message I got from my old friends with their *miss you* note scrawled underneath.

I miss them too. So much.

But neither of those things pull me back from the ledge.

No.

I need to do this.

I need to feel something. Something other than… *this.*

My finger hits enter, and I hold my breath as the screen changes to a tick with *profile uploaded* written underneath.

Fuck.

I've really done it.

I click on the link to my new *sex hookup* profile and take a breath as I see my picture staring back at me. It's really there. *Live.* The green circle at the side of the image tells the world I'm online right now.

The words look even worse somehow now they're out there to be seen.

I'm seeking my monster in the darkness.

I'll run but you'll run faster.

We'll play cat and mouse until you catch me.

I won't know you, and I'll pretend I don't want to.

You'll pretend you don't care.

I'll tell you I don't want it.

You'll tell me you'll take it anyway, and then you will.

And it'll be rough.

One wild night where anything goes, and then we'll never see each other again.

I feel like such a crazy as I read it back. My message sounds... off. Too confident maybe? Too callous? Reckless?

I click to edit, and when I feel the lump in my throat I know I really am on the edge. I'm tired. Tired of trying, tired of playing *normal*. The urge to bare my soul is too strong to ignore this evening, to be authentically vulnerable just once, even if only a handful of strangers use it as masturbation fodder.

My fingers are jittery when I type.

Please... I might sound crazy, but I need this. I've always needed this.

Please help me feel alive again.

I'm not seeking a psycho, just someone who can help me feel alive again.

I can't face looking at my updated profile with its little green online icon, so I close the laptop as soon as I'm done. I sit on my bed in the tiny apartment I hoped would feel like home by now, my knees pulled up to my chest as I stare at the patterns the streetlights make on the wall.

And then my phone pings.

Once, twice, and then again.

My email is on fire. My nerves are burning as I scroll through the early responses. But they're shit.

Hey babe. Ur hot.

Wot you up to sexy?

Love your pic. Gonna fuck you up good.

No.

No, no and definitely *no*.

How big are your tits?

bait

You wanna get fucked real good?

Wanna cam?

On and on they keep coming. A sea of idiots who haven't even bothered to read my profile.

My outpouring feels pointless, my confession nothing but a potential in for jerks looking to get their dicks wet.

I flop back onto my bed with a sigh, and then I laugh. It's one of those self-deprecating laughs that almost makes me reach for the *how to heal your broken heart* book on my nightstand.

What the fuck is happening to me? Really?

My dick is ten inches. Wanna see?

You like girl on girl?

And then I get my first dick pic. It's blurry and from a crappy angle that make his balls look too big. *Show me your pussy.*

One day, when life is good again, I'm going to confess this stupid evening to whoever my new best friend here happens to be, and they'll laugh and I'll laugh and I'll show them these messages and all the crappy requests I got. They'll call me crazy and I'll smile and say I was, and this will all be a distant memory.

He'll be a distant memory too.

But not today. Today these messages are all for me.

Maybe these messages are the universe's way of answering my deepest fantasies. At least the universe has the sense of humour I've been lacking lately.

Ur one hot dirty bitch.

Do you take it up the ass?

Maybe a Friday night wasn't the best time to post a new online advert.

I head through to my tiny kitchenette in my PJs and flick on the kettle to make myself a tea. I should've gone out with the girls from work, maybe I'd have found a real friend here. Hell knows I need a real friend here.

I'm about to put my phone on silent to stop the endless pings when it pings again.

I'm figuring it's another cheap one-liner, maybe even another dick pic, but the message surprises me.

Phoenix Burning the username reads. *What happened to you?*

My heart skips at the question.

I've been waiting for it to come for so long. My tongue is parched, desperate to speak the truth. My soul screams for someone to hear me.

His picture is in darkness. There's only a hint of his face. He looks stern. Serious. Brooding.

Maybe I'm seeing what I want to see.

I take my tea back through to the bedroom and fire my laptop back up. I read them again on screen, those four little words. I stare at his picture like it could be my salvation, weighing things up. Weighing up how much I really want this.

And then I type…

phoenix

I've been on this site sporadically for the past three months. I've never messaged anyone. Never even found anything that offers a passing interest.

The profiles are a blur to me – pictures all blending into one.

None of them ever make me pause.

Until now.

I guess the weekends are the hardest. The nights when I've finally got Cameron settled to sleep after a long week, when I've said goodnight and prayed this is the night he'll say it back. When Serena has gone to bed and I'm still wide awake, alone with my own company.

Lonely.

I haven't been out socially since Mariana passed away, not between taking care of Cam and getting the business back up from its knees. I've not once taken Serena up on her offer of staying up late in case Cameron wakes up while I'm off out somewhere.

I haven't wanted to meet anyone. Not like that.

I still don't want to meet anyone like that.

I just want…

Fuck.

I slouch back in my chair, the profile still on my screen.

I just want…

I just want to feel alive again.

I've never been one to hide from the truth, and the truth is that a woman like Mariana was never going to be my forever. I'd have given anything to make it so, but even if she hadn't run off that night it would've been some other night down the road.

A woman like Mariana was never meant to settle down in this sleepy town with a man like me. She was never meant to play happy families in sweet suburbia.

The fact that she tried it was a beautiful miracle. Beautiful *madness*.

That woman, Mariana, with her wildness and the flames in her eyes, and her reckless impulses and the soul she wore on her sleeve – that woman ruined me for all others.

I gave her my heart and she gave me my boy. I gave her everything I could give, but still she wanted to run. Harder. Further. Faster. I could only chase her so far.

Turns out that wasn't far enough.

The profile on screen isn't like the others. Raven hair obscures most of the girl's features. She's staring at the camera with one beautiful wide eye, her high cheekbone stark against the shadows, her expression so… lost.

Beautiful.

Wild.

I don't know what it is that feels so familiar about this one random woman's picture. She looks little like Mariana. Mariana was tanned and strong-featured, with dirty eyes and a dirty laugh to match. The woman in the picture reminds me of a black swan, elegant and etheric. Deep. I can't stop staring at her.

Maybe that's what's familiar about her – the fact that I can't stop staring at her.

The darkness in her eyes. The way it feels like her soul is calling through the screen.

Maybe I'm finally breaking down. Maybe this is the moment the clockwork reality I've created to get Cam and I through this horrible nightmare crumbles into chaos.

I can't crumble into chaos.

I read her words again, just to be sure I'm understanding them.

They seem too fucking good to be true.

I'm seeking my monster in the darkness.

I'll run but you'll run faster.

We'll play cat and mouse until you catch me.

I won't know you, and I'll pretend I don't want to.

You'll pretend you don't care.

I'll tell you I don't want it.

You'll tell me you'll take it anyway, and then you will.

And it'll be rough.

One wild night where anything goes, and then we'll never see each other again.

The girl may not look like Mariana, but Mariana could have written that profile. Mariana was the one who begged me to bring *her* fantasy to life.

She was the one who got me hooked on the chase. Addicted to the darkness. The thrill of the hunt.

I shouldn't entertain the idea of one wild night where anything goes. There's me and Cam and a business that needs me on top form to navigate the financial pressure of a pending insurance claim.

Maybe this profile isn't even serious. Maybe she's just a girl who gets off on flirting with danger – because that's what this profile is, just one big beacon of recklessness for the dregs and the crazies and the desperate out there.

The thought concerns me more than it should do. She's at least twenty-five – plenty old enough to make her own dumb decisions. The string of potential assholes I can only assume are flooding her inbox are none of my business. Not my problem.

I'd force myself to click on *next* and forget about her if it wasn't for the extra lines of her profile that appear when the screen refreshes.

Please... I might sound crazy, but I need this. I've always needed this.

Please help me feel alive again.

I'm not seeking a psycho, just someone who can help me feel alive again.

The words hit me in the gut. Hard.

Mariana's ghost laughs in my ear.

I've always needed this. That's what she said to me in the shadows the very first night I caught her.

I stare again at the screen. *Please help me feel alive again.*

Alive again.

Melancholy grips me by the throat. *Alive.*

It's been too long.

I wonder what happened to the black swan that took the life from her. I wonder why she needs this.

I wonder how many assholes will be beating down her door for a cheap shot at getting their rocks off.

Many, I'm sure.

My question is simple. Impulsive.

What happened to you?

I'm almost certain she won't reply. I'm positive I'll just be one of the masses of messages she sends to the trash bin when she realises this site is full of douchebags.

I'm a heartbeat away from signing out from *adult hookup* and talking some sense into myself when the message pings.

And I'm one breath away from crazy myself when I bring up her reply.

four

There are two ways of spreading light: to be the candle or the mirror that reflects it.

—EDITH WHARTON

phoenix

The green *online now* circle is illuminated next to black swan's profile photo. Her username is simple and stark, and yet it says so much.

Bait.

Her tagline is new. Her profile unfolding in real time.

Just a girl wanting to feel.

Bait.

She's bait alright. The predator in me stirs, adrenaline pumping as old memories come flooding back.

Her message comes through in segments, one line at a time.

I've been waiting a long time for someone to ask me that question.

I loved hard. I lost harder.

And then I lost everything along with him.

My job. My home. So many people I cared about.

Then I lost the baby too.

I bled my soul out with the life inside me. Bled so hard I nearly disappeared too.

My world spat me out and kept on turning without me.

It was too painful to stay, so I ran.

And here I am, just trying to make a new life.

It's hard.

It's really, really hard.

The simple honesty in her words makes my stomach lurch. My own sadness is thick in my throat as I type a reply.

The world has a habit of spitting us out and leaving us behind. I'd like to say you can catch it up again if you run fast enough, but I'm not so sure. I live in hope.

I'm staring at the online icon when the tick appears to say she's read my message.

I see her typing.

What happened to you?

I smile to myself. Smile at this simplistically honest communication with a random stranger.

And then I type.

I loved hard. I lost harder.

I pause. And then I type again.

Your fantasy is dangerous. Be very careful you don't find more than you bargained for. You don't want to put your trust in the wrong person.

I'm torn between the strange urge to unload my pain onto a stranger and the urge to chase her blindly through the wilderness.

Her message is almost instantaneous, feeding through one line at a time…

The one person in this world I trusted implicitly sold me down the river to save his safe little portion of suburbia.

I cried and screamed and begged for him before they took me down to surgery to save my life, but he never came.

He never even called.

So yeah, I know I won't be able to trust anyone, especially not some random stranger online.

But that's okay.

I know how dangerous this fantasy is, it's been haunting me my whole life.

But I need it.

Believe me, I need it so bad.

I should talk her down and back away, but my fingers have a life of their own...

So did the woman I lost.

She replies in a heartbeat. *She did? She needed this too? Like I do?*

I shouldn't say it. But I do.

Yes, she did.

Another heartbeat. *And what about you?*

I stare at the skyline through the window. The orange glow from the town nestled down below. I hold back from answering, afraid my own darkness will swallow me whole.

Another message pings...

You've done this before, yes? Could you do it again? Is that why you messaged me?

My scars itch. My heart pounds as I realise how hard I am.

Another ping...

I'm sorry, I just. I've been having these dreams since forever. They're the only thing that feels right to me anymore. I know how fucked up that sounds, that something so dark could be the only thing I'm sure of.

And it does sound fucked up. It sounded fucked up from Mariana too.

I was as hard then as I am now, as tempted by the darkness as much then as I am tonight.

I fight the urge to palm my dick through my pants.

The girl is skirting disaster. My black swan has no idea how close she is to danger. A little bird flapping on the ground as the predators circle.

If I'm the one who answers her call, she'll come out the other side to tell the tale at least.

Maybe this time will be different. Maybe this time I can…

I bury the thoughts as they arise.

She's not my problem. I'll do my bit, take what I need, give her what she's craving, then walk away without even a backward glance.

My words glare from the screen at me before I press send.

Crazy. This is crazy.

Two weeks.

Prove to me you're serious about this over two weeks.

Prove to me this isn't just a moment of recklessness, or some crazy self-destruct mission.

Prove to me you really do need this. That you really do know what you're getting into.

If you do that and mean it.

Really mean it.

Then maybe I'll be your monster.

abigail

I feel so raw. So exposed.

But I *feel.*

I take a breath, and for the first time in months my words don't feel trapped in my throat. It's strange how such a simple confession, one tiny moment of truth amongst the pretence, can mean so much.

Phoenix Burning could be anyone, but right now he's the closest thing I have to hope.

I read his latest message back through, over and over as I form a response.

Then maybe I'll be your monster.

Questions swirl. When? Where? How do I prove it?

I don't know how I'll show him I'm serious via nothing but an anonymous hook-up site, but I already know I'll do whatever it takes.

Two weeks, I type. *I'll prove I'm serious, just tell me how.*

My heel taps against the bed at the prospect this could really happen. Really, really happen.

I type another response before I've received anything back.

What happens then?

I watch the *typing* status at the bottom of the screen.

My stomach flips when his message comes through.

You won't know me, and you'll pretend you don't want to. You'll tell me you don't want it, and I'll pretend I don't care. It'll be rough. Really rough. You'll never know my name and you'll never see me again. One wild night where anything goes.

I can hardly breathe, staring dumbly at the screen as another message sounds.

And then you'll delete this profile and promise me you'll never do this with a stranger again. You'll stop running, you'll pick your life up and make it mean something again.

Tears sting, threaten to spill.

And you? I type. *What will you do?*

He replies so quickly.

Maybe a little darkness will turn us both back toward the light.

I stare at his shadowy profile picture, trying to get a measure of the man. His features are strong. His hair looks dark and wild. His eyes too.

It's at least partly an illusion of my own making – the photo gives very little away. I'm seeing what I want to see, and I know it.

I know it, but I like it.

A shiver dances along my spine. Maybe this man, this online stranger, really could be my monster. My saviour.

Maybe he's really going to be the one to chase me down.

What do you want me to do? I ask.

Tell me your name, he says.

I consider giving him a fake one, but don't.

Abigail, I type. *What's yours?*

My clit flutters. I close my eyes in relief as I slip my hand down my knickers.

Another ping. *You'll never know.*

The thought thrills me. His words thrill me.

He thrills me.

My fingers are circling hard when he messages again.

I'll sign in tomorrow night, and by then you'll have told me about your dreams.

The green circle next to his name disappears, just like that. *Phoenix Burning* offline.

The envelope at the top of the screen tells me I have twelve new messages, but I don't give a shit about any of them. I close my laptop and hitch my legs up, my heart bursting with the dark thrill of a fantasy grappling for life.

It'll be rough. Really rough, he said, and I believe him. Fuck knows why, but I believe every single word he said.

I'm riding on the wings of insanity, but I don't care. I'm teetering on the edge of the precipice, but I don't care about that either.

My belly is tight, but it's wracked with something more than pain.

Excitement.

Relief.

A bit of both.

Fear.

Nerves.

Trepidation.

Need.

Fuck, how I need this.

I bite my knuckles as my fingers strum my clit, hips raised as I contemplate the unthinkable.

Two weeks and he'll make this real.

Two weeks and he'll be my monster. A monster of flesh and bone and breath. A monster who won't disappear when I open my eyes.

He'll chase me, and hurt me, and fuck me, and I'll pretend I don't want it. But I will.

Oh fuck, I will.

And then I'll never see him again.

It's been a long time since I've given myself an orgasm without seeing *his* face.

A long time since I've been able to give myself over to fantasy without *his* memory ruining everything.

But tonight it's easy. Tonight I gasp and whimper and squirm under my own fingers. Tonight my toes curl and my breaths come out in hisses, and it feels so fucking good I hit the sky.

Tonight it's just about the monster and me.

And tonight is the first time in an age I fall asleep without crying.

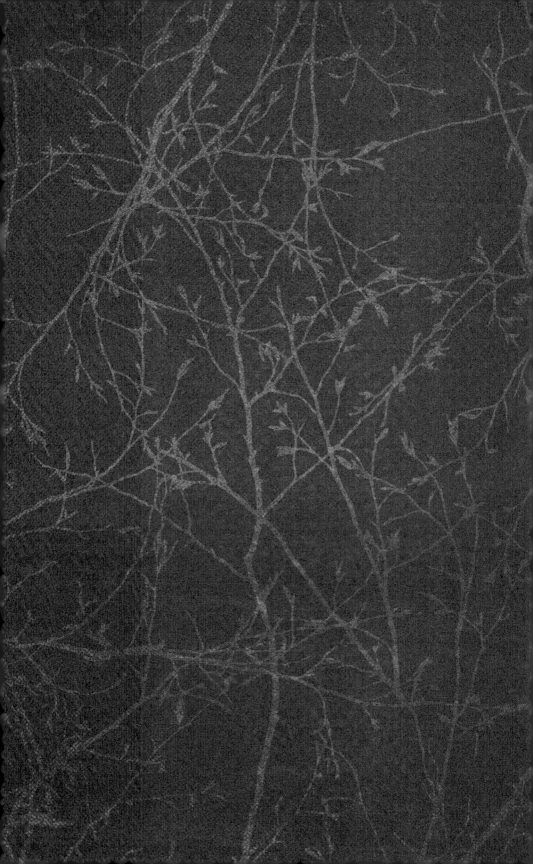

five

When you look into an abyss, the abyss also looks into you.

—FRIEDRICH NIETZSCHE

phoenix

The very first night I chased Mariana, I swore it was one moment of madness.

And this is another, right here and now.

There's that familiar wildness behind my eyes as I press my forehead to the glass of my bedroom window. It makes my temples pulse. My nostrils flare. And I feel it. I feel it right the way through me.

The rain is lashing outside, one of those freak passing storms as summer rolls in. Water bounces against the pool cover in the yard down below. I can hear it drumming. I can *feel* it drumming.

It was raining the first night I chased her. My boots squelched thick through the mud as I powered up the hillside after her. She was fast, even barefoot.

But I was faster.

She didn't go down easy, Mariana.

Sometimes her nails drew blood. Sometimes she was feral enough that I became a beast for real, simply because I had to. Sometimes I even believed her screams.

Sometimes I didn't fucking care.

My breath mists up the glass as I tug down the zip on my jeans. My fist curls around meat and metal, the barbells on my dick shooting sparks straight to my balls. Another of Mariana's legacies.

But it's not Mariana I'm thinking about tonight as I work my dick. It's not Mariana's eyes I imagine staring up at me wide and scared.

Excited.

I'm imagining a stranger. Creating a fantasy from nothing but one obscured online photo.

My adrenaline is pumping.

My fist is too.

It's enough.

More than enough.

My balls ache and tighten. My jaw is gritted hard.

I wonder if she'll be ready for it when I catch her. I wonder if she'll be ready for the way my body slams hers and steals her breath. Steals everything from her.

I wonder if she'll beg me to stop.

Abigail.

A broken little bird.

It would've been so easy for her to lie, but she didn't. I know she didn't.

I feel it.

Her.

The strangest connection through nothing but text. Desperate and flawed.

Fucked up.

Two strangers circling each other's darkness as our demons said hello.

I want to break her.

It'll feel so good to fucking break her.

To punish her like I should have punished Mariana.

I want to pin her down and take her body until her soul finally stops running.

I want to force my way inside her, deep enough to make her scream. I want to pound her until she can't breathe, until there's nothing but me. All me. Only me.

Me, me, fucking me.

No sadness. No ghosts. No fucking regrets. Just my body inside hers.

I won't let it be painless. I won't let it be easy. And I won't let it be quick, either.

I'll hurt her until she thinks she's been hurting forever, until she screams so much she can't scream anymore.

Until she's done.

Until she's mine.

Fucking mine.

I hear the wetness of my dick in my hand. It's slick. Hard.

Dangerous.

My cock is a fucking weapon. Mariana made it so – begged for it to be so.

But it's not Mariana I want tonight. It's Abigail.

Two weeks and her skin will feel every inch of mine. Two weeks until she'll whimper and beg and scream for me. She can fight me with everything she's got, but it won't matter.

She'll suffer for her salvation, just as I'll suffer for mine, cursed with needs I can't ignore. Needs no man should have. Mariana jacked me up and got me hooked, an addict to her filthy fetishes, damned to hunt like a beast in the darkness.

My hand tightens around my cock. The piercings ripple under my skin. I grip so hard it hurts, just like Abigail will.

Scared pussy always hurts so fucking bad.

Scared pussy always fights.

And scared pussy always tastes the best.

Forcing my way inside her will be fucking divine. Leaving marks on her pale skin will be divine.

Breaking her open will be my divine fucking pleasure.

And then, when she's nothing but tatters on the floor, her face a mess of soil and tears, her pussy used and gaping. Raw. Exposed. Maybe then she'll be broken enough to pick up the pieces.

And maybe I'll be broken enough to pick up mine.

The catharsis is addictive. My breaths rough and shoulders braced as I stare into the black world outside.

The twinkling lights disappear as I slip into the abyss.

My cock is throbbing, the barbells hurting so fucking good.

I love the way my ridges feel against my fingers.

I love the way they'll feel inside her cunt. I love the way they'll hurt before they feel good.

I'll make her come regardless, even if she doesn't think she can. Even if her pussy cries in protest. Even if she hates how dirty it makes her feel.

I'll make her feel so fucking dirty.

One night.

One wild night. Crazy night. Desperate night.

I tip my head back, stifling my grunts with Serena so close next door. My fist is frantic, brutal as I shunt my hips toward the glass.

Gonna leave my handprints over her pretty pale tits.

Gonna lick the tears from her cheeks.

Gonna make her beg me to stop.

Gonna hurt her so bad she won't stop coming.

I grunt as my cock jerks. The first stream of cum jets onto the window glass.

And another, and another as I swear under my breath.

Gonna make her realise that beasts come after bait.

Gonna make her realise that meeting some stranger online was a stupid fucking mistake.

For both of us.

abigail

I wake up late.

I sit upright as I fathom the unthinkable.

I slept through.

My breath is even. My pillows are dry.

My pussy…is…. *not*.

I'm soaking through my knickers. My thighs are clammy.

My clit tingles.

Fuck.

I reach for my phone. My email notifications show twenty-five unread messages. I scroll through them all, not giving a shit about any of them.

I scroll all the way until I see his picture, just to check he's really real.

Phoenix Burning.

There it is. I breathe in relief.

His username suits him. He looks like he could set the world on fire.

Set *me* on fire.

My smile feels goofy and fucked up but I don't care.

It's one glimmer of hope in the darkness. One tiny glimpse at authenticity.

bait

My soul soars from the ashes.

Phoenix.

The bird from the fire. The bird who rises from the flames.

My heart still feels like lead, but it's beating.

And I want it to. For once, I want it to.

Two weeks.

I scroll back through our messages, my mind whirring at the sight of my confession in the cold light of day.

He asked and I told him. I told him my secrets and he answered right back.

I zoom in as much as I can on his profile image. I try raising my phone screen brightness, and that helps a little.

His features really are dark, but there's more. His skin looks inked. A hint of shapes on his neck. So many shapes.

Maybe I'm imagining it.

Maybe.

I force myself to stop before I see too much. I shouldn't see anything.

He's just a monster in the darkness. He's just a hand around my throat. Muscle against my back.

He's a long, thick cock forcing its way inside me.

He's filthy words in my ear as he makes me take him.

I put a hand on my belly, but there is no ache there today. I pull my knees to my chest and the stupid gesture doesn't make me sob.

Two weeks.

Two weeks to prove I really want this.

Him.

A monster.

My monster.

I call up a fresh message on my laptop. The circle next to his profile picture is grey. *Offline.*

My fingers move so easily. My words are at odds with the summer sunlight beaming through the blinds.

It used to be a monster. Fur and fangs and claws. I never saw him, but he was big. He'd chase me through my dreams until I'd wake up screaming. Every night.

I tried everything to get rid of it. Early bed times. No TV. No stupid horror stories.

It didn't make any difference.

Panic and excitement are two sides of the same coin, so they say. I don't know when I started getting confused between the two. Puberty, I guess.

Have you seen Bram Stoker's Dracula? That film with Gary Oldman where he turns into a big wolf creature and fucks the girl in red on a gravestone?

I saw that before I should. Not at my house, but at a friend's. It was dark enough that I could hide my blushes. Dark enough that I could hide the way I was rocking in my seat and couldn't stop.

I was lucky, because I don't think I could have stopped if I'd wanted to.

That was the first thing I ever came over. Biting into a pillow with my heart racing, feeling so fucking disgusting at the thought of being taken by some evil half-beast.

Maybe that was the beginning of this whole thing, I dunno. Those years were pretty confusing.

I felt so guilty after that, that I'd make sure I screamed louder when I woke up, just to convince myself I still hated them. But I didn't.

I don't know when the monster stopped having fur and fangs and claws. I don't know when I first knew he was a man.

I don't know exactly when I started waking up in the morning with wet knickers and my fingers on my clit, but when it started it didn't stop.

I've thought so much about what the man will do to me when he catches me, but in my dreams it's never happened. Not yet.

I'm sick of fighting what I want. I'm sick of pretending I don't crave the things I crave.

When these dreams came back a few months ago it was the greatest relief of my life. But they aren't enough.

Not anymore.

I need this for real.

Even if it's just once.

I take a breath. My insides feel exposed. Awkward.

Uncomfortable.

But I like it.

Please, I type and my belly flips.

Please give me what I need.

I sign out before I can obsess about him coming back online.

And then, for the first time in weeks, I call my mum.

p h o e n i x

When the alarm wakes me up on Saturday morning, I'm not sure what I'm most afraid of – whether she'll message or whether she won't.

Maybe she'll come to her senses and bail on the reckless idea. Maybe it would be for the best if she did.

It's only when I'm lying there pondering the outcome that I realise the sky is blue outside my window.

I don't usually notice the sky is blue.

It's a strange observation.

My dick is hard enough that it aches. I've wrapped my fingers around it without a second thought, and that's a strange observation too.

A run.

I need a run.

My chest doesn't feel constricted as I lace up my running boots. My strides don't feel pained as I spring out from the porch and skirt the side of the pool. Today I even look at it on my way past.

Today I wonder what it would be like to get it serviced again for Cameron and me.

I hate the pool. It usually seems so... soulless. Just another painful reminder.

But not today.

For the first time in months I take my time at the top of the Malverns. I pause a little bit longer, breathe that little bit deeper. I watch a car weave its way through town below and out the other side. My eyes follow it all the way.

I nod at a couple on the footpath. I point a man in the direction of his runaway dog as he races on up to the Beacon.

And then I send off a message to my dispatch manager to tell him I won't be in for the Saturday morning shift today.

I'd chide myself for recklessness if I wasn't well aware of the truth – I normally convince myself I'm needed there, but it's bullshit. It's been bullshit for months.

There's less of an anti-climax when I head back down the hill track for home this morning. Cameron is already up when I get in, sitting in his high chair as Serena pours his cereal.

"He was an early riser today," she tells me, and she isn't kidding. I figure he's at least an hour early until I check the clock.

No. Forty minutes of that is down to me.

My boy looks happy with himself, scrolling through the channels on the TV remote even though his favourite is on channel one. I normally do it for him.

Seemingly that was an error on my part.

I watch him pressing the buttons, more than capable of navigating the menu.

Choices.

He's making active choices.

Baby-steps outside the norm.

And why wouldn't he? He's perfectly capable of making his own TV choices.

If only I'd let him.

"Hey, champ. Daddy's staying home today," I tell him. "We can go feed the ducks. Maybe grab an ice-cream. You'd like that, right?"

His smile is bright and easy. His dimples take my breath.

My equilibrium wobbles but holds.

"Not going in?" Serena asks, and I shake my head.

"It's a nice day. They can cover it."

She raises an eyebrow. "Are you feeling okay?"

It surprises me to find that I am.

Or I am until she flashes me a guilty expression.

"What's up?" I ask on instinct.

She doesn't answer, just flicks through the pages of her Saturday newspaper on the worktop. Like that shit's gonna cut it.

"What's that look for?" I prompt, and she sighs.

She fishes her phone from her dressing gown pocket and hands it over. My mood shrivels to nothing as I see the message icon flashing.

"You didn't? Just tell me that you didn't."

But she won't. Of course she won't.

She can't.

I click to read her messages, and sure enough there's a string from Jake.

Ash.

He calls himself *Ash* now, for the sake of my prolonged misery as much as his own.

"He had a right to know about the offer," she insists, but I shake my head.

"He has no right to anything," I snap. "Nothing, Serena. Not one goddamn thing."

I keep my tone in check for Cam's sake, gritting my teeth behind him as he remains oblivious.

"He wants to talk," she hisses, like I'm the one who's fucking unreasonable here. Maybe I am.

"*I* don't," I tell her. "I made my decision. I told them I'm not selling, and I'm not. End of story. Job done."

"And what if Jake has other ideas?"

I shrug. "Not my problem. I'm the main signatory."

Serena's eyes are dark brown oceans of *fuck you* when she folds her newspaper up. She props her weight on one hip and flashes me the lip curl.

"You two need your heads banging together," she tells me and then she sighs. "Please, Leo. Please just speak to him."

I shake my head. "It's Phoenix," I point out, but she closes her eyes.

"Leo, please. *Please*. Just speak to him. We can't go on like this. None of us can. Not you, not me, not Jake, either. Or Cam."

I flinch as she says my boy's name.

"We're good," I snap, even though it's a lie.

Cameron finally decides on a channel. It's not the one I was expecting. Monkeys run up a tree. Some documentary thing.

Hell, the world has jumped an inch on its axis somewhere.

"We need to start living again," Serena continues, oblivious. "Please, Leo. Please let us start living again."

The pain is back in my gut at the thought.

The flames are back under my skin as our eyes meet across the room.

bait

Determined meets furious, but this time I bite my tongue. This time I stay exactly where I am, with Cameron's documentary playing in the background, and the sun still shining in through the kitchen window.

Let us start living again.

My phone vibrates in my pocket. My heart jumps in my chest.

"Leo?" Serena prompts again. "Will you talk to him?"

I call up my notifications and sure enough there is a little number 1 next to my *hook-up* message inbox.

Let us start living again.

Serena's eyes are pleading. Desperate.

Cameron turns up the volume on his documentary.

And I stop. Think.

Living again.

Maybe she's right.

I call up my contact list before I can think better of it.

six

Death is not the greatest loss in life.
The greatest loss is what dies inside us while we live.

—NORMAN COUSINS

abigail

I've been in my apartment three months already without so much as waving to a neighbour, but today feels different. I've seen her in the communal hallway before – an older woman with short blonde hair. Up until now I've always hung back and kept my distance.

She's fishing her keys from her handbag with her shopping on the floor when I step outside and pull my door closed behind me. She looks my way and smiles, and I smile back.

And then I say it.

"Hi."

"Hello," she says. She pushes her key in the lock. "I'm Sarah."

"Abigail," I tell her.

She smiles. And then she's gone.

It's strange how the tiniest little actions can feel so significant. There's a strange tickle in my chest as I head downstairs and step out onto Church Street.

Sarah. A neighbour. A neighbour with a name.

And with that my fate feels sealed – I really do live here.

I take a deep breath as I head into High Town, walking with purpose. Walking like I belong here.

Maybe for now I do.

Today the world looks a little bit different. I feel a tiny shift in the universe. It's barely noticeable, but it's there. A sliver of life amongst the numbness.

A ribbon of excitement.

I'd almost forgotten what excitement felt like.

There is one thing to be said for having no life but misery for months on end. My bank balance is healthy, even on a massive pay cut. My apartment is smaller than the one I left behind. My diet here has been minimal and basic, without the added cost of social dining racking up over the weeks.

Strangely enough, if I'm honest with myself, there is something to be said for a minimal existence. I miss so much, but I don't miss *things*. I don't miss my overflowing wardrobe, or the entire rainbow collection of nail varnishes displayed on a rack. I don't miss the drawers full of old paperwork and junk mail and odds and ends. I don't even miss the scatter cushions I'd compulsively update every season.

I arrived here with nothing but the bare bones for starting over. Right now that seems okay.

Bare bones can surely be the building blocks for something new.

I find myself walking past the homewares stores I'd have squealed over once upon a time. I skirt by a stationery shop that would have been an Aladdin's Cave to me back in Hampshire. I don't know where I'm going, or what I'm looking for, but I keep on walking, keep on heading *somewhere*.

Anywhere.

And for the first time in an age I notice the people. Walking, talking, checking their phones, oblivious to the world around them, just as I was.

I notice the smell of fresh bread drifting from the bakery on the corner.

I notice the way the sun breaks through a lazy streak of clouds.

The way the cobbles turn to tarmac under my heels as I take a left at the end of the street.

The sound of the pedestrian crossing bleeping up ahead.

The way it feels to breathe.

And I smile.

I smile because a stranger asked a simple question, and then he heard me.

I smile because someone found me in the darkness and didn't try to switch the light on.

I smile because a man who calls himself Phoenix Burning offered me something I've never had.

And then my smile is all gone.

I guess it's the way the guy's hair blows from his eyes. The way his nose is Roman and his eyes are blue. The way he moves, so familiar. So much like Stephen.

I guess it's the way he's looking at her – the girl at his side. Looking at her the way I thought Stephen looked at me.

I guess it's the pushchair – the one I'd picked out for myself.

Their baby is wearing white knitted booties. His eyes are tight shut. His fingers so small.

They pass by so closely I can smell her perfume.

It smells like everything I ever wanted.

It hits the back of my throat and then it chokes me. I'm retching in broad daylight on a crowded street, with a womb full of hurt that pains when I breathe.

And I'm alone.

Lost.

Reeling.

I back into a solid wall before my spine buckles. I close my eyes to everything around me before the light pricks my tears.

Lullabies at the top of my lungs, a hand on my belly as I drive through the night with tears running down my cheeks.

I'm battling an ocean of pain with my bare hands because of tiny toes in a pair of white booties. And I've been here before. So many times.

A baby-cry on the train cutting me like glass. A new-born sleep suit discarded in the wrong aisle of the supermarket. A man holding his little boy's tiny hand as they cross the road.

The looks passing between my ex-colleagues as they try to find the words to tell me Stephen was the one to clear my desk. That he hadn't even asked after me. Not once.

I feel like I'm bleeding out all over again, but today I fight the ocean and I win.

I open my eyes before the tears fall. I take a deep breath, push myself from the wall and force my legs to keep walking. I walk until I get to the river and I follow it for miles, through the meadows and out the other side, until the sunny afternoon turns into a warm evening and my heels are blistered. Until I notice the sky is pink and that I've never really listened to a duck quack, not properly. Not like now.

And then, finally, when I know the bare walls of my apartment won't break me, I go home and wait for my monster.

phoenix

People used to think we were twins, Jake and me. They wouldn't think it now.

He's lost weight. A lot of weight.

His broad shoulders look sunken. His arms look lean and wiry. His eyes are darker than ever as he slams his truck door behind him and I slam mine.

We meet in no man's land. In the middle of the car park we used to pull into every morning. The tower is a black hulk looking over us, the burned-out roof jagged in the shadows.

I contemplate the odds that he's going to charge me down before we've even said a word. That we'll end up grappling on the cracked tarmac while Mariana's ghost screams. *Or laughs.*

The seven months since we last faced off haven't been kind to either of us, that's for sure, but today he keeps his fists in check. At least for now.

He reaches inside his jacket and pulls out a cigarette. I don't move an inch as he lights up. He takes two long drags before he jabs a finger in my direction.

"Take the fucking offer."

"Fuck the fucking offer." My voice is calmer than I feel.

He gestures to the maw of concrete and rubble behind us. The doors are warped and gaping. The ground still littered with broken window glass. "What fucking good is it to you? She's fucking dead! Let this fucking place die with her!"

"I'm not selling."

"Why the fuck not?!"

I don't have an answer to that. I don't fucking *need* an answer to that. I stare past him to the darkness inside.

I can still feel the heat. Still smell the stench as the pallets went up. Still hear my choking screams as I bellowed her name.

"The business is almost back on its feet. If I was gonna sell I'd have done it a long time ago, when we fucking needed it," I tell him.

"Nobody fucking wanted it then."

I shake my head. "Think what you want, Jake. There's always some fucking vulture looking to make a quick buck. It would've sold."

His shoulder lands square against mine. "It's *Ash*."

I turn my face to his. *"I'm the one who lost her."*

I recognise the rage in his glare almost as much as I recognise the pain behind it. His emptiness stirs mine. Grief bubbles in my gut.

"She was *mine*," he hisses. "You fucking know she was. *I'm* the one who fucking lost her."

My fists clench on instinct, a whisper away from pounding my hate into the sack of shit who shares the same fucking blood as me.

I'm one man battling a fucking storm, shaking my fists at the fucking lightning. I've been here before, so many fucking times.

But tonight I am victorious.

Because of her.

Because of a stranger.

Because I feel alive.

I step away. I loosen my fists. The grief stops bubbling.

"I'm not selling," I say, calmly. "I'm going to redevelop."

"Redevelop? What the fuck?"

"You heard me."

He looks like I jabbed him in the jaw. Part of me wishes I had.

I notice how tired he looks, even in the half-light. I notice how much longer his beard is now than mine.

And in this one long moment, I wonder if it's really grief that's still crippling my older brother, or whether it's guilt.

"Why were you really here?" I ask him. "What was she doing in that storeroom on her own?"

He doesn't miss a beat. "I don't fucking know. I came here to work, she was already—"

I cut him off with a shake of my head. "Enough of the fucking bullshit. You tell me the truth, and I'll talk about fucking selling."

My heart pounds but I stand firm. My pulse is in my temples, but I don't move a muscle.

Not until he does.

"Sell this fucking place, or I'm selling my shares," he says, and he's already retreating to his truck.

It's so tempting to go after him, but I don't.

Cameron and I had a great time feeding the ducks today. I'm not going to be explaining to my boy why Daddy's got torn-up knuckles in the morning, not for anything.

"Don't be a fucking dick," I shout as Jake starts the truck up, but he doesn't even look back.

I watch until his taillights turn the corner at the end of the drive, and then I take a breath.

I lean against my truck and allow myself a minute, just me and this burned-out hole, and Mariana's secrets. The ones she took with her.

And then finally, when I know I'm calm enough to look Serena in the eye without tearing her a new one for bringing Jake into my shit, I go home.

bait

abigail

I've been staring at my inbox for an hour when the circle next to his name finally blinks and turns green.

I chew my thumbnail as the tick appears against my message. *He's reading. Right now.*

It's almost midnight and I've allowed myself a couple of glasses of wine to finish up my Saturday evening. It's made me brave. Brave enough to wait online so boldly for him to arrive.

I can see the ending line of my last message, bold as brass on the tab.

Please give me what I need.

I may have cringed if it wasn't for the alcohol.

I wait with tickling nerves, feeling like my broken soul is on parade while a total stranger reads about my nightmares. I wonder what he's thinking.

If he's hard.

If he wants this even half as much as I want this.

My pussy is aching, my belly fluttery with crazy fantasies. I'm already playing with myself when the typing icon shows on screen.

My breath is ragged when the message pings.

I enjoyed reading about your dreams.

I'd be lying if I told you they didn't make me hard. I'd be lying if I told you this conversation hasn't woken something deep.

I'd be dishonest to claim I'm not planning on fucking you like a beast while you beg me to stop.

You're toying with a monster. If you're not careful, I'll bite you hard.

Be very sure you're ready for that.

My reply is easy.

I've been sure forever.

I rub my clit as he carries on typing.

Tell me what your monster does to you when you think of him late at night. Tell me how you need to be broken. How you need to be hurt. Used. Taken.

And then I'll tell you what you're going to be given.

My pussy throbs when I take my fingers away to type.

I don't hold back. Not a single thing.

The monster always catches me from behind. He's strong. Strong enough to pick me up as my legs flail. I'd scream if his hand wasn't over my mouth.

He tells me to stay quiet. Tells me he'll hurt me if I cry out.

I'm tempted to scream just so he'll make it worse for me.

Sometimes he forces me onto the ground, sometimes he drops me to my feet and throws me against a wall, his body pressed tight to mine.

And then he whispers. He always whispers.

He tells me that maybe he'll let me enjoy it if I don't fight him.

Fuck, I've been waiting for this. My clit is thrumming hard. My thighs clenching.

I wait for a response before I carry on.

His reply is just two simple words. All the encouragement I need.

Go on.

I go on.

He pins me tight and tugs my skirt up. He tears my knickers down and pushes his fingers inside me. It's always rough enough to make me cry out.

I'm never ready for him.

I never want to be ready for him.

bait

It always hurts and he always makes me take it.

He grabs my tits so hard it takes my breath. He tells me that I'm a dirty little bitch who asked for this.

Who wants this.

And I am.

I am a dirty little bitch who wants this.

I tug my bra down until my tits spill over the cups. I pinch my nipples until I moan.

I don't need to wait long for another message.

You're a dirty little bitch who's going to get what's coming to you.

My response is instant.

Please.

Please make this real.

Oh fuck, please.

I tug on my nipples and pretend that it's him. I'm desperate for a response as I stare at that screen. Squirming on the bedsheets as my clit begs for release.

It throbs as I get the ping.

If you've any sense you'll stop this right now.

Walk away before you're in too deep.

I don't know quite what he means until a photo icon flashes up.

My heart is in my throat as I click to open.

And fuck.

Fuck.

I'm sober in a beat, shuffling up to sitting as I maximise the image.

No.

It can't be.

There's no way. Just no way. He can't really…

I can't stop staring. My mouth is open wide.

And he's right.

Oh my God, he's right.

If I had any sense I'd stop this right now.

seven

The fishermen know that the sea is dangerous and the storm terrible,
but they have never found these dangers sufficient reason for remaining ashore.

—VINCENT VAN GOGH

phoenix

If she has any sense in that pretty head of hers she'll reply with a *thanks but no thanks.*

Part of me hopes she does.

The other part has my palm straining around the monster I just sent her a picture of. The angle didn't hold anything back – the ladder of barbells on the underside of my cock glinting in metallic horror. The ridges are thick.

Threatening.

I don't need any special camera effects to big up the scale. It's no illusion that sees this weapon of hard flesh and steel towering high above my bellybutton. My hands are big, but they don't look it, not as my fingers stretch around the girth.

Mariana said Christmas had come early when I first dropped my pants.

She changed her mind regularly.

But Mariana was also crazy enough to want more. Always more.

bait

Six bars along the length of me. A thick curve of steel spearing the head.

It always hurt her. Sometimes it drew blood.

Sometimes it even hurt me too.

It'll hurt Abigail. She'll whimper at every fucking inch.

The green circle by her image remains. I wait for a ping that takes an age.

I'm glad she takes her time.

This isn't the place for horny bravado. This isn't a time to feign bravery and hope for the best.

Her reply is simple. Obvious, really.

That's going to hurt.

My fingers grip tighter. I reply with one hand.

Yes. It will.

I grip so hard it pains, my eyes closed at the memory of sublimely tight pussy.

I type slowly. Clumsily.

You need to think about this. Carefully.

My balls are tight enough to blow.

I'm relieved when her reply is at least halfway sane.

I know I should probably slam this laptop closed and write this off as a lucky escape.

A step too far into the crazy.

But I can't.

I still want this.

A pause before the *typing* status shows up again.

I think want it even more than before.

Fuck.

My cock throbs in my grip.

She's not alone on the crazy train. I guess we're both riding all the way to its final destination.

I force myself to slow this runaway down, grappling for at least some semblance of restraint.

I grunt as I loosen my grip. Grit my teeth as my cock protests.

My fingers jab at the keys.

Sleep on it.

Consider it in the cold light of day.

Think about it until you have second thoughts.

Think about it some more after that.

And then, if you still want it, let me know.

I'll look for your message tomorrow night.

A simple yes or no will suffice.

Just make sure it's the right call.

It's me who slams the laptop closed with the green circle still next to her picture.

It's me who moves into the bathroom just to get some distance.

I turn the shower on full blast and kick off my jeans. I'm under the flow in a heartbeat, the jet bearing down on my scalp as I lather up the body wash.

I don't know what I'm trying to scrub away. I don't know why I think cleanliness will make me any less of the monster I feel inside.

I soap down inked skin she'll never see. Years of hopes and fears and dreams etched onto my body for all time.

You can't hide work like this under collars and cuffs, but you can hide it in darkness.

I'm inked from my fingers to my scalp, plenty enough for the world to see. My darkness is palpable. Always has been.

But there's more than ink marking my body. My scars stretch from my shoulder to my spine on my left side. Sometimes I still feel them burning.

Sometimes I still smell my own searing flesh.

Body wash makes no difference. It doesn't touch what's inside.

bait

It doesn't change what I am. *Who* I am.

I grunt as I take my dick back in hand.

It's brutal. Quick. Painful in my grip as I shoot my load all over the tiles.

This girl, Abigail – *bait* – is edging me towards insanity. *Or salvation*. Reawakening a beast I thought died along with the woman I couldn't save.

I nearly died trying. But not *nearly* enough for Jake.

I see it in his eyes every time we're unfortunate enough to cross each other's path.

I saw it tonight. I see it in the mirror too.

Sometimes I fight the regret. Sometimes I don't.

Sometimes regret is all I can feel.

But right now I feel nothing but the urge to pound Abigail's tight cunt until she screams.

I twist the shower setting to cold and groan as the water punishes my skin.

Sometimes, in my dreams, I still hear Mariana screaming on the other side of that door.

Sometimes, late at night, I ask her ghost why she did it.

Why she left our little boy behind. Why she left me.

Why she was there that night in the first place. Why the fire took her and not me.

Why she was in that room alone. Why she was there at all.

Why Jake was there with her.

So many fucking questions.

I turn off the water.

I grab a towel.

For the first time in a while, I contemplate the possibility that maybe I'll never have all the answers.

And for the very first time in forever, ignorance doesn't feel quite so bad.

abigail

I can't stop staring at the picture on screen, even though I know I shouldn't be.

I can't stop playing with myself, even though I shouldn't be doing that either.

I'll never be able to take him.

I can't imagine anyone could.

Stephen was big enough that I had to loosen my jaw to get his dick past my teeth, but he'd be dwarfed by the monster in front of me.

Phoenix Burning is definitely inked. His figures are etched with dark symbols. It looks like there's a rose on the back of his hand. I can only just make it out.

I've never been with a guy with tattoos before.

I've never been with a pierced guy, either. Never even seen a pierced guy.

But I want to.

Oh fuck, how I want to.

I push three fingers inside, and it's tight. Regardless of the fact I'm soaking through my knickers, it's still tight.

I'll never take him. Not unless he…

Fuck.

He'd have to be so brutal.

So rough.

A shiver dances through me, because somewhere, somehow, I know he would be. Could be.

Will be.

Because I already know how this story ends.

bait

I already know I'm riding this wave all the way until it crashes. I already know he's the only thing I want. The only thing I *need*.

Everything else fades away into blissful ignorance, my mind closed off to anything other than the way he'll feel inside me.

There's nothing on my mind but the thought of his palm clamped over my mouth as he whispers filth into my ear.

I wonder how his voice sounds.

I wonder what kind of accent he has.

I minimise the photo long enough to click on his profile again. Malvern, it says. Maybe thirty minutes by car from here. Forty-five tops.

He's close. Really close.

I do have a car, I just rarely use it. It's been in my parking space for weeks, untouched.

I try to imagine driving into the night on my way over to meet him. I imagine parking up somewhere and knowing everything will be different by the time I make it back to the driver's seat.

If I make it back.

The thought is just a whisper, but it's there. It has to be there.

I know nothing about the man on the other side of the chat window. I have no assurances other than the words of a stranger in the ether.

It shouldn't be worth the risk. *Shouldn't.*

I imagine how bandy my legs will feel as the moment draws close.

My heart is pounding. Nerves tight.

My legs loll open as I fuck myself with three deep fingers.

Yes.

I know the answer I'll be giving him already.

I've known the answer since he messaged me for the very first time. It'll take more than one graphic picture to divert this collision.

The circle next to his profile picture is grey when I type out my response.

I don't need to sleep on it.

I'm not impulsive enough to need time for the doubts to creep in.

They are already here. They've been dancing behind my eyes since the moment you messaged me. They are always here and always have been, but they make no difference.

Your picture is enough to scare me, but fear changes nothing. It never has.

If anything it only makes me want this more.

My answer is most definitely yes.

I pause.

I read it through with shallow breath.

And then I hit send.

eight

Don't judge each day by the harvest you reap but by the seeds that you plant.

—ROBERT LOUIS STEVENSON

phoenix

The message is waiting for me in the morning, well ahead of schedule. It's listed in my notifications, ready to greet me when my alarm goes off. I feel an unfounded sense of acceptance as I power up the hill track and admire the rising sun. She saw, she feared, and still she wants.

This surreal sense of intimacy with a stranger is full of surprises. The spring in my step. The lightness in the air.

The beautiful promise of one wild night to dwarf all others, and the bittersweet inevitability that we're destined to go our separate ways when we're done.

Maybe it's the impermanence that feels so beautiful. Maybe it's the knowledge that our collision will be short which promises such a potent explosion.

I breathe in the view at the top and today my eyes are on the horizon, scanning the Herefordshire countryside.

She's down there, somewhere. I wonder what she's doing. I wonder where she is.

bait

Sleeping, if she's got any sense on a Sunday morning.

Training her pussy to take a decent girth if she has any sense at all.

Her profile is limited. A simple *Hereford* and nothing more listed as her location. As of yet I know so much but so little.

The shadowy promise of dawn breaking as I uncover all her broken pieces.

Dawn's always been my favourite time of day with good reason.

I wave to the same couple as yesterday on my way across the top. I tip my head to the same guy and his dog on my way back down.

I shower quickly, then make my boy his breakfast and watch him choose his own TV channel.

I pull my sister tight to my chest and kiss her head, because gestures are easier than words sometimes.

And then, as another first of all the firsts these past few days, I sit down at the kitchen table and breathe. Just breathe.

My feet feel planted on solid earth for the first time in months. My place here feels real again.

I wonder if it feels the same for her, wherever she is. Whether the universe is looking a little brighter through her eyes this morning, just as it is through mine.

I'll need to know her, *Abigail*. I'll need to know so much more than she'll ever get to know about me.

The things she craves. The tiny details of her fantasy she isn't even aware of herself. What she looks like to a passer-by on the street. What her footsteps sound like in the darkness.

I'll need to know enough to safeguard me against a crazy encounter gone bad. I need a message trail that shows irrevocably that she wants this just as much as I do.

That she's a girl I know indulging in a fantasy we planned out, not just some random I accosted in the darkness.

But for now I push those more sobering thoughts aside.

I'm buoyant on the hum of life, and nothing is going to steal this moment from me.

Not today.

abigail

I usually cringe inside when the office girls ask after my weekend. I hate the way my polite vagueness always feels so hollow.

But not today.

There's excitement simmering in my belly as I smile in the kitchen before work starts. I feel bouncier than usual as I tell them my weekend was good, and for once I'm not lying.

For once it's true.

It seems midnight is the magic hour for Phoenix Burning. Last night was the most magical of all.

I'm not sure how much more I'll have to do to prove my intentions are serious over these coming weeks, but I think I'm well on my way already.

He wanted pictures, and I sent them. Happy pictures from days long past. An old work portrait. A couple of riskier selfies that I took on a whim.

And now it seems he wants more. Always more.

He's tugging my soul from the depths and holding tight. He's whispering in every dark corner of my mind.

An unexpected ping on my mobile lets me know I've got a message mid-morning. I know exactly who it is before I've even checked.

I call it up at my desk with the handset cradled in my lap out of sight.

bait

What is your full name?

The question takes me aback enough that my head swims.

My full name.

This crazy fantasy has never felt so real as it does when I tell him. The fear is there. Palpable. Creeping around the edges of my consciousness as my heart thumps.

Abigail Summers.

Abigail Rachel Summers.

And then silence. Nothing but a tick as he reads my response.

So I busy myself. Throw myself into a job I usually pass off as nothing.

I restructure my filing system for purchase orders and automate some of the processes. I act as if I care, and slowly, over the course of my Monday, and my Tuesday after that, part of me begins to believe it.

I pick up the overflow calls when they come into our back office. I speak with clients with a telephone voice I'd long forgotten.

I find myself laughing with colleagues at the photocopier.

I find myself agreeing to their office social later in the week.

I don't know when the pretence falls away and my actions take on a reality, but they do. By Wednesday afternoon I've even taken on a backlog of invoices from a colleague fresh in from sick leave.

At night I share my deepest fantasies with a total stranger, and by day I find myself taking tiny steps toward being human again.

I don't ignore messages from old friends back home. I call my parents as I walk home from the office. I shop for real food rather than ready meals and I buy myself a decent set of pans.

Life always prospers on fertile ground. Slowly but surely, seeds burst into tiny shoots and the barren pit of me stirs with my soul and sparks anew.

My nightmares have never been so vivid nor so welcome.

Busy days have never been such a happy time-killer.

I never again expected to enjoy a work night out for what it is.

But I do.

I never expected to race home for midnight with a heart full of excitement for a faceless man at the end of an internet connection.

But I do.

And I really never expected tonight to be the night he says goodbye.

But it is.

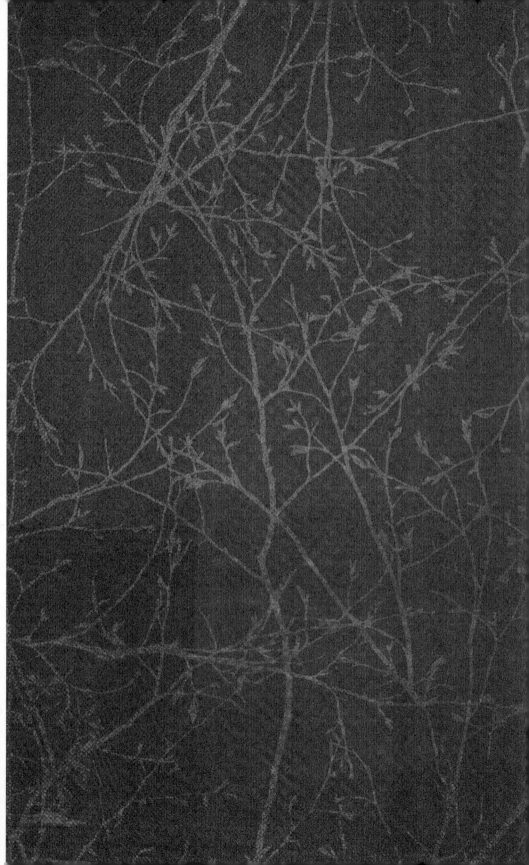

nine

The return makes one love the farewell.

—ALFRED DE MUSSET

abigail

A few glasses of wine with the girls from work turns out to be a fine way to pass the time until midnight calls. I actually enjoyed myself. And now, I'm back in my apartment and logged in when the light turns green on his profile.

I doubt he can be left with any uncertainty by now as to how sure I am that I want this. The thought makes my skin prickle.

I'm already so used to this strange sense of closeness. I know nothing, and yet I feel so much. I don't even know his name, and likely never will, but that doesn't matter. It's only taken one short week for this time of night to feel like my everything.

My stomach flutters as the first ping comes through. I wonder if I should tell him I'm drunk.

I wonder if I should tell him that my life has become liveable again since he came along.

bait

Even in my inebriated condition I know that would be a stupid thing to confess.

His message gives me shivers,

There's only one nightclub in Malvern.

It's on an industrial estate down by the Link train station.

Next Saturday evening you will park at the station.

You will cross the road and take the path along Spring Lane, and then walk through the estate until you get to Fireflies.

You will be on soft drinks only, but you will have a good time.

You will dance, even though your nerves will be spiking like crazy.

You will stay as long as you like.

And then you will leave.

You will walk back slowly the way you came.

And you will be careful, keeping an eye over your shoulder the whole time.

If you feel scared, you will run.

His messages pause and I can't hold back. My fingers are a flurry on my keyboard.

And you'll be there? You'll be there to chase me? Next weekend for real?

My heart is racing as he types a response.

You will meet your monster, just be sure you really want to be acquainted.

I do. Oh fuck, I do. My whole body is thrumming.

His messages keep coming before I can reply.

You can turn back whenever you wish.

You can decide against coming at all.

You can call a taxi from the club to your car and never step foot in the shadows.

Changing your mind would be easy, but still, if you want a safe word you can have one.

My response is instant.

I don't want one and I won't be changing my mind.

I'll be there.

His reply comes right back.

So will I.

I can't believe this is really happening. A strange bubble of emotion brings a lump to my throat. But it's not sadness.

It's relief.

Excitement.

Or it is until he messages again.

This will be the last time we speak, but before we say goodbye, I want you to know that I've really enjoyed our conversations.

I hope this turns out to be everything you were hoping for, and that it brings you to life again.

My stomach falls through the floor. I'm not ready for goodbye. Goodbye hasn't even been on my radar. Not even close.

I know this is a one off. I know it was always meant to be.

I know that saying goodbye is inevitable. I just… I don't want… not now.

I'm struggling for words when another ping comes through.

For what it's worth, I think the guy who left you alone in your darkest hour is the weakest kind of asshole. Please don't let him steal more of your soul than he already has. Believe me when I say he's not worth it.

The lump in my throat spills into a stupid tear. But strangely it's not Stephen I'm crying for.

I force myself to type.

Wow. Goodbyes always feel so shitty, hey?

I swat my tears away as he pings again.

So I've found.

I'm dreading the circle turning grey, but the typing icon stays solid.

And then more.

bait

I'm sorry for everything you've been through. Truly.

His words make my heart pang.

I'm sorry too.

I'm sorry for the things in my life I wanted and will most likely never have, but mostly I'm grateful for him – the stranger who's giving me back my heart, even if it's still bleeding.

I'm not ready for the next message.

I'm not ready for the circle next to his picture to blink out.

Goodbye, Abigail.

I'm still typing when the text box dulls to grey along with his icon. My fingers are still slamming the keys when *Phoenix Burning* changes to *user unavailable*.

And then he's gone.

He's really gone.

My bleeding heart bleeds some more, but this time I'm still smiling.

This time goodbye is bittersweet.

Because this time the best is still to come.

phoenix

Severing our intimacy across the ether hits me deep. Really fucking deep.

Saying goodbye to my black swan is a tragedy, but it's a beautiful one.

It feels harder than I thought, but it has to be this way.

When, *if*, we meet in the darkness, we will meet as strangers and nothing more. I will be a monster and she will be my bait.

Silence feeds the thrill and excitement. It also feeds fear.

There will be no daily contact to offer reassurances. No running commentary to put her demons at ease.

If she really does arrive at the club next weekend it'll be because she was right all along – she really does crave this fantasy too much to leave it alone.

And if she doesn't?

My gut turns at the thought.

And if she doesn't the world keeps on spinning.

I don't know why that feels like such a bullshit lie.

I stare at the logout screen for an age, fighting the urge to reactivate my profile and feign an unanswered question. Something of importance. Anything to keep the channel of communication open just a little bit longer.

My cock is aching in my jeans as I stare numbly ahead.

I have her photographs saved to my desktop. I also have her current address, and the one in Hampshire she lived in before that.

The electoral roll software at work has more benefits than scoping out bad client credit risks, it seems.

I had her history at my fingertips, right there for the taking.

Abigail Rachel Summers. Twenty-seven years old. Six years younger than me.

Born in Fleet. Excellent credit rating.

I found her on the business connect website, keeping my search anonymous. She hasn't updated her profile with her new position, whatever that may be, but in her old life she was doing well for herself.

Head of Customer Relations at some business services company. Her profile picture was smiley and professional, her dark hair in one of those fancy buns. Her work pictures show a woman who is comfortable in her own skin. Comfortable with her place in the universe.

I feel so fucking sad for her that the universe chewed her up.

Stephen Hartley is a listed contact in her organisation overview. Sales Director. Handsome guy. Longish hair. Maybe a hint of throwback goth if you took the suit out of the equation.

Somehow I know he's the douche in question. Call it instinct.

I feel all her broken pieces. I feel her sadness. Her hopelessness. Her despair.

I'm no fool. I know she's mirroring my own. I know it's my own hopelessness reflected right back at me.

It doesn't make it any less real.

Stephen Hartley is every kind of spineless. I have the urge to hunt him down and give the prick some payback, which is all the confirmation I'll ever need that deactivating my profile and treating this fantasy as the one-time-only affair it's intended to be is the only rational move available.

It's definitely rational.

Painful.

Uncomfortable.

Sad, almost.

But rational.

I allow myself one last lingering look at my black swan before I close my laptop.

And then, with my cock in my hand, I imagine the next, and only, time I'll ever see her again.

ten

We need the sweet pain of anticipation to tell us we are really alive.

—ALBERT CAMUS

abigail

I've never known a week pass by so slowly.

All the time-killers in the universe couldn't make the days go any faster, and no amount of fantasising in the world makes up for the void I feel every night when midnight comes and he isn't there.

I keep my profile active, just in case. I log in every night just to stare at his greyed-out profile.

I read our previous messages until they give me shivers.

I stare at the photo of his beast of a cock and imagine how it will feel to have it forced inside me.

I wonder if I'll beg him to stop. I wonder if he'll make me bleed.

I come at the thought of both.

I'm fucked up and I don't care. I'm flying high, unhinged and free.

Insane.

I'm clearly fucking insane.

I come until I'm exhausted. Over and over and over again.

I barely sleep.

And when I wake, the first thing I do is log on to stare at his greyed-out profile again.

And read those messages again.

And stare at that monster cock, the horrific piercings, and come again, imagining it pumping inside me, so hard, so rough, so bad I'm screaming.

Insane.

Clearly insane.

The days of silence bring distance. His earlier familiarity easily fades, leaving only the promise of darkness.

I'm not ready for him and I never will be, but I'd be a fool not to at least try to ready myself. I buy myself a vibrator online, one they aptly call *The Monster*, and open the parcel with shaking fingers just three days before I meet the monster for real.

I have his cock on screen and my fingers on my clit when I try my new purchase.

Beautiful dread hits hard as I strain to get the head in. I'm panting like a whore when my pussy finally gives in enough to take it. The stretch hurts so bad that I have to grit my teeth.

I imagine it's him. Imagine that I have no choice.

I'm sobbing at the ache. Flinching at the way every inch hurts like hell.

But I keep on going. I make my pussy take it, just like he will. I whimper a mantra of *no, no, no,* and I like it. I hope he likes it too.

I hope it makes him fuck me harder.

Oh fuck, how I want him to fuck me hard.

I push onto *The Monster* and cry out as it fills me.

I fuck myself until I'm raw just thinking about him. I fuck myself until I'm thrashing in my own sweat and my pussy is a burning squelching mess.

And so it goes on.

Every waking moment my thoughts are for him.

And in those scarce moments where I'm not either working or playing with myself, I'm planning my date with my nightmare.

I left most of my evening wear in a charity shop back in Hampshire. It makes my choices easier at least.

I'm going to be wearing my one remaining little black dress and it's a good one.

It's tight. Flattering. Short enough that my bare legs will feel noticeably exposed.

Wearing it makes me feel good. Even a little bit slutty.

My highest heels will make running difficult. The bait will be easy to snare when the time comes. I doubt I'll outrun him even ten paces.

And it's crazy.

This whole thing is too crazy for words. Too crazy to ever survive being spoken aloud, so it's a good thing I have nobody left to share it with.

I'm going to be attacked by a stranger on a dark night in a strange town. Once I leave that club I'll have no way out. No safe word. No friend waiting on standby to come to my aid.

Just me and him – the monster and his steel-sculpted dick and his promise to fuck me up bad.

I might be walking into the biggest mistake of my life, but I'll be doing it with a smile on my crazy face.

I'm rational enough to contemplate the possibility that Phoenix Burning is some kind of serial killer psychopath, and I'm painfully aware that my night with him could be my last.

I know the risks. I feel them in every fibre of my body.

They make me feel more alive than I've ever felt in my life.

bait

The thrill must be contagious. In that one working week alone I'm invited out on three different socials. I'm included in more photocopier gossip sessions than I've been party to in the entire four months previous. I'm buzzing on an insane high.

And then finally, after the longest week in all eternity, I'm standing in front of my full-length mirror in my little black dress.

My hair is washed and straightened. My eyes have a cat flick that's right on point. My lips are ruby red.

My bra is black lace and barely covers my nipples. My thong is a scrap of lace that will grant no modesty.

My perfume is Dior and my handbag holds nothing but my phone, keys, and purse. No hidden weapons. No emergency panic alarm should things get out of control.

In honesty, if tonight turns out to be my last, and Phoenix Burning turns out to be the one who ends me, I'll just be bummed that he delivered so much colour to my life before he took it away.

My legs barely carry me to my car when the time comes. My knees tremble all the way through my drive into Malvern. My heart is in my throat when I see the sign for Malvern Link train station.

I pick a space by the ticket booth. I steady my breath before I dare to risk getting out and standing.

It's still light outside, plenty bright enough to lend the illusion that I'm just a girl on a night out. But the illusion lends me no confidence. My eyes dart all around me with every step, my body braced to run every time someone appears in view.

But I keep it together.

I keep on walking, and underneath the fear I'm wanting this just as much as I always have.

The road leads through an industrial estate, just as he said it would. The buildings are tall and looming, even in the evening light.

No doubt they'll be terrifying in the darkness.

Even though my mouth is bone dry and my legs feel boneless, my bare thighs are noticeably clammy as I wait in line for entry to the club. My clit tingles every time I shift position in the queue.

I'm a jittery mess as I take a seat at the edge of the bar, scanning the gathering crowds for any sign of him.

I sip my Coke and I wonder if I'll recognise him. If somehow his dark intentions will shine their light right back at mine. I look for what I know – dark features and inked skin, but it's busy. Too dark and crowded to stand a hope in hell of identifying some random guy in the room.

I wonder if he's watching me. I wonder if he's been following me all along.

He told me to dance, so I do. My body feels clumsy and my heels make me feel like I'm twirling on toothpicks. Every breath feels tight, but I don't care.

I hope he can see me.

I hope he's hard.

The week leading up to this took a thousand years. The hours in the club pass by in a breath.

I freshen up in the bathroom and flinch as I check the time on my phone.

Shit.

Midnight has been and gone already. Two hours left before closing and I know it's time to go.

It's obvious why he chose this place. It's remote – so far from the main High Street that the surroundings will be deserted. Dangerous.

Just a few short steps from the safety of the club and I'll be easy prey.

I clench my thighs tight to help with the nerves, and it's there. The need is right there. It's never been more there than it is right now.

I thought my nightmares were as real as waking life, but I was wrong.

bait

This is waking life. Waking life feels hyper real. Waking life is petrifying.

My terror is in my throat, even though I haven't even left yet. My palms are clammy and my eyes look wild in the mirror as they stare back at me.

But I want it.

Even though I feel like a crazy person, I still want it. *Him.*

I try to calm myself in a cubicle, but it's pointless. I've reached critical mass, fight or flight, so when I move again I do so with purpose – straight through the throng of dancing bodies and out the other side. I grab my jacket from the cloakroom attendant and smile politely at the security staff on the door.

I resist the urge to confess my stupidity and beg them to call me a cab, but it's close. I daren't even look back at them as I leave the lights of the club behind me.

So I walk.

Quickly.

Toward the darkness with my heart in my throat and my life in the hands of a stranger, until there are no lights left at all.

phoenix

She's terrified.

So terrified that I doubted she'd ever leave that club on foot, but she did.

She's been looking for me for hours. I enjoyed every frantic turn of her head. Every little jolt her body made when someone came too close.

Luckily, I know the shadows well enough that she'll never see me, not before I want her to.

She didn't see me in the truck in the car park. Didn't see me hanging back far enough to remain out of eyeline as I followed her across the industrial estate.

She walked right past me on her way to the bathroom, brushed my arm on her route-march out of there.

As I follow at a distance, I wonder if she'll fight. If she'll spit and curse and scream. If she'll claw at my face like Mariana did.

But she's nothing like Mariana.

Abigail wears her vulnerability so perfectly. So easily.

Her steps are quick and frantic. I can feel her fear right through me.

The security of the club is long behind her when her pace begins to slow. The lighting around here is sparse at best, and her heels are perilous. She knows it.

I hang back, enjoying the view as she spins a 360 under a street lamp.

My cock is throbbing. The barbells grind against denim with every step I take. The beast is behind my eyes, straining to run wild. It takes every scrap of self-restraint to let her go just a little bit further.

And then I quicken.

I let her hear my footsteps on the tarmac in the shadows behind her, and then I stop.

She freezes. Listens. Pauses on the edge of flight.

Her terror captivates me.

My black swan is beautifully petrified.

There's still a part of me that wants to watch her safely back to her car and leave her be, but I'm in too deep.

I need this just as much as she does. Maybe even more.

Fuck, how I fucking need this.

I savour that final perfect moment of stillness as I pull a coin from my inside pocket. My eyes are right on her as I flick it in her direction.

I wait for the ping as it lands.

She jumps. Starts. Freezes for one frantic heartbeat.

And then she runs.

Fuck, she fucking runs.

And so do I.

I know where she's headed, even though she doesn't. The adrenaline of the chase turns me into the monster she craves, and I know she hears me. I know she feels me.

I head to her left and she runs to the right. Runs further into the darkness.

The bait is snared.

Mine.

She's herded like a lone little lamb and she has no fucking idea.

The ground turns rough under her heels. I watch her stumble and catch herself. There is elegance in her misstep.

She corrects herself quickly to keep on running, but she's too late.

Much too late.

I go in for the kill.

The force of me knocks the breath from her as I slam into her back.

My hand clamps over her mouth and steals her scream.

I'm rough as I grip her tight to my chest. My arm is crushing as it snakes around her waist. I'm brutal as I lift her feet from the ground.

She sucks in air through her nose as she struggles for breath.

And I'm waiting. Ready for the fight. Waiting for the nails on my scalp and the assault as she flails.

But it doesn't come.

eleven

I would rather be a superb meteor, every atom of me in magnificent glow, than a sleepy and permanent planet.

—JACK LONDON

abigail

In my fantasies the monster always catches me from behind. He's strong. Strong enough to pick me up as my legs flail.

In real life the monster is too.

This monster is huge, his arm so tight around my waist that I struggle to breathe. He's the solid wall of muscle against my back. He's the firm hand over my open mouth.

He's heat, and breath, and terror.

He's my most beautiful nightmare.

And he's real.

Tonight, he's real.

His arms are thick and tense, hoisting me from my feet as though I weigh nothing at all.

My fingers dig into his forearms and find them unyielding. My legs grapple for grip but find nothing.

I have no breath to scream, nor strength to fight him. I thought the struggle would come naturally, but it doesn't.

I'm paralysed.

I wonder if he can feel my drumming heart as he carries me further into the darkness. I wonder if he feels how my wired nerves spiral away with me.

I'm rigid in his grip, but I don't struggle – my eyes wide in the pitch black, straining to find bearings where I have none. His boots crunch on gravel underfoot. We're in the shadow of brickwork, one of those looming buildings hides us from the deserted street.

Alone.

There is numbing liberation in the way I know no one is coming for me. I feel myself falling into myself, all of my pieces contracting to protect my broken soul.

But I don't want protecting.

I don't need to be protected from this.

It's everything I ever wanted and more than I ever feared, all at once.

The monster speaks.

"Don't make a fucking sound. I'll hurt you if you do."

His voice is low. Deep and dark and threatening.

And I'm every bit as fucked up as I ever feared. Underneath the terror and the dread and my racing heart, I realise my clit is fluttering.

My pussy clenches, and it aches. It fucking aches for him.

My nipples are stiff against the lace of my bra. My hands are clammy and desperate as they grip at his skin.

"Understand?" he whispers.

I nod and the hand across my mouth moves with me.

I whimper into his palm as he slams my body into a doorway. Shutters rattle loud enough to make me squeak.

He drops me to my feet and pins me against the door with a heavy arm against my back, forcing me against it so hard it hurts my tits, my face squashing against cold metal.

"Quiet," he tells me and I nod again, barely able to breathe he's holding me so tight.

I flatten my palms against the door and push back hard in the quest for even an inch of space, but he doesn't budge.

He hitches and grinds, and I feel him.

Oh fuck, I feel him.

Bigger than the monster toy I used at home. Bigger than I ever feared. *Hoped.*

I whimper under my breath as he finds my wrists and raises them over my head. They're so small in his hands. Breakable.

I'm so small. Breakable.

He pins both of my arms in position with just one of his, and the other snakes around my front and tugs my slutty bra down with my dress. My tits flatten against cold metal. My nipples are tight and tender, sparking against the chill.

He kicks my legs spread with his boots, and I sink lower, teetering precariously from his solid grip on my wrists.

Cool air hits my clammy thighs. I roll my tits against the metal door and I like it. I'm more petrified than I've ever been in my whole entire life, but I hear myself moan.

Thick fingers slide between skin and shutters. Thick fingers grab at my tit and squeeze until I whimper.

And I can't help myself. I tip my head back against the ridge of his collarbone and let myself ride the craziness.

"You fucking asked for this," he whispers, and I smile a crazy smile in the darkness.

Yes.

I asked for this.

I fucking *begged* for this.

Dreamed of this my whole life.

He pinches my nipple so hard it takes my breath, then tugs me back from the shutters enough to trail his fingers over my goose-pimpled skin.

I arch my back and hope he gives me more. My body begs for more.

And then I lie.

It comes so easily.

"No… please don't…"

He grips and twists, mashing my tit flat against my ribs.

"No…" I breathe again. "Please stop…"

His breaths quicken with mine. He presses tighter against my ass.

He likes it.

He wants it like this.

Part of me comes undone – a stray part that feels alien to the rest of me.

It's that part that whimpers as he tugs my dress up around my waist. It's that part that's begging him to let me go as he slides a rough hand between my legs.

I'm offering my pussy to his fingers even as the protests are tumbling from my mouth.

"No… *don't*…"

I'm delirious and fucked up. Euphoric and horrified all at the same time.

My pussy aches so good at his touch, my clit a desperate little bitch.

His thumb hooks inside my thong and presses right on target.

"Please no…" I hiss. "Please stop… stop…"

He yanks the scrap of fabric so hard it tears from my hips. When his fingers force their way inside me there's three of them at once with no warning.

He's rough. Fast.

Brutal.

"Your cunt is so fucking tight," he grunts.

I cry out as he forces his fingers in deeper. My eyes water as he makes me take it.

"I haven't even fucking started yet," he tells me, and I know it.

His thumb rolls against my clit. I hear the wetness and I feel so vulnerable I want to die in his arms.

Maybe I will.

He lets go of my wrists and flattens me tighter against the shutters. His fingers slide around my throat and squeeze hard enough to make me rasp.

His mouth is on my neck. His breath is all I can hear.

I don't know what to do with the freedom he's just granted my wrists. My arms hang lifeless at my sides until I feel daring enough to touch him. To feel him.

I'll never know the stranger in the darkness, but my fingers will.

So slowly I reach up behind me, my fingers trail up the back of his neck. Solid.

He's fucking massive.

My fingertips graze soft hair, *shaved sides*, then tangle in longer lengths on top. I'd give anything to see him.

I'm grunting as his fingers piston deep, begging him to stop with every breath. I shuffle my legs just a little bit wider, praying he keeps rubbing my clit the way he is right now. Just like that.

But he doesn't.

I groan as he pulls his fingers away.

He takes hold of my hair and yanks me from the shutters along with him. My heels scrabble against the gravel as I stumble after him.

He pulls me further from the road. We turn a corner at the rear of the building, and I see a row of huge trucks as a security light blinks on in the distance.

I could scream. Part of me wants to.

But I don't.

He shunts me in front of him as we dip between two trucks. I twist to face him, but I've missed my chance to see. It's dark again. My adrenaline is spiking all over.

And then he pushes me to the ground. I cry out as my knees hit the concrete. I feel them graze as he shoves me forward on all fours. The ground is rough against my palms, but rougher against my face when he forces me flat.

Oh God. Oh my fucking God.

He positions himself behind me, lifts my dress and slides his fingers all the way back in. I know what's coming when I hear his belt buckle. I panic when I hear the zip of his jeans.

I struggle but go nowhere. My pleads feel thick in my throat as hot fear takes over me.

I feel pitiful.

Sad.

Beautiful.

Happy.

Joyous.

Out of fucking control.

I'm surprised when the tears prick at my eyes. I'm embarrassed how I spread my legs even as the first sobs come.

I flinch as I feel the head of him. He's too big. Too hard.

"Please..."

And I'm crying as his cock rubs back and forth between my pussy lips. I feel the ridges of metal and know he's going to fuck me up.

"Please..."

I let out a strange feral sob as he pushes the tip inside.

"This is gonna fucking hurt," he says.

phoenix

It takes some serious fucking resolve not to slam my cock balls deep into Abigail's beautifully tight cunt in one thrust, damned be the consequences for me as well as her.

Luckily, resolve is something I've long cultivated.

Still, I really do feel like a monster as I deliver the nightmare she begged me for.

She's a mess on all fours before me, her breath raspy with tears as her whole body trembles. Her adrenaline is off the charts and has been for a while.

But she stays still like a good girl. Like she was born for this.

Maybe she was. Maybe she was right all along and she really does need this. Maybe she always will.

Like Mariana.

Abigail is nothing like Mariana. Mariana was fiery and sensational and easy to read. Mariana liked to hiss and spit and go down hard.

Abigail is a delicate blend of pure fucking crazy. Elegant and dirty and needy and vulnerable.

Insane.

Fucking insane.

And I feel insane right along with her. This lunacy has been a long time coming. Maybe too long.

Her legs stay nice and wide for me, even though they're shaking. Her back is arched, her soaking wet pussy offered readily for the brutality she's convinced is coming her way.

I admire the way she thinks I'm going to tear her apart and she still doesn't try to run.

I admire the way she's really all in with this, even though she must be fucking petrified.

"Please…" she whimpers.

I shunt my hips enough to sink the tip, and even though she's sopping fucking wet, it still takes some force.

She breaks enough to sob a little. It's pitifully beautiful enough that my balls tighten.

"This is gonna fucking hurt," I tell her and she cries out as she braces herself for the impact.

It doesn't come.

I wrap her hair around my fist in a heartbeat, the thick end of my cock still snug in her perfect cunt as I tip her head back.

She's close enough to kiss. But I don't.

Even though I want to, I don't.

She's close enough that I could tell her she's gonna be just fine if I wanted to. But I don't offer any assurances.

My breath is a whisper in her ear. "Don't fucking fight it."

Her cheek is wet with tears. She nods again and takes a ragged breath.

She holds it in and grits her teeth as I inch my way inside her. It's slow. Tortured. Tight enough to burn. And she hisses as I crush her with my full weight, my legs pushing hers wide and holding them. I pull her hair into a high pony and brush my lips across the back of her neck.

Her moan is divine.

It's even better when I bite her.

My teeth nip and hold, my grunts low in my throat as my cock gains ground.

In and out, claiming her slowly, firmly, as she hisses out a breath with each thrust.

I'm steady with each barbell, careful as I edge them inside her, but there's a desperation in the way I move. I can't stop. Can't hold back.

She tenses and groans underneath me as her poor pussy takes it all, but this isn't the assault she feared and we both know it.

There's no way I can bottom out in her, not in one go, and that's a damn fucking shame. A real damn fucking shame.

I just can't.

I take what I can, pushing for just a little bit more with every thrust, well aware this beautiful nightmare is speeding fast towards its closing act.

Its only ever act.

"I want that cunt," I whisper. "Give it to me."

I change angle just enough that the metal inside hits the right spot, and she can't fight it any more than I can.

She squirms and moans.

Wriggles and whimpers.

Bucks as much as she fucking dares.

Her legs part wider of their own accord, and I know I'm going to give her the most painful fucking orgasm she's ever had.

"That's it," I grunt. "Good girl."

Her breaths are pained but needy.

She wants more and I know it. I feel it.

I fuck her as deep as I can without tearing her. She takes everything she's given.

Her hair smells like coconut.

Her neck smells like a beauty counter.

She tastes like I never want this to be over.

"Please…" she whimpers. "More…"

And I smile against her skin. I smile at the crazy.

I smile at how two random strangers can be a million degrees of fucked up and still feel so right.

"Come for me," I hiss. "Come for your monster."

And she does.

I let go of her hair, grab her tits hard and fuck her like the nightmare she wanted me to be.

With my beast of a dick stretching her pussy to gaping and metal bars grating her deep, she comes for me as she cries out.

It's wild. It's hard.

And it's fucking everything as she jerks and whimpers.

It takes my all not to flip her over and fuck her eye to eye.

It takes every scrap of restraint not to plant my mouth on hers and kiss her like I mean it.

And I'd mean it.

I realise that she's inside me as deep as I'm inside her.

She's supposed to cry *no*, not *yes,* when my balls tighten and I thrust in hard.

I'm not supposed to finish off in her pussy.

I'm not supposed to come inside her.

I'm not supposed to grunt and shudder and unload deep as she pants for me.

It shouldn't feel like heaven as her sweet crazy cunt milks me dry.

She shouldn't make me feel the way she's making me feel right now.

My black swan is supposed to be fighting to get away, not lying sated underneath me with her cheek on the tarmac as I pull my barbells free one by one.

My breaths are heavy on her neck as I lift myself free.

I'm reeling as I shove my cock back in my jeans.

She still doesn't move. Not even an inch.

She's a wreck in the shadows with her legs spread wide, glancing over her shoulder as though she wants round two.

But I'm already retreating. Already backing away into the darkness.

I register her confusion. The disappointment in the way her eyes search, until she moves enough to feel the mess she's in.

She's taken enough. So much more than enough already.

She winces as she rises. Cries out as she registers how rough she just had it.

I watch her ease slowly to her feet, so slowly. Tenderly.

I watch her find her bearings and come to her senses.

She staggers before she finds her balance – a few precarious footsteps before she's on her way barefoot, her heels lost in the dark.

I watch my black swan back through the trucks and out the other side. I watch her feel her way along the building and back to the main road.

I watch as she finds the handbag she didn't even realise she'd dropped earlier.

I watch her all the way back to her car and out of my life.

There's a terrible knot in my gut as she drives out of sight.

And a terrible sense of regret that I'll never see her again.

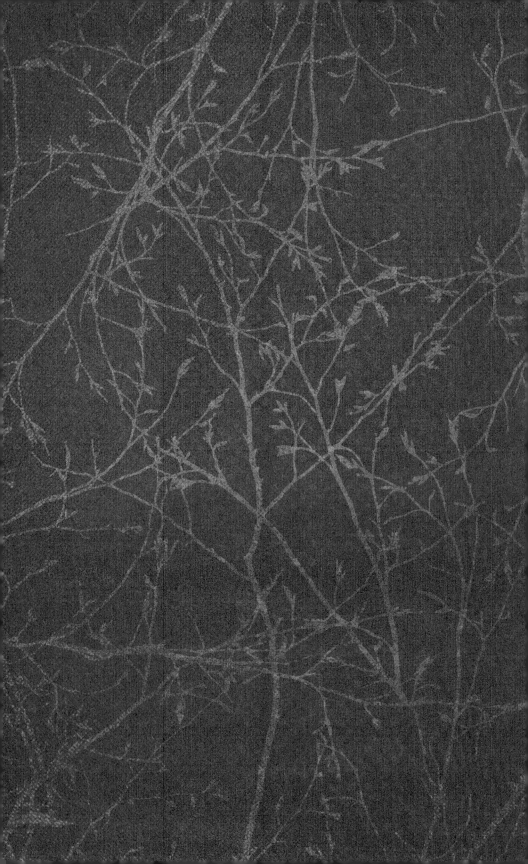

twelve

Whenever a thing is done for the first time, it releases a little demon.

—EMILY DICKINSON

abigail

I'm knickerless and barefoot, my clammy fingers trembling against the steering wheel as I head back to familiarity. My heart is still racing, my brain is fried, and I feel like I've just been donkey-kicked in the ovaries, but I'm smiling. Grinning from ear to ear, in fact. I feel like a caged animal seeing sunlight for the first time in years.

I find myself laughing, high on relief and euphoria and the crazy urge to turn the car back around and do it all again.

My thighs are slippery and my knees are stinging. My toes feel cold and clumsy against the pedals and my hair is a tangled mess. And as far as my pussy goes, I'm a burning mess down there.

But it doesn't matter.

None of it matters.

I did it.

I met the monster and came out the other side.

I met the monster and I *loved* it. He was everything I dreamed and more.

He was everything, everything, EVERYTHING.

I wish I had someone to blurt it all out to, even just so they could call me crazy. I wish I had somewhere to scream out my overflowing endorphins.

I have neither, so it's just me and my tumble of thoughts and the memory of his brutal touch against my skin. *Inside* me.

I was reckless. Irresponsible. Asking for trouble. Crazy as all living fuck.

But the risk paid off.

Fuck, how it paid off.

I indicate into a layby once Malvern is behind me and turn on the interior light to check out my injuries. Grazed knees, a scuff on my palm. Filthy feet. I think I've cut my heel, too.

Even tugging my skirt up my thighs makes me wince. *Ow, fucking ow.*

This is going to hurt tomorrow. Bad.

Insanely enough that feels like a good thing, the memory worth clinging onto just as long as I can. It was really real. More real than anything I've ever done.

I'm brave now, so much braver than I was back there. Brave enough that I'd do it all again in a heartbeat.

And then it hits me like a punch in the ribs.

I won't be doing this again in a heartbeat. Or ever.

I don't have the slightest idea how to contact him again if I wanted to. Wouldn't recognise him in a line-up. I don't even know his name.

I force that unwelcome thought aside for the time being. Why ruin a great experience with practicalities? It's not as if they've worried me so far.

No. Now's the time to revel in the beautiful aftermath.

My demons are running free, dancing with the devil on my shoulder. My sensibilities are long put to bed, and in their place is a wildness I don't yet recognise as me, but I want to.

I hope this wildness stays. This freedom stays.

I want to feel this high forever.

And before I'm even safely back across the Herefordshire border I'm already praying I'll see the monster again.

phoenix

I locate one of Abigail's shoes under a truck. The other is upturned on the gravel nearby.

I find her torn scrap of knickers on the ground by the shutter doors. The discovery makes my cock twitch all over again.

I stuff the mementos in my glove box for safekeeping, then open up the warehouse to clear the security footage before anyone else finds it first.

She'll never have any idea that we were playing on my turf. Never know how meticulously I planned this.

It's almost a shame. *Almost.*

I watch the recording through before I hit erase. Just as I planned, there isn't so much to see from that angle, just me and a figure in my arms before I slam her into the shadows.

It's still enough to ensure I have my dick in my hand before the recording is done. I can smell her on me. Taste her on my fingers.

I can still feel her pussy around my cock as she strained to take me.

And I'm wanting more.

I'm already wanting fucking more.

One-time-only never felt so tragic as it does right now.

I hit delete and shove my dick back in my pants before I go any further with this insanity.

It's done. Finished. One filthy splurge to fulfil a stranger's fantasy and nothing more. I just hope it was everything she was hoping for.

I lock up and head home. It's both very late and very early when I slide my key into the porch lock and step inside.

My jeans are filthy on the knees, my cock is slick with everything she had to give me. I feel gloriously fucking filthy and that's enough to bring a smile to my lips.

A big fucking smile.

Crazy girl. She really is a fucking crazy girl.

I'm heading upstairs for a shower and bed when I notice the bottle on the coffee table. It stops me in my tracks.

No glasses, just the bottle of vintage scotch from our drinks cabinet. My fucking finest.

Serena doesn't drink scotch.

No sign of a glass, which means some asshole was necking it straight from the bottle. But that surprises me none.

I find an ashtray outside the back door. Five butts mashed inside.

Well, fuck.

My first fucking night away from this place since Mariana passed and that sonofabitch comes calling. Waltzing in like he's still fucking welcome here.

I take a breath before I clear the cigarette butts into the trash and put the scotch back where it belongs. I take another as my pulse races and the anger spits in my gut.

I'm fierce in the shower, scrubbing away every trace of my beautiful stranger while I simmer at the thought of the motherfucker who used to be my brother being loose in my fucking house.

So close to my sleeping boy. *My* sleeping boy. *Mine.*

Because it was *my* fucking girlfriend who died in that fucking fire. *My* fucking life that burnt up with her.

There's enough tension for a whole fucking lifetime in my wrist as I jerk my cock and force myself back to happier moments from this evening.

So many pleasures to sample and not nearly enough time. I didn't taste her, didn't pin her legs high and feast on that wet cunt of hers until she screamed. I didn't get to see the whites of her eyes as I fucked her face to face. Didn't feel her moans against my lips. Didn't stretch that tight little asshole until she begged me to stop for real.

Fuck.

I'm out of the shower just as soon as I've shot my load.

It takes everything not to reactivate my profile and thank her for a good time. I'm tense in bed and thinking of her, of her sweet sad soul and the train wreck of baggage she carries on her shoulders as the whole damn world plays ignorant.

Just like they do with me.

She's a fractured mirror reflecting my own fucking brokenness.

A beautiful demon in the darkness whispering my name.

Her tragedy could eat me up and hold me tight, but mine...

Mine could bury her alive.

Burn *her* alive.

Light is breaking on the horizon outside, but it's fading on the glorious distraction I've been living these past few weeks.

I know how the story ends if two fucked up souls play at life together. I know how the story ends when two people's demons hold hands.

Abigail Rachel Summers is everything I need, all at once.

And absolutely nothing I should ever do again.

bait

•

It's bright when I open my eyes; so much for hearing the alarm.

It takes me a moment to register I'm not alone. The tiny body next to me is barely a lump under the covers. His hair is a dark little nest on the pillow.

He's pretending to be asleep. He'd have fooled me if I hadn't seen the twitch of his head.

"Morning, bud," I greet, and scoop the lad under my forearm. He's smiling as he presses to my chest, giggling silently as I tickle him under the arms and pretend to be a monster for the second time in recent hours.

I can't remember the last time I stayed in bed long enough for him to join me. I'd forgotten how good it felt to have his tiny body so snug against mine.

Tiny fingers trace the ink on my chest then rise to beep my nose. I know this game.

"Want some breakfast?" I ask, but he shakes his head.

I wish he'd just find the words to tell me what he's thinking. What he's feeling. What he wants from me.

I take a chance on it, wrapping him in arms that could crush him to dust but would do anything to protect him. It's the right call. Little arms wrap around my neck and squeeze right back. My fingers tickle his scalp and I breathe in the smell of his sea monster shampoo.

"I love you," I tell him, and I'd give anything in the world to hear it back.

What I get instead is another beep on the nose.

That'll have to do for now.

I know the twinkle in his eyes when I ruffle his hair. I know he's ready to get up when he kicks the covers up in the air to make a fort out of them.

"Ready for breakfast now?" I ask, and he nods.

I grab a t-shirt and tug a pair of jeans on over my boxers while he looks at the picture of himself on my bedside table. He's so small in that picture, barely more than twelve months old.

I wonder how far his memory goes back. I wonder how much of the horrible shit that went down last year really managed to go right over his head.

Not enough, that's for sure.

I check him for wetness before I scoop him up and head downstairs. There's nothing there. It's a good sign.

A good sign things are finally getting better.

They won't be getting better for Serena as I catch her eyes across the kitchen. She's already drinking coffee, the morning news blaring in the background.

I put Cameron in his chair and hold up cereal boxes for him to point to. I keep the smile on my face even though I'm fucking seething.

"Morning," she says. "Good night?"

I don't even grace her with an answer. I give Cameron the TV remote and pour his cereal with a smile, and then I gesture her to the living room, heading through and leaving the door open just a crack.

She takes the cue.

My voice is a raging fucking hiss as I jab a finger at the drinks cabinet.

"One fucking night, Serena. I'm out one fucking night and you let Jake come calling. What the fuck does he want with my fucking house?"

Her eyes are fiercer than I expected. "I *invited* him."

It's like a slap in the face, sobering enough that I take a step back. "*You* invited him? *Here?* Why the fuck would you invite him here?"

Her voice is a hiss right back at me. "He's my *brother*, Leo. Where the fuck else have I got to invite him to? Did you know he sleeps in his fucking truck nine nights out of ten? The heating in his place packed in a few months back, the place is a shithole from what I hear. He won't let me come to him."

I shake my head as she talks. "And this is supposed to make me feel guilty, is it?"

She groans. "I'm just telling you the truth of it. I'm here all the time, with you and Cam. You never go anywhere. You've never been anywhere! I used the opportunity to see my other brother, is that such a big fucking deal?"

I don't believe her that it's not a big deal. Her eyes drop too quickly from mine.

"What did he have to say then, *your* brother?"

"Stop," she says, but I don't.

"I don't suppose he had any wisdom to impart seeing as he's holding back a whole fucking jigsaw puzzle of fucking answers from me?"

"He doesn't remember…"

"Bullshit," I hiss. "That's fucking bullshit."

"The night of the fire is repressed…" she begins, but I hold up a hand.

"He remembers enough to fucking hate me for pulling him out first. He remembers enough to blame me for her being there in the fucking first place. The rest is what? Mysteriously forgotten?"

Her lip trembles and it's enough to knock me off my axis. She gestures toward the kitchen with tears in her eyes.

"So it's okay for little Cam to play mute for twelve months straight? It's okay for little Cam to play baby while we all tread on eggshells? It's okay for everyone else to struggle with all of this, but Jake is a liar? Nothing but a liar? No trauma for Jake? No? None at all?"

I suck in breath, reeling as she keeps on rolling.

"It's not as if he loved her or anything, is it, Leo? Not as if he was crazy about her? Not as though you fucking knew it?"

"Shut your mouth," I hiss, but she shakes her head.

"You're in denial and you can't even see it!" A tear rolls down her cheek, and I hate it. I hate seeing her cry.

"*He* wants to sell the old premises," I snap. "*He's* the one who hates *my* fucking guts, Serena. *He's* the one who's threatening to sell his shares to anyone paying."

"And why do you want to keep them? Why do you want to keep any of it?!"

I shake my head. Smile at the ridiculousness. It's ridiculous. This whole thing is ridiculous. I hate that sack of shit even more for addling her fucking mind the first opportunity he gets.

"I'm refurbishing the premises," I say, even though I'm not sure I am. "It's a better size than the unit in town. We can expand."

"Expand?!" Her eyes widen. "Leo, the business is on its fucking knees. The insurance isn't going to cover it and you know it, even if you won't say it. *You're* not even sure it was an accident, and you think they're gonna toe the line? You're driving yourself into the ground after her, all because you won't just stop and face the obvious."

But she's wrong. She's fucking wrong. The business isn't on its fucking knees, not anymore. Not after twelve months of blood, sweat and pain. So much fucking pain.

And it *was* an accident. It has to have been a fucking accident.

My soul can't fucking take it. Not any fucking more of it.

"What's the *obvious*?" I ask her, even though I don't want to. My voice is weak. Hell, I feel fucking weak.

"The *obvious* is that you aren't over any of it, Leo. Not even close. The *obvious* is that you're using all these problems as a crutch to stop you facing your own grief. The business... Cam... *me*..."

There's a lump in my throat that I struggle to choke back down. "Cam needs me to be this way. He's been through too much..."

Tears track down her face. She shakes her head. And I don't want to hear whatever she's about to tell me, but I can't walk away.

"He can talk," she whispers. "I hear him when he's alone. I hear him through the door when he thinks I'm not listening…"

"It must be the TV…" I interrupt, but her head is still shaking.

"It's *him*, Leo. You think I'd make this up? You think I'd have any doubt before I said this aloud? He can speak, I swear."

"No–" I protest, but she cuts me off.

"*Yes*," she says. "I'm sorry, Leo, but *yes*…"

"But the speech therapists…" I argue. "Why would he?" But I know it. I know it too. It sucker punches me, right in the fucking pit of me. I don't know how I keep my footing. I force some tiny scrap of composure. "Why bring this up now? Why didn't you say something earlier?"

"Because I needed to be sure…"

"And you're suddenly *sure*, are you? After inviting Jake round for the first fucking time last night?"

"It's not the first time…" she admits, and I let out a choked laugh at how this keeps getting better and better.

"Jake's seen Cam, has he? He's seen my boy?"

"*Mariana's* boy too, Leo. He loves Cam. Cam loves him."

And how it breaks my fucking heart.

I stalk the room like a fucking beast, my pulse in my ears as I struggle for composure.

My voice is a spit and hiss. "And Cameron speaks to *Jake*, does he? Does he call him fucking *Daddy* as well?"

She rushes forward but I hold up my hands. She stands with wide eyes, shaking her head. "No! Of course not! Of course he doesn't! That's not what I meant!"

My eyes are daggers, right on hers. "You think it, though, don't you? You think Cam is his. Is that what Jake thinks too? Is that why he comes here?"

She chokes for words.

"That's what you think, isn't it?!" I bark. She points at the kitchen puts a finger over her lips and I curse myself. I lower my voice. "Tell me the fucking truth. Please just tell me the fucking truth."

She shrugs and still the tears fall. "I'm saying *none* of us know, Leo. Not you, not me. Mariana's gone, and Jake…"

My demons are playing inside me and they are vile. The darkness is behind my eyes and no amount of running, or early mornings at the office, or choosing my son's TV channels has the power to quash any of it.

"You're leaving," I tell her. "Today. You'll be gone from here by the time I get back from the park with Cam."

Her wide eyes are like saucers. "What?! No! Leo, no! You can't!"

But I can.

I don't want to recognise the woman in my living room. I don't want to know the sister who kept so many cards this close to her chest.

"Go live with your other brother," I whisper. "You can see him all you want. I'm sure you'll be very happy together."

And she cries. Oh how she cries.

"You don't mean that!" she sobs, throwing her hands in the air. "Leo, you can't mean that!"

But I do.

I do mean it.

I choke it all down, just like I always have. Force my demons back in their little cages.

All apart from the one that escaped last night.

The one Abigail coaxed from me.

I let that one stay free.

bait

"Cam will be done with his breakfast," I say, as though it's just a normal day. "You'd better start packing your things."

I leave her sobbing, her heart breaking as she cries.

But I don't feel a fucking thing.

thirteen

abigail

For the first time ever, after years of waiting... *hoping*... the monster catches me in my dreams.

He catches me and hoists me off my feet... and his cock is thick and studded with metal...

And then he kisses me...

The monster kisses me and I want it.

I've always wanted it...

And then I wake.

The room is empty. The sunlight making patterns on the wall through the drapes, just like always.

But nothing is just like always.

My belly is still aching, my thighs still clammy from the promise of him, and

I'm more desperate for the beast than ever.

I flinch as I grab my laptop, my heart in my throat as I log in to my profile.

I said I'd delete it, but I won't. I can't.

His messages are still greyed out. His profile is still listed unknown.

Fuck.

I take a breath, trying to contain my running thoughts.

It's over. Done. Just one crazy experience for the memories.

I wince as I get to my feet. Wince again as I hobble to the bathroom.

The monster really got me good.

I grit my teeth as I take a piss. Ow, I'm fucking sore.

I should be thinking about getting tested for nasties, but somehow I know I'll be alright. I couldn't justify why if my life depended on it, I just know it.

Unfortunately, I don't have to be thinking about getting the morning after pill, either. The operation that saved my life took my fertility away in the same breath. Scarring. An unfortunate complication, they said.

Even the thought brings tears to my eyes out of nowhere.

The odds that I'll get pregnant again are… slim.

Virtually nil.

There's still a chance… more surgery… but no guarantees. Nothing even close to a guarantee.

I've transferred my medical notes to the local practice from back home, but the hospital referral… that's still in the process of moving to another health authority. The waiting lists make it not worth thinking about imminently, so I don't. Or try not to.

Just like I try not to do so many things.

Walk amongst families. Hear a baby cry. Watch a little kid run after their parents.

I avoid it all.

Another part of the reason I left. Selfish, but true.

Friends getting married, having kids. Friends with kids meeting friends with kids and inviting me along – the woman that can't have one.

I wipe myself and flush. There is a tiny flash of pink on the toilet paper. A minor injury all considered. I expected worse.

I expected him to be a lot less... considerate.

I expected him to tear me in two without a moment's hesitation.

I fantasised he'd take my ass once he'd done with the rest of me. I imagined him pressing his forehead to mine while he took everything I had.

I'm half glad he didn't when I have to use the handrail for leverage to get up. The aftermath of what he *did* do requires enough recovery to be going along with.

I grab myself some toast and eat it in bed. I flick on the TV I haven't watched in ages and keep my profile open on my laptop, just in case.

And finally, when I dare risk it, I rub my clit until I come for him all over again.

It's different today.

The way I come is different today. The way I picture the monster in the darkness is all about him.

It always will be.

From now on, it always will be.

My fantasies couldn't go back to yesterday if I tried. They're different. They feel different.

And that's alright.

It has to be alright.

Because today *I'm* different, too.

p h o e n i x

I usually carry Cam everywhere out of habit, but today I let him clamber down from the truck on his own. I take his hand and let him walk alongside me. Encourage him to open the park gate on his own.

I push him on the swing with a lump in my throat. Push him higher and higher, faster than usual, just to see if he'll squeal.

He doesn't.

He doesn't make a single sound.

I watch him on the slide with a fake smile on my face. I hoist him onto the springy metal horse with a *giddy-up* and a laugh.

But I'm breaking inside.

I wonder if Serena is done packing her things. I wonder if she's already called Jake to ask for a ride.

She's been staying with us for twelve months, my domestic crutch through a workload that would have swallowed most people alive.

It nearly swallowed *me*.

I trusted her. Needed her. We both did.

Still do.

Fuck.

I force that under the surface with the rest of the shit down there.

And I stare at my boy. *My* boy.

My boy who looks like his mother and not like me.

My boy who has the same cow's lick as Jake had when he was a boy.

Cameron looks my way and smiles, rides that metal horse a little bit harder. He's mine.

He has to be mine.

Because if he's not…

I force the demons back in the pit. Kicking back on a bench as Cameron keeps playing.

I pull my phone from my pocket and call up my *hookup* login, and I'm so close to reactivating my profile. So fucking close.

But I can't.

I don't trust my demons. I don't trust hers either.

I don't trust where this insanity will end.

I don't trust where I'd want it to.

When I look back at my boy, he's going too fast. Rocking that horse as though he's in a fucking steeplechase.

His eyes are on me, his mouth unsmiling, and I don't understand why it hits me so hard in the gut, until I do.

I'm already poised for action when I realise the obvious.

My instinct is to run to him and sweep him off there before he hurts himself.

My instinct is to baby him like the baby I've let him be these past twelve months.

The baby I've *made* him be.

But today I don't.

Today I let him keep rocking.

He's tall enough that his feet easily reach the foot bars. His grip is strong and his balance is good. He could dismount if he wanted and I know it. He knows it, too.

His expression turns to a grimace as I don't react to him. He rocks so hard that the metal springs squeak and lurch and my stomach squeaks and lurches with them.

And then he falls, loses his footing and tumbles onto the woodchips below. He rolls onto his back with his face scrunched with tears that make no sound, and I hate myself.

I hate myself and I hate Serena for opening her stupid fucking mouth with her stupid fucking theories.

If only they were fucking stupid.

I've scooped Cameron from the floor in a heartbeat. He's tight in my arms before the horse has even stopped rocking.

He's tense, flailing, his face screwed in agony as the tears roll down his face. But I see no injuries.

I tug his trouser legs up and there's not even a mark, there's not even a graze on his elbow. Nothing.

"What hurts, Cam?" I ask him, but he keeps on silent-crying. "Tell me what's hurting, champ," I try again, but he doesn't even point.

I sit back on the bench and hold him tight, and I'm asking him with my eyes right on his. My soul is on my fucking sleeve as my world goes to shit, and I'm begging him. I'm fucking begging him.

"Please, Cam, please just say something. Please, just say something, bud. Anything. Just talk to me. Make a noise. Anything."

I'd feel like an idiot if it wasn't for the way his eyes sharpen on mine. I'd call Serena out for spouting bullshit if it wasn't for the way his fake tears dry to nothing.

"Cam, please…" I try again. "Talk to Daddy. Please, just say something. Come on, champ, please."

But he doesn't. He sniffles and stares at his muddy boots, and then he points at the pond behind my back, accident forgotten.

"Ducks?" I ask. "Say it, Cam. Ask Daddy for the ducks."

He stares blankly ahead.

He acts as though he doesn't hear a word.

Deaf as well as mute today.

I sigh and brush his hair from his forehead. "Alright," I say, "let's do it."

And we do.

I lead my little boy to the duckpond and dig the food from my pocket. I squat on my haunches to help him throw the pieces. I smile like this is just another day, just like yesterday, just another fun day at the park like all the other times we've been here.

But it's not.

This isn't yesterday.

Today my demons have broken from their cages and my eyes are open wide.

Things will never, ever be the same again.

And *I'll* never, ever be the same again either.

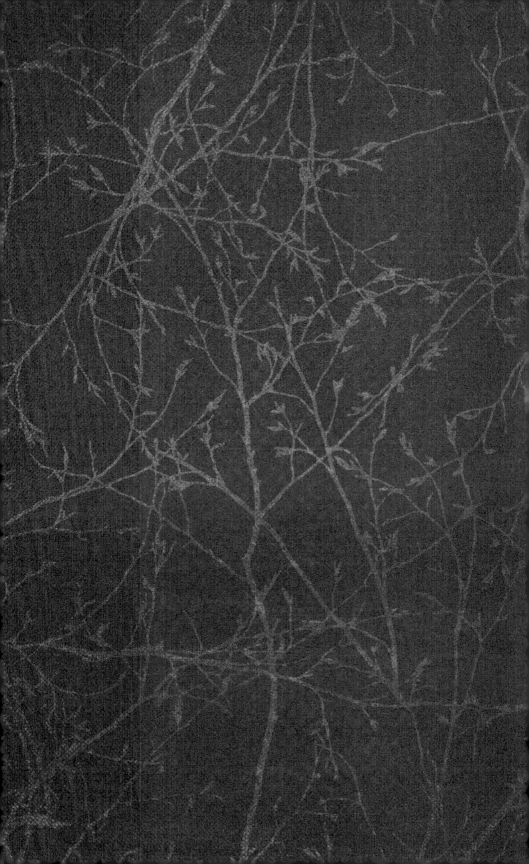

fourteen

I will not be a common man. I will stir the smooth sands of monotony.

—PETER O'TOOLE

abigail

I try with everything in me to stick to the plan.

I try to let that one wild night fade into memory and start living my new life with a full heart.

I'm still smiling with colleagues. Still giving my all to my ever increasing workload. I'm still calling my parents and letting them know I'm doing just fine.

But it's not enough.

I should've deleted my profile like I promised. I should've drawn a line in the sand and moved on from our one crazy night in the shadows.

I wish I could.

I think it's the monotony that's killing me slowly. *Wake up, shower, head to work. Smile at the same faces, pretend I'm just another girl in the office, make sure I offer a round of coffee at least once every day.*

I try to break it for myself. I go out twice for drinks after work in that one next week alone. I start watching TV shows as though I might have an interest in continuing them.

It's all a lie.

All I want is more of the monster.

My monster.

All I want is another night with his breath on my neck and his terrifying cock inside me.

He doesn't log in and I stop expecting him to. The sliver of hope that he'll come looking for me has long dulled to nothing by the time the weekend comes back around.

And then, late on Friday night after a couple of glasses of wine, the crazy in me notches up another gear.

I feel the insanity churning in my gut as the idea hits me.

If he won't come looking for me…

I have nothing to go on and I know it. I've got a deactivated profile which listed Malvern as his location and nothing more. He could've been lying about that.

The nightclub could be miles from anywhere he knows. He could have scoped out my route on street view for all the sense my scheming makes.

He could be living miles away and I could be a distant memory. He could be regretting ever agreeing to meet me.

But I need to know.

It scares me how much I need to know.

So I make a decision.

A batshit crazy, based on nothing concrete whatsoever decision.

And then I sleep.

For once at least this week, sleep comes easy.

phoenix

Life without Serena is bullshit tough.

Cameron is restless, back to wetting the bed at night, and I feel a dick for ever sending her away.

I feel a dick for taking Cam into work every day and trying to amuse him with a laptop full of cartoons. I feel a dick for being in work at all.

But the world keeps on spinning, and I keep on spinning with it.

It feels like shit. This whole fucking week feels like shit.

I take the speech therapist outside the therapy room on Friday morning and fight the urge to slam the prick into the wall.

"He can speak," I hiss. "My sister heard him."

The asshole nods. He fucking nods at me. "That's entirely plausible, yes."

"*Plausible?* You're telling me that's fucking *plausible?*"

I could tear his head from his body when he sighs. Shrugs. "Trauma is difficult to treat, Mr Scott. Cameron may be *choosing* not to speak. There's little we can do about that. There's nothing *physically* wrong, it's the *emotional* condition we are working to understand."

My eyes burn. "You're the speech therapist. Make him speak."

He laughs a little, until he sees how serious I am. "I can't *make* him speak, Mr Scott. With all due respect, maybe you should be talking to his counsellor."

And I do.

I talk to everyone who'll hear me before the day is done. His doctor, his child psychologist, the bereavement counselling service. They all say the same bullshit thing.

bait

In his own time.

Slowly, slowly.

This is a complex situation, Mr Scott.

A complex situation in a sea of the same old fucking bullshit.

I'm struggling to keep it all afloat. Floundering in the riptide. I work my ass off, just like every other week, and dedicate the rest of my time to Cameron. I take him everywhere I go. I try everything I can think of to get him to speak to me.

And in the end, I achieve nothing.

The business is still chugging along, just as it was before. Cameron is still the same mute boy who wets the bed at night. Serena is still gone. Mariana is still dead.

And I'm still drowning. It's a slow death, slipping deeper into the icy depths of monotony. It's water torture, one cold drip at a time, stripping my soul from my bones.

My demons are screaming at their bars and I don't even have the freedom of running up the hills to keep their cries at bay.

By the time Friday evening finds me I'm as exhausted as I've ever known. Cameron is asleep on the sofa at my side, his cartoons still blaring on screen as I stare numbly at the wall.

My phone is on the coffee table, calling me, *begging* me to reach out to my black swan, but I don't.

I can't.

I jump a mile as the handset starts vibrating, my heart thumping like crazy at the irrational thought that it could be her.

It's not. Of course it's not.

Serena's number flashes up.

I ignore her for the hundredth time this week, but she calls back, then calls back again after it.

"What?" I bark when I finally relent enough to answer.

Her sobs knock me sideways. "Please, Leo. Please just let me see Cam. I understand you're angry. I get it. But please let me see that little boy." She pauses, and in that moment of self-hatred I wish I'd have been in that fire until the end. "I miss him so much," she whispers.

And he misses her.

I wish I could tell her I do too.

"You can see him," I offer. "When?"

Her sobs take her breath. I wait. "Tomorrow?"

I clear my throat. Hold everything back. "Sure," I say. "Morning?"

"Please."

I look at my sleeping boy, and I know it has to be this way. "See you in the morning," I tell her.

And then I hang up.

I carry Cam up to his bedroom and kiss his head as I tuck him in. "At least you won't have to tolerate another morning in the office, champ," I whisper.

We can't go on like this. Not any of us.

Somehow, at some point, we all need to start living again.

Me, Serena, Cam...

Even Jake.

I guess that's why I find myself out in the yard at gone midnight.

I guess that's why I take the cover from the pool and start the clean-up process I've been putting off for months.

I guess that's why I make the decision that I either need to refurbish our old burnt-out premises for real or let them go.

I guess that's also why I fold Cameron's baby chair up and put it in the utility room, and why I decide that tomorrow is the first day of his new life with new possibilities.

Mine, too.

abigail

My nerves are jumping right through me as I take the car into Malvern on Saturday morning. It feels a ridiculous idea in the daylight, but not ridiculous enough that I'm not parking up in the station car park at barely past ten.

I was worried I wouldn't find my bearings, but as soon as I step away from the station I know exactly where I'm going. I cross the road, just as he told me to. I follow the street through the industrial estate, just like he told me to.

I don't know what I'm looking for in this direction. Too many buildings and they all look the same.

I reach the nightclub so quickly it takes me by surprise. It looks so innocuous in the summer sun. There's no sign of life whatsoever.

No sign that this was the place I finally brought my fantasy to life for real.

The way back is the real test. I don't know what I'm looking for. I have nothing to ask a passing stranger. No photo prompters other than the shot of his monster cock saved to my phone. Somehow I don't think I'll be using that one.

I navigate by streetlights, recalling every glow of light I found solace in. I'm reaching a bend in the road when I see the one that sets my heart thumping.

I remember the ping of metal in the road. The sound of footsteps behind me.

My belly flutters and my clit sparks, senses on high alert as I position myself underneath it.

Here. He was here. Right here.

I scan the surrounding buildings in the daylight.

A refrigeration company, a furniture importer, an IT support company.

I keep going.

The headquarters of a local housing association, a removal firm.

No and no.

And then I see a dip in the tarmac. A dip and then a kerb.

I remember tripping, correcting myself on shaky legs… and then him. At my back.

I keep walking until the next business comes into view. Scott Brothers Logistics. It's big. Set back from the road.

Trucks.

The tarmac turns to gravel on the driveway, and I remember the crunch under his feet.

I feel like an idiot as I head closer, my cheeks burning when I notice they're open for trading on a Saturday morning.

Fuck, I feel like a fucking crazy.

And then I see the shutter doors. My whole body trembles.

I feel like I've hit the jackpot, which is ridiculous. Totally ridiculous.

I'm staring up at them when a voice calls out.

I start so hard I gasp, and I'm staring dumb with wide eyes at the man who comes over.

Hoping… praying…

But it's not him. Of course it's not.

This man is too short. His hair is cropped all over. He's carrying a clipboard and there are no tattoos to be seen.

"Can I help?" he asks, and he's so friendly. So nice.

"Sorry?" I ask, as though I haven't heard his question.

"You looking for something?" he asks. "Need a pallet moving?"

I smile at the absurdity, then shake my head. "No," I say. "Sorry, I just…" I decide half-honesty is the best policy. "I was clubbing last weekend, I lost my shoe. *Shoes.*"

"Like Cinderella," he laughs. "Sorry, haven't seen any glass slippers lying around." He looks down at my feet. "Must've been quite some walk home."

"It was." I find I'm laughing back. "Sorry, this is… crazy."

"I'll keep an eye out," he says. "You got a phone number?"

I'm too far embedded in the pretence to back out now. "Sure," I say, and reach in my handbag for a pen, but he beats me to it. He hands me his clipboard and plucks a pen from behind his ear with a flourish.

I scrawl my mobile number with *Abigail* over the top. "They're black. High. Satin."

"I'll be sure to let you know if anything turns up," he says.

I feel like such a fool as I walk away. I'm laughing at my own stupidity as I abandon this crazy errand and opt to head back to the car. Yet, I'm already considering using the cock picture after all before I drive off anywhere.

Needs must.

And I definitely have needs.

phoenix

Jimmy has a smile on his face when he brings the forklift truck back inside. He climbs down and flashes his clipboard to a couple of the other guys. They laugh.

I don't give a shit what they're joking about, just keep on checking generator stock with my head down.

He seeks me out anyway.

"Ain't seen a glass slipper, have you, boss?" he asks.

"A what?"

He holds up his paperwork. My heart fucking thumps as I see *Abigail* scrawled on the top. A mobile number.

It can't be.

"Some girl lost her shoes here. Was looking for them outside. Pretty thing she was. Wouldn't mind finding them just so I can give her a call."

My demons go fucking wild, rattling their fucking cages. I'm already staring beyond him to the open door as he tells me these glass slippers are high and black.

"Satin, she said."

"I'll be right back," I tell him, and I'm off in a beat.

She's already out of view when I reach the street. No sign of her in either direction.

I pull my keys from my pocket and jump into my truck, knowing full well she can't have gone far.

I reach her at the end of the estate, just as the street heads down toward the station. I know she must be parked up in the same place.

She looks just as stunning as I remember, wearing a simple red summer dress with her black hair shining in the sun. She's wearing sandals with open toes. Barely any makeup.

Her walk is hurried but easy. Her head is high.

And I want her.

Oh fuck, how I want her.

My resolve shrivels to nothing. I need this too much to turn back.

I locate her car in the car park long before she arrives – the same red Mini Cooper I watched her get out of last weekend. I pull up into the nearest space for a clear vantage point, with no fucking idea what I'm going to do when she gets here.

Her shoes are still in my glove compartment. I consider handing them over, just like that. Asking her out for a coffee. A walk.

A hunt in the darkness.

Anything.

bait

I'm still debating my approach when her car alarm bleeps. I'm still tripping over my options when she slips into the driver's seat and pulls away.

It's instinct that makes me follow her. My cock is throbbing hard by the time she pulls into a petrol station and I pull in after her.

She fills up and I do too. There's a fuel pump between us and she remains oblivious.

I love how oblivious she is.

She's ahead of me in the queue and she has no idea. I can smell her coconut shampoo as she stares straight ahead.

She's close enough to touch. To taste.

I fight the urge to hoist her from her feet and abduct her in plain daylight. It takes everything I have not to call her name.

Two cashiers become free at once. She steps up to the counter and so do I.

I hand my card over just as she looks away. She crouches and picks up a packet of fruit sweets from the display stand.

And then she registers my shadow.

Her eyes move up slowly, from my boots to my eyes.

Hers widen. Mine hold firm.

She doesn't know me, but she thinks she does.

Some deep part of her *knows* she does.

The cashier hands my card back across the counter and I take it.

My black swan's mouth drops open as she sees the back of my hand.

The picture. Of course.

I sent her the picture.

She drops her sweets with a gasp. They literally tumble right out of her fingers. They crash to the floor and I'm straight down after them.

"Butter fingers," I say with a smile. Her hands are shaking as I give them back to her.

Her whole body is shaking.

"Miss?" her cashier asks, but she doesn't move. "Miss, if you could pay for your fuel…"

She stutters, fumbles.

I smile at her beautiful awkwardness.

And then I clear my space in the queue.

"Wait!" she calls, but I don't respond. "Wait, just a minute!" she calls again, and I look back in time to see her frantically keying in her PIN number.

And now it's my turn to hear *her* frantic footsteps behind me as I step out through the door.

fifteen

Stranger, if you, passing, meet me and desire to speak to me, why should you not speak to me? And why should I not speak to you?

—WALT WHITMAN

abigail

I t's him.

It has to be him.

I *know* it's him.

Every nerve is firing, every intuition I've ever had paling into insignificance next to this one.

I can't pay for my fuel quickly enough. It's desperation that makes me call out to him.

"Wait!"

He doesn't even slow down.

"Wait, just a minute!" I call again, but he doesn't look back.

I swear under my breath as I shove the stupid sweets into my handbag. I'm forcing my purse in after them as I dart through the queue and throw myself through the open door.

Fuck.

I scan the cars at the fuel pumps but don't see him. It's only when I take a step to the right that I see him heading for a truck at the far side.

Opposite me. He was at the pump opposite me. I must've been right next to him.

My sandals make a slapping sound on the forecourt as I dash over. I may be wired like a fucking crazy, but there's no way I'm letting him leave. Not without knowing for sure how I can see him again.

If I can see him again.

I approach from the front of his truck, standing like an idiot to block his way out of here. He'd have to mow me down to get out of my sight.

And then I look at him. Really look at him.

He's as dark as I imagined. Dark hair, dark eyes, heavy brows. His hair is long on top, just as I remembered. His beard is fucking perfect. He looks fierce, wild. He's dressed in black. Black jacket, black t-shirt, black *everything*. My legs are quivering and I don't care. My whole body is thrumming, and it feels like life itself.

The tattoos on his neck are obvious. Glorious.

He's fucking glorious.

And he's staring right at me.

"It's you," I tell him, even though my voice is weak.

He doesn't even flinch, just raises an eyebrow. "It is?"

I'm nodding, even though I'm second guessing myself. I contemplate the possibility that I'm crazy, and this guy – this beautiful creature – is just a *coincidence.*

But no.

I know this isn't a coincidence.

I remember the way his skin felt under my fingertips. I remember the graze of the hair on his scalp.

I remember *him*.

He takes a step forward and my breath catches in my throat.

"What's me exactly, sweetheart?"

Another step forward and I'm so aware of the bulk of him. So aware of how easily he picked me up.

There's a tension in the air between us, and I'm not imagining it. His body knows mine, just as mine knows his, and I'm not imagining that either.

"It was you…" I whisper. "I know it was you…"

He tips his head. His smile is dirty.

Divine.

Everything.

He could run me down with his truck for real before I'd move an inch.

"You're looking for someone?" he asks.

I nod like a fool.

He shrugs. Playing with me. He *has* to be playing with me.

"And where did you meet this *someone*? Are they from around these parts?"

"Online," I whisper. "I met him online. I ran through the darkness and he caught me. I had a fantasy and he brought it to life. He made it real, and now I can't stop. I don't want to stop."

"So you came looking for him?" he asks, and I see it. He can't hide the glint in his eye.

"I couldn't think of a better option."

He smiles at that. "In that case I'd suggest you go looking for him back where you found him."

"He's deactivated his profile," I say, deadpan.

He shrugs. "Maybe he'll turn back up."

"You think?" I ask.

He nods, just a little. "Worth a shot, right?"

I watch mute as he climbs into his truck. I'm still standing there as he turns on the ignition.

He puts down the window and leans out on his elbow. I see the ink snaking up his arms and wonder how far it goes.

All the way.

I imagine it goes all the way.

"Must've made quite an impression, this stranger," he says.

"You could say that." My smile feels ridiculous. *I* feel ridiculous. I step closer, as close as I dare. I could reach out and touch him. I wish I was brave enough. "He's all I can think about."

He smiles back at that. "Should be careful what you wish for. You might just get it."

"I'm counting on it," I tell him.

His eyes eat me up but I hold mine firm. The darkness there takes my breath. My demons wave at his, and I swear they wave back.

I feel the ghost of a shiver up my spine.

My whole body wants him to wrestle me into his truck and drive me away.

"Goodbye, Cinderella," he says and my heart stutters.

My shoes. He remembers I lost my shoes.

It's still stuttering when he puts the truck in gear and drives away. The truck rumbles, loud. His elbow is still resting on the open window as he pulls onto the street and disappears from view.

If I wasn't a puddle of everything, I'd drive after him.

If I wasn't shaking like a leaf, I'd try to tail him all the way to forever.

But I'm both.

It takes every last scrap of composure I've got left just to drive my car off the forecourt.

phoenix

I'm done fighting.

I drive home without going back to the warehouse. I take the scenic route up the hills only to make sure she isn't following me.

If she was, I'd head her off long before I ever got there. I'd coax her into the middle of nowhere and punish-fuck her for her boldness until she screamed.

I'm at least partially disappointed her Mini doesn't appear in my rearview, but that's okay.

We're well off fucking script all round, but that's okay too.

It'll have to be.

I barely acknowledge Serena when I step through the door at home. Cameron heads on over and I scoop him up for a bear hug, just like usual.

"Good day, champ?" I ask and he nods.

Serena's made lunch for the both of them. Potato salad with mayo. She holds up the bowl and I nod.

I take a seat at the table and pat the place next to me for Cam. He climbs up without protest, doesn't even look for his high chair. That's got to be progress. Got to mean something.

I'm clutching at straws, but I don't care. Not right now.

I'm still fucking angry, but it feels easier not to show it. Everything feels easier right now.

Serena spoons me out a bowlful and slips into the chair opposite. She looks at her food and not at me.

I thank her and she nods.

I hold back from helping Cam with his cutlery, and sure enough he does it for himself.

"It's nice to be back," Serena offers finally.

I don't have a response for that, so I say nothing.

"I've enjoyed the day with Cam," she continues. "We had a good day, didn't we?" she prompts and he smiles.

It's a good move on her part. I can't argue with a smile from my boy and she knows it.

"What are your plans?" I ask and she shrugs.

"I want to come back, Leo. Please let me stay."

I sigh. Smile to myself. Smile at how crazy my world is.

And then I breathe.

I just fucking breathe.

Open-toed sandals and a red summer dress. Her beautiful confusion.

Her shaking fingers.

The want in her eyes.

"Stay for dinner," I say to my sister. "Cam wants you around. Right, champ?"

He nods. Grins.

I just wish he'd fucking say something.

"And you?" she asks. "Do you want me around, too?"

Too much, too soon. I feel my eyes darken on hers.

She holds up a hand. "Sorry, my bad."

But it's mine.

It's all mine.

I eat my potato salad and keep my mouth shut. I tell her it's delicious and clear up the bowls.

And then I head upstairs to let my demons run free.

abigail

I race upstairs to my apartment. I curse my laptop for taking so long to start up.

I log in with bated breath, but there's nothing there.

Just the same old greyed out profile staring back at me.

Crap.

Holy motherfucking crap.

I try it again, logging out and back in just to see if it makes any difference.

It doesn't.

I drop onto my sofa and keep the window open on screen.

He's got to be there. Got to be.

But he isn't.

And then, in a heartbeat, he is.

Oh my poor heart, how it thumps.

In a flash his greyed out profile comes back to life. His picture appears right where it should be. *Phoenix Burning* online.

I stare at the little green circle as my soul expands and soars free.

My fingers have a life of their own, but his message pings through first.

You're pretty reckless, hunting down a monster in a strange town. You'd better hope the monster doesn't creep up on your tail.

He has no idea how much I want him creeping up on me. No idea how fucking crazy I am for another round in the darkness.

I press enter and send him my message, niceties be fucked.

I need to see you again. Please.

I watch the icon as he types.

Be careful what you wish for. This beast isn't tame. It's wild. Dangerous.

It fucking bites.

I remember his teeth on me. The way he nipped my neck. The tickle of his beard. His breath.

How much I wanted him.

I wish for everything, I type. *Scare me. Chase me. Hunt me down. I don't care.*

I keep on typing before he has a chance to respond.

You brought me to life again. Being with you gave me hope when I had none. I can't go back.

My heart is racing, mouth dry. I feel like an addict going cold turkey, desperate for a fix.

His message pings. I can barely look.

This is crazy. Dangerous.

Out of hand already.

I can't argue with that. I don't even try.

Please. Just tell me where to go.

I cross my fingers and toes. I cross my legs too, clamping my thighs closed just to feel the squeeze against my pulsing clit.

His reply takes an age, and it feels different now. I can picture him now. His brooding darkness, the gorgeous bulk of him.

Be ready at midnight. I'll tell you where to go.

If you change your mind, just stay offline.

It you've any sense, you'll change your mind.

I haven't any sense. I've come to terms with that already. I'm at peace with these reckless decisions and the rocky road I'm travelling.

I just hope he is, too.

My reply is easy. Obvious.

I'll be ready at midnight.

He's already offline when I hit enter.

phoenix

I'd have told Serena she was welcome to stay over regardless of whether or not I had somewhere to be tonight. I'm not such a prick that I'm only offering for my own ends.

She sorts out Cam's bed time, and he's happy for it. She reads him his story as I listen from the landing outside.

It's the one about the ducks and the caterpillar. I know the words by heart.

I'm desperate to hold her tight and make things up. The words are stuck in my throat, begging to come out and thank her for everything she's done for us. To ask her to come home.

This is her home now.

But it's not that fucking simple. If only it was.

Her words are still ricocheting around my soul. Those festering questions that hang in dusty corners, they're all right there, spoken aloud between us.

Things can't just go back to the way they were before.

She looks uncharacteristically meek as she steps out to join me.

"He's fast asleep," she whispers and closes his door gently.

"I could do with heading out for a while," I say as we head downstairs. "But I can stay in. I don't want to impose."

She falls over herself to tell me it's ok. Her eyes are curious but happy. Asking silent questions that I'm not ready to answer and maybe never will be.

I'm not sure meeting a stranger online for brutal sex in dark alleyways classes as potential relationship material.

Relationship.

Even the word brings me out in a cold sweat.

"Go," Serena says. "Take a break. Enjoy yourself. I'll take care of Cam. I'm just happy to be back home." She pauses. "Even if it's just for a night."

I have no answer to that.

I wish I could cut through my own baggage enough to tell her I'm happy too.

I wish I could forget that she had that sonofabitch in my house behind my back.

Like she's the first woman to have Jake here behind my back.

I shunt that little gem of bitterness right back into the depths.

And then I grab my jacket.

sixteen

Once upon a midnight dreary, while I pondered weak and weary.

—EDGAR ALLAN POE

phoenix

Hereford isn't familiar turf. I rely on satnav to reach the address I found listed for Abigail Rachel Summers on the electoral roll, and then I lap the block a few times to get my bearings.

Her apartment building is a rickety period place, just a stone's throw from the town centre. I park up in an unloading bay around the corner and scope it out on foot. The communal entrance shows six apartments listed. Six apartments, three floors. The view through the glass door is just enough to see the numbers on the the bottom two apartment doors.

Number one is on the left. Two on the right.

It's easy to assume they continue up in the same pattern.

Hers is number four.

One floor up on the right hand side.

I step back and look up at the window. Twilight makes it easy to tell the light is on, but I see nothing to confirm my suspicion it's her place. The walls look plain through the window. No trinkets on the sill.

I hang back, staring right up there from across the street.

So close. She's so fucking close. I want to see her. Catch a glimpse of her.

I want to taste her, impale that sweet little cunt again and again.

I have no rein on the beast in my belly as it throbs and stirs. My dick is already straining in my jeans, my pulse already quickening.

Part of me considers heading up there and beating her door down before midnight is anywhere near.

It's tempting, but no. I save that idea for another day.

Another day.

I'm already thinking about this crazy arrangement as if it has some kind of longevity.

It should freak me the fuck out, but it doesn't.

I focus back on the night ahead of me. Of *us*. Tonight is all about the hunt. The chase. The thrill of the pulse in my ears as my boots pound the ground after her. Grabbing her in the dark, muffling her screams. My dick twitches in sweet anticipation.

I call up a map on my phone, examining how the streets branch out from here. To the left is the main bulk of civilisation. Streetlights and clubs and cameras. To the right is the cathedral. Cobbled lanes and shady grounds. Beyond that looks to be parkland. I zoom in closer and realise it's a sprawl of playing fields.

The river runs next to them.

The river path ends up on the outskirts. I follow it with my finger and zoom in where the streets have thinned out. A pub on the corner. A few houses nearby from the looks. Not a lot else.

My senses prickle. This is perfect.

I'm back in my truck in a heartbeat, destination set. Sure enough, the streets thin out as I drive. The pub is still open when I get there but won't be for long. The car park is deserted.

I park up in the spot closest to the river and grab a torch. The path is just where I expect. A gap in the fence leads right down to the water. It's dark here. Treacherous. Perfect.

I'll herd her right the way through the shadows, straight to my waiting truck. She'll have no fucking idea until it's too late. I'll just have to grab her at the right spot.

I do a 360.

Right… here. I make a mental note of it. Of the tree looming overhead. The dull streetlamp positioned over the pub fencing.

Yeah, I'll recognise it, sure enough. I'll grab her right before the entrance to the car park.

And then she'll meet the monster for real.

I head back to the truck for my final preparations. I take Cameron's safety seat from the backseat and store it out of view in the trunk. I check what work supplies I have to hand while I'm in there.

The tow rope seems both drastic and tempting, and I like it. I coil it on the passenger seat for easy reach.

I lock the truck and set off on foot. I check for any junctions in the river path on the way back, any potential spots I could lose her. There aren't any worth worrying about. This route is straight, a rat run of shadows and uneven ground. She'll be too busy keeping her footing to worry about veering off course.

Perfect.

Twilight has turned to darkness long before I've made it back to her apartment block. The glow of the city is ominous across the meadows. Bitter orange and dirty enough to be sinister.

The water ripples and splashes in the blackness down below. The banks are high and thick with undergrowth. A group of kids with bikes hang out at one spot, but they're already clearing off for the night as I pass by.

I clear a couple of empty drink cans from the path and snap away the occasional branch that hangs down too low.

I feel empowered as I reach the cathedral grounds. She'll be able to run. Fast. Largely unhindered. Run straight into the trap and she'll never even know it's coming.

My balls tighten. My muscles already wired and ready for the chase.

I make sure my boots are fastened tight before I call up my login screen on my mobile, and then I wait.

I watch.

I think about her.

I think of all the things I'm going to do to her sweet little body once she's too exhausted to run another step.

I know it's her apartment for sure when a shadow passes across her window. I see the shape of her against the wall inside. Back and forth. Over and over.

Pacing.

She's pacing.

And my heart is racing.

She's waiting. Readying herself.

Feeling the fear.

It's a beautiful observation.

The last fifteen minutes crawl by, but that's good. I'm lost in the rhythm of her pacing, riding the tremors of anticipation. I can't wait to sink my dick into that tight little cunt all over again.

I log in at midnight and she's already signed in.

She stops pacing. Her shadow darts away.

I don't bother with small talk.

You will leave your apartment. You will be barefoot.

You will head for the cathedral. You will walk slowly through the grounds until you reach the river path.

When you are scared, you will run.

One simple question pings back at me.

Barefoot?

I smile to myself.

Yes, Cinderella. Barefoot.

I wonder if she's smiling too.

Now? she asks.

I back into the shadows. My eyes firmly on her apartment entrance.

Now.

abigail

Now.

I'm dithery as I shove my phone in my handbag. I shove my keys in after it.

I'm dressed in a baby blue summer dress, which I know is stupid at this time of night, but it seemed a good option when I tried it on. It shwooshes as I run and looks so pretty as I twirl. I want to look pretty for him, even though we'll be in darkness and he probably doesn't give a shit either way.

My belly flutters as I realise just how much I want to look pretty for him.

My knickers are skimpy and white. My bra is white lace and pokes up over the neckline of my dress.

I don't bother with a jacket. I somehow suspect I'll work up quite a sweat.

No shoes.

I take a breath as I head down the stairs, and pause for just a second before stepping onto the street, the pavement cold under my feet. I know exactly the route he means. The view towards the cathedral looks clear.

I wonder where he is. If he can see me. Of course he can. He's in the shadows, somewhere near.

The thought makes me shiver.

I walk with purpose, eyes wide and head up, flinching at every shadowy doorway, even though there's nothing there.

Church Street is narrow and dimly lit. I keep right in the middle between the buildings, focused on nothing other than saving my breath for what's ahead.

I'm going to need it, and I know it.

I slip through the bollards into the cathedral grounds, and my soul lights up in the darkness. It's magical. Beautiful.

The cathedral is a beacon of wonder. Lit up in a grandeur I've never really appreciated until now. Imposing and petrifying and brilliant all at the same time, looking over me as I stand barefoot in the middle of the night, just waiting to… sin. A crazy bitch sinner.

I'm smiling at the thought and I savour this moment. I want to remember it forever.

I walk on the grass to save my toes, and it's easy to pick up pace as I cross the grounds toward the river path. I flinch as grass turns back to tarmac, then flinch again as my toe scuffs a stone.

Ow.

Tonight could be really fucking painful.

In more ways than one.

I realise now that he could appear at any moment. I scan the shadows, my heart suddenly racing. Will he throw something, like last time?

Or will he just jump me and throw me to the ground?

I'm petrified and excited all at once, to the point that my heartbeat is in overdrive. Everything about this screams crazy, but I couldn't talk my body down from this if I tried. Every single muscle is wound tight and ready to go.

I'm ready to go.

But he said to walk slowly, so I do. I walk as slowly as my jittery nerves can bear, the harsh ground underfoot not helping.

I breathe as steadily as I can. In through my nose, out through my mouth. I clutch my handbag tight just to keep hold of something.

The drop to the river path is dark. Really dark.

I hesitate at the top, my eyes blinking and searching. *Waiting.*

Waiting for the monster to jump out of the shadows. Waiting for him to hoist me from my feet and drag me away.

Tiny steps, so tiny. Edging closer. I'm so expectant. So alert.

But he isn't there.

Fuck.

I was so sure. So fucking sure.

But no. I descend without incident. My feet hit the grit and soil of the river path and all I hear is water down below.

My senses run riot down here, imagining horrors all around me. Hands in the undergrowth reaching out. Hot breath on my neck.

It's the crunch of a stick behind me that sets me running. A squeal and I'm away, racing along the riverside without even so much as a glance back over my shoulder.

My hands swing at my sides, handbag long forgotten. It bounces against my ass, making a strange slapping sound as I go. My breath is wild in my ears. My heart is on fire.

My feet don't feel a single thing.

I know this way well, but at this pace it feels laced with peril. I'm dipping under imaginary branches, veering away from imaginary demons. In danger of going tumbling just to escape the one behind me.

It's a while before I know for sure there are footsteps pounding after mine. He's at a distance, but he's closing. I feel it.

My body screams with it.

I'm sprinting on wild instinct and nothing else.

My lungs are burning. My breath rasping in my throat. My heart thumps loud.

But not as loud as the boots of the beast behind me.

I fly like the wind, as fast as I've ever run in my life. My belly lurches with the thrill of being captured, but my flight instinct doesn't agree. All I can do is keep on going, adrenaline so high, it's fucking incredible.

I don't know how long I've been running when the undergrowth gets deeper to my right. I don't know how long it's taken to reach the part of the path where there are barely any lights left at all.

I have to slow down here, so I do. I curse under my breath as my foot squelches in wet mud, and I know I'm too close to the river.

Shit.

I head further up the bank, but when I do his footsteps are nearer. Louder.

Faster.

He's right on top of me.

My heart booms and so does my clit. My thighs are slick even though it's fucking insane.

I'm desperate for him, even as my body finds its reserves to keep on running.

I'm making desperate noises as I breathe and I can't stop.

I can't stop because I fucking love it.

I'm a tumble of emotions with no structure. No backbone.

It's all I want to do to fall on the ground and beg that he doesn't hurt me. Beg that he does. Fall at his feet and beg him for anything; beg him for everything. *Everything.*

But then I see a light up ahead.

I know this place. I've been here before.

My heart soars as I recognise the pub from my crappy date with pink-shirted Jack.

The car park there is dim, but it's lit. I'll see the monster coming.

Oh fuck, how I want to see him coming.

I want to see every inch of his brutality as it comes my way.

Every inch of his beautiful face.

I make a final sprint for it, even as I feel him at my back.

The world stops spinning.

It slows to nothing as I feel the heat of him.

A thump of his boots and I hear his breath.

And then he grabs me.

Hard.

He steals the last of my breath from my lungs as he slams into my back. My bare feet are still running in the air as he lifts me clean off the ground.

I've no air to cry out, but he clamps his hand over my mouth anyway.

I've nowhere left to run, but still he crushes me until it hurts.

"Quiet," he growls, and I try to nod.

He doesn't take his hand away. Part of me hopes he never does.

The monster carries me easily up the track to the car park. I wonder if he's going to fuck me over the railings, but he passes them by.

And then I see the hulk of his metallic black truck in the shadows.

"Don't make a fucking sound," he growls again as he pins me to its side. My cheek presses to window glass. I see my own misty breath. My wild eye looks at itself in the dark reflection, and behind me I see him.

And he's beautiful.

He looks wild. Even wilder than me.

Dark and angry and coiled tight.

Dangerous.

He opens the passenger door and I wonder if I'm supposed to get in.

I'm not.

That's obvious enough when the rope comes out.

I've never been tied up before. I protest before I can stop myself.

I'm a whimpering mess, begging *please, no*, but he doesn't even look at me.

My handbag comes off over my head in a flash and he tosses it into the footwell. I try to pull my wrists from his grip, but he tugs them up behind my back and binds them tight.

He wraps the rope around my waist, around my thighs too. My pussy clenches as he threads the rope between my legs.

My clit throbs as he pulls it tight and I swear I almost come.

He pulls it again on purpose, I know he does, and I moan for him. I fucking moan for him.

I wish he'd touch me. Wish he'd use me right here, with my cheek pressed to the window.

I wish he'd fuck me so hard I'd scream for more, for less, for hurt.

He shunts me aside unceremoniously and opens the rear door. I'd stumble if he didn't have such a solid grip on my arm.

He's going to leave bruises.

And I'm going to love them.

He wrestles me roughly into the rear footwell. I squeak as I realise where this is going – just me, trussed up in rope, wedged behind the front seats.

It's tight. Claustrophobic enough to make me beg.

"Please…" I whimper. "Please, not like this… I'll get sick…"

"Shut the fuck up," he says and the door slams at my feet.

The driver's door opens soon after. The seat moves against my back as he climbs up. I hear the groan of the leather as he settles into position.

I curse as the ignition comes on. Beg some more as he reverses out of there.

I don't stop begging for miles – lost in this crazy footwell hell. Scared and battered with feet sure to be bleeding. They feel like they're bleeding.

My imagination runs riot, wondering if he really is some kind of psychopath.

I have no idea how he found me. I have no clue how he knew exactly where I'd be.

Still, my clit keeps on throbbing. My thighs are slick even though I'm freaking out so hard I could vomit.

I know we're out of town, even without windows. I feel every cattle grid. Every winding turn in the road.

And then we stop.

The quiet is ominous once he kills the engine.

My breath whistles in my ears. My heart pounding like crazy all over again.

He clambers out of the front seat, and I'm whimpering to myself before he's even on me.

Cold air grazes my thighs as he opens the rear door.

I kick out on instinct as he grabs at my feet, but he's stronger. He drags me out easily.

And then he lets me go.

He unwinds the rope from my wrists before I've even got my bearings. He tugs it from between my thighs so quickly it burns.

153

My eyes blink and focus.

Darkness.

So much darkness.

Just the moonlight overhead.

And fields. So many fields. Fields upon fields.

I twist my head as he tugs the last of the rope from me.

Fields and soil and trees in every direction.

We're in the middle of nowhere.

"*Run.*"

One word. That's all he says.

He shunts my shoulders and says it again.

"Run."

And I do.

I run through soil and grass and heather. I scrabble up a hill on my hands and knees and take off again at the top.

My rational mind is too fucked up to keep a grip. I'm lost to endorphins and adrenaline and terror. This isn't a quick sharp shock like being slammed into the shutter doors. This is drawn-out. Exhausting.

More terrifying than anything I've ever known. And that's because I'm doubting him.

He's going to kill me.

He's going to fuck me so hard and leave me to die.

I can't hear him behind me but I keep on running, images of my dying self, sprawled naked on a hilltop, flashing through my mind, my pussy an unrecognisable mess. I run and run until I stumble and fall. I drag myself up and curse myself through tears, knowing full well I'm losing any grip on my own crazy reality.

I'm crying, sobbing as I run.

I'm crying at how bad my lungs are aching. At how pointless this is.

How scared he's made me.

How fucked up I am.

I don't want to run anymore.

I've barely made it a couple of fields when I'm a whimpering mess on the ground. I'm barely crawling when I hear his boots thump the ground behind me.

Strong.

Steady.

Menacing.

"You done?" he asks, and I shake my head.

I keep on crawling, scrabbling for grip enough to get to my feet.

But they hurt.

My toes are freezing cold and raw.

It hurts too much to keep on going. I have no breath left in my lungs.

I sink to my knees and I feel so degraded as his boot comes to rest on my back. Humiliated as he presses me to the dirt.

And I love him for it.

"Are you done?" he asks again, and I nod.

I'm done.

I'm a mess.

A fucked up mess with jangling nerves and clammy thighs.

Who hates how much she wants this.

Who loves how much she wants this. *Him.*

I can't believe how hard I've run. How far I've come.

How fucking crazy I am.

How my thighs are opening in invitation, even though I know I could die tonight.

And I can't believe how terrified I am when he drops to his knees behind me.

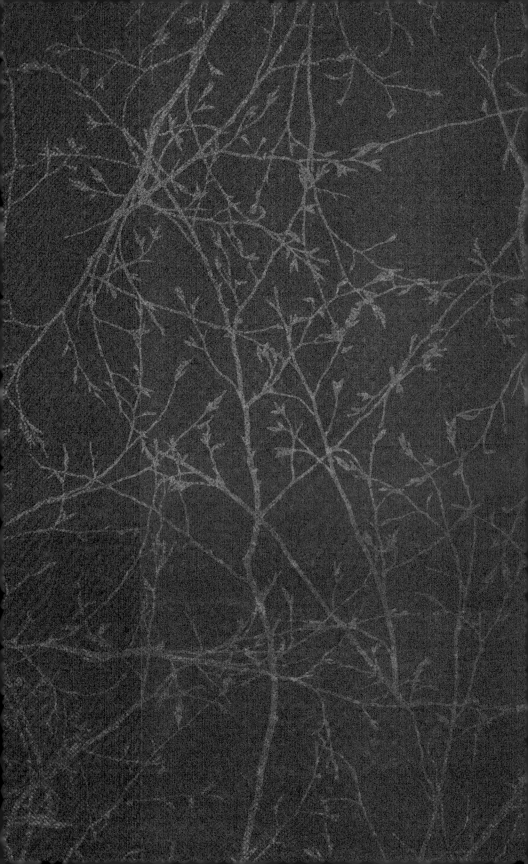

seventeen

Every man has a wild beast within him.

—FREDERICK THE GREAT

phoenix

She's even more of a wreck than I thought she'd be.

She ran much harder than I ever expected.

And now she's broken.

Part of me wants to scoop her up and make it all better. The other part...

The other part wants to make it so much worse.

I teeter between two torn sides. I'm in no man's land as I drop to my knees in the dirt.

And then she decides for me. Even as she whimpers, she reaches down and tugs her skirt up her thighs.

It's an invitation.

The most desperately fucked up invitation I've ever had.

I almost hate myself for wanting it.

Almost hate myself for the way she makes me feel. The way she summons all the broken parts of me and makes them sing.

She's shivering as I run my fingers up her bare leg. She rolls back against the heat of me as I lay down in the dirt behind her.

I barely need to coax her leg up and over mine. She tips her head back willingly as I snake my hand around her throat.

She's terrified but wanting. Broken but seeking.

"You're gonna give me whatever I want," I whisper, and the words keep coming. "Whatever I want, whenever I want. I'll be around every fucking corner. In every fucking shadow."

My fingers slip around her waist and down. I hitch her ass back against my throbbing dick and she grinds like a wanton little bitch.

"I'll be your monster," I whisper. "I'll be every dirty fucking nightmare you ever had."

She's offering her pussy to my fingers even as they slip inside her knickers. She's wet. Wet enough to take three straight in with a groan.

"*You* came looking for *me*," I hiss. "Remember that."

Her voice comes out choked. Her whisper just a breath on the breeze. "I *found* you."

"And *I* found *you*. I found you at the train station. I followed you to the petrol station. I was at your front fucking door."

I sound like a crazy stalker. *Feel* like a crazy stalker.

I feel like a beast without boundaries. She's trampled them all.

I finger her sopping cunt and close my eyes and all I see is her. The blue of her dress trailing behind her in the darkness. The whites of her eyes in the window reflection as I bound her wrists.

"Be the monster..." she breathes, and I slam my fingers all the way inside.

I take my hand from her throat and take her hair instead. I hold her tight. Hard. Her head against my shoulder, the scent of her so close.

And then I push a fourth finger all the way in.

She groans. It sounds pained, even though her ass bucks back at me.

My mouth finds her neck and tastes her skin. She tastes of dirt and sweat and dreams. She flinches as my teeth pinch. Her hand reaches back for my ass, coaxing me tighter against her.

I can't get any fucking tighter against her.

I fuck her deep and fast, fingers buried to the knuckles in that sweet tight pussy. I breathe into her ear as she moans for me.

I need this.

I need *her*.

She tips her face as far as I allow, almost enough that I could kiss her.

Her eyes are dark in the moonlight. Her hair is like black ink on the ground.

"Be my monster..." she breathes again, but I'm the one calling the shots.

My fingers squelch as I pull them free. My thumb is wet on her clit as I press hard. Brutal circles, her thighs spread wide.

I let go of her hair and wrap my arm around her neck. It's the most delicious headlock, her fingers gripping my forearm and squeezing tight.

She's trapped. Restrained. In the grip of a beast who won't give her an inch.

And she fucking likes it.

I'm as brutal with her clit as the rest of her, but she fucking likes that too.

She's on the edge in a heartbeat. It barely takes a fucking minute.

My black swan makes such pretty noises as she comes. The most desperate little gasps, so choked. She shivers and squirms and bucks that tight little ass against me, and it's enough to send the beast in me fucking wild.

She's barely even done when I force her onto her back. I pin her wrists above her head with enough weight that she squeals, and then I tear that sweet blue dress from her tits and rip the lace of her bra down with it.

The white catches the moonlight, just like her skin. Her nipples are dark little bullets, screaming for touch.

She should be begging me to stop when I feast on her tit. She should be screaming as I pinch one of those sweet little nubs tight between my teeth.

Her legs shouldn't part this easily as I grind my crotch against her puffy little slit. I tear her knickers off at the seams and wrestle my dick free from my jeans with clumsy fingers.

The head goes in in one, and it's heaven. Crazy fucking heaven.

I press my forehead to hers as I force the first barbell inside. Her eyes are on mine. Her hitching breaths on my lips.

I could kiss her, but I don't.

I can't.

Kissing her demons would free my own. Every single one of them.

She wraps her legs around my waist and urges me on, even though her face is pained and her eyes are wide.

I give it to her.

Deep, hard thrusts send me deeper.

My hips slam forward to claim it all.

Our eyes stay open. Hers flash with pain just as mine do.

Her pussy clenches hard enough to fucking hurt.

I grunt as I pull out of her.

She groans as I push straight back in.

"More," she whispers. "Give me everything."

She's crazier than I fucking thought, and so am I.

I shunt in hard and she cries out.

I do it again and she screams.

But she takes it. And I take her.

Her forehead is clammy against mine. Her breath playing against my lips.

She relaxes underneath me as we fall into rhythm. Her thighs loll open and her pussy welcomes me home.

I'm as close to bottoming out as I've ever been, my balls slapping loud against cold skin.

I want so much to land my mouth on hers, but fear it would end us both.

She takes it hard. So fucking hard.

I close my eyes against hers just to enjoy the sensation.

And *she* kisses *me*.

Gently.

Tenderly.

Her lips a ghost against mine.

My eyes open wide and hers are right there. I grip her around the throat and pound her pussy harder to punish her.

Tears spring as I watch. Her glassy eyes don't waver.

"Hurting?" I growl.

She nods.

"Tell me to stop."

She shakes her head.

I taste her tears before they've spilled. I slam my cock in all the way and the screams again.

And then I hitch myself up to change angle. She cries out as the pressure changes.

She's hissing like a wildcat as my piercings grind the right spot. *Just like Mariana did.*

The similarities end right there.

My black swan's eyes are full of sweet dark soul. Full of tenderness along with pain.

bait

I release my grip from her throat and drop my full weight onto hers. Her fingers spring to my face and brush my jawbone as though I'm a thing of wonder.

"Come," I growl. "Show your monster how much you like it."

She moves her hands to my bare ass. Her fingers are as chilled as my skin. She squeezes hard, then raises her legs, grunting as she takes what she needs.

"Good girl," I hiss. "Show me."

She must be fucking exhausted, but she's still going strong. Her feet must be killing her as they thrash against my legs.

When she comes undone it's explosive. She's louder than I expected, screaming at the moon as she goes.

I don't do anything to quieten her. There's no one for fucking miles.

I wouldn't care if there was.

I don't even wait for her to catch her breath. She's still panting as I tear myself out of her. Her mouth is open in a scream when I scramble up and fill it with cock.

It won't fit. It never does.

Not until I hook my fingers in her teeth and open her wide for me.

She splutters as I push my way in. Her throat bulges as I make her take it.

Her tongue feels so fucking hot against my piercings. Her eyes look so pretty as they strain.

I unload straight down her throat, cursing and straining. I leave nothing but a thick string of cum and spit between us when I'm done.

Fuck.

The beast calms.

The red mist starts to clear.

The ravaged girl underneath me rolls over. She winces as she tries to rise to her knees.

She's fucked.

Battered, bruised, exhausted.

Freezing cold.

She shivers without my body heat, her teeth chattering as she stares at me.

I tug my jeans back up and rise to my feet.

She rearranges her dress to cover her tits. I wish she wouldn't.

She scrambles but falters. I see the pain in her eyes as she struggles for balance on sore legs.

It's the easiest thing in the world to scoop her up off her feet.

She doesn't say a word as I hold her, just wraps her arms around my shoulders and presses her face to my neck.

This is all kinds of fucked up.

The way my heart pangs is all fucking kinds of fucked up.

The way I carry her so carefully, defies every rule of crazy.

But I can't let her go.

eighteen

When death, the great reconciler, has come, it is never our
tenderness that we repent of, but our severity.

—GEORGE ELIOT

abigail

My monster carries me so tenderly. Securely, even over rough ground. His shoulders are firm, his breath even. His grip is strong and steady, his body heat divine.

I'm aching. Exhausted. Sated beyond anything I've ever known.

My feet hang limp all the way back to his truck, my face buried into his neck for the warmth.

I can still taste him. My throat is raw with the memory of his intrusion. My pussy, too.

I can't bear the thought of another bumpy ride in the footwell, but he opens the front passenger door and drops me onto the seat before I even protest. I can barely rest my feet on the floor they're so sore.

I buckle myself in as he heads around to the driver's side. I have no idea what to say as he turns the key in the ignition.

I wonder if he meant it – taking what he wants whenever he wants it. I wonder if this is a thing now.

As fucked up as I am right now, I want nothing more than this to be a thing.

He turns on the heater and reverses up the lane. He turns at the top and we speed away.

I take the opportunity to look at him again in the darkness as we go. His features are so strong. So brutally rugged.

He's the hottest thing I've ever seen. Being close to him makes my skin prickle.

I wonder what he looks like under his clothes. I wonder if I'll ever find out.

I can feel the giddiness now, building up under the adrenaline. I'm as high as a kite, a few stupid jokes away from laughing until tears roll.

And yet I feel so lonely.

I've never wanted someone's touch so badly as I want his right now.

He drives and I watch.

He stares out of the window and I stare right at him.

I'm sad when signs for Hereford appear in the road. My heart is pained when I recognise the streets passing by. We're back in the city centre so quickly, parking up in a loading bay just down the street from my front door.

I wonder if he was here earlier. I look up at my living room window and the open curtains. He could have been spying on me for hours.

I feel like such a wimp as I contemplate having to put my feet back on solid ground. They're freezing and sore. Grazed to all living shit from the feel of it.

I grit my teeth as I swing the car door open, bracing myself for the impact of dropping down onto the tarmac. But he blocks my exit before I can move.

The closeness of him takes my breath as he reaches past me to flick on the interior light.

I flinch as I see the state of myself in the glow.

I'm filthy. Caked in mud and bits of hedgerow.

I've torn a toenail. I've scratches all over my ankles. The soles of my feet look like they've spent an hour on an industrial sander.

I'm still staring at them as he reaches into the glovebox. The packet of wipes rustles in his fingers as he pulls one free. He props his foot on the sill and lifts mine up over his knee. I stare dumb as he works the wipe over my skin.

I flinch as it stings, but he doesn't stop.

"I didn't expect you to run so fast," he says. "I'd have let you wear shoes."

I shrug. "Guess I surprised you."

His eyes meet mine. "Guess you did."

He's surprising me too, but I don't tell him that.

I watch him wipe my foot until the wipe is filthy and he pulls out another. I love the way his fingers can be so tender after being so rough.

I love the way the ink patterns look on his skin.

He switches my clean foot for my dirty one. I should point out that they'll be filthy again before I reach my apartment, but I don't want him to stop.

"You need to put these in a hot bath," he tells me.

I smile as I tell him I only have a shower. A small one at that.

His eyes are dark on mine. "A bowl then."

I nod.

I figure he's just putting the wipes away when he reaches back to the glovebox.

My eyes widen when I recognise my shoes.

"You found them."

"One of them was under a truck," he says.

I don't know why I'm smiling so hard to see them again, but I am.

I don't know why I have the urge to brush my thumb across his jaw when he slips one onto my foot and buckles it up so gently.

Walking on these is going to be marginally better at best to walking barefoot, and that's being optimistic. I don't want to tell him that, though.

He fastens up the other and I thank him. His eyes burn me as I grab my handbag from under the seat.

"First floor, right?" he asks and I nod. He glances across to the building and points at my window. "Yours?"

"My living room."

He looks from my feet to the communal entrance. "I'll help you up the stairs."

He holds out his arms to help me, but I don't move a muscle. I'm frozen like a fool, floundering at the kindness of such a brutal stranger.

His dark eyes are dirty. Amused.

"Even a monster can be a gentleman," he says.

I think of Stephen back home. His slick ways. His posh suits. His cocky smile.

And I guess it's true enough that a monster really can be a gentleman.

After all, I already learned the hard way that a gentleman really can be a monster.

phoenix

I feel like a prize asshole as I help Abigail up to her apartment.

Her feet were a wreck and they're barely any better now. She'll be sore on them for days.

The rest of her probably won't feel all that great, either.

She's elegant even in pain. There's a finesse about the way she limps. A beauty in her grace of movement.

She ran like a nymph, her hair streaming like a siren.

She is a siren.

I'm still holding her as she digs her keys from her handbag and pushes the door open. I step inside without hesitation, closing the door behind us as she gets the light.

Her place is small, neat, organised.

Barren.

It surprises me.

"I haven't long moved in," she says, as though she's embarrassed.

She's been on the electoral roll for months and I know it. There's a sadness in her eyes that doesn't go unnoticed.

She lowers herself onto the sofa but I don't join her. I'm not sure I should even be in here. Unsure I'm even welcome.

"You promised you'd delete your profile," I remind her, and she smiles.

"I didn't think I'd be so desperate for a repeat performance."

"And how about now? Are you still so desperate to go again?"

Her eyes sparkle. "Maybe not right this second."

It makes me smile. "A rain check, I think. See how you feel in a few days."

She shakes her head. "No rain check necessary. I want to go again."

My demons are fucking joyous.

And so am I.

"You'll delete your profile like you promised," I tell her, then hold out my hand. "Give me your phone."

She looks up at me curiously, but hands it straight over from her bag.

She doesn't have a lock code. Her backdrop is the factory default.

I suspect that hasn't always been the case.

I log into my work GPS portal and download the logistics app to her handset. She stares up at me but doesn't say a word. I set the app to update in real time, just as I do with the drivers' PDAs. I'll feed data straight through to my phone.

I clear the browser listing showing my company login. The app still stands.

I hold my own handset up. "Your phone will talk to mine," I tell her. "I'll know where you are in real time. Nowhere to hide. You have your phone, I'll be able to find you." I pause. "Speak now or forever hold your peace."

She takes her phone back from me. "Anytime?" she asks. "So you'll just what? Show up?"

"Written notice kind of ruins the chase, don't you think?"

"And if I want to get hold of you?" She drops her gaze. "I guess *you'll* be the one getting hold of *me*, right?"

"Maybe when you least expect it."

Her breath is shallow. Her eyes soft.

I have to get out of here before I lose the power to walk away.

I slip my phone back in my pocket. "I'll see myself out."

"Wait," she says, but I don't. She doesn't follow me, not in those heels. "I don't even know your name."

And that's how it's going to stay.

I take one last look around the place before I leave, taking in the layout – the window positions, the small kitchen table, the bathroom off to the right. I assign it all to memory in a heartbeat and then I make my move for the exit.

Then I see it, the bowl on the counter. Coins. A couple of charity badges.

And a spare key.

I turn it over in my hand.

Definitely for the front door.

I slip it into my pocket.

And then I get the hell out of there.

nineteen

phoenix

I've got her front door key in my pocket, the scent of her pussy on my fingers, and a storm of shit to work out at home.

The sword of unanswered questions hangs by a dangerously fine cord over my head, but tonight I'm charged enough to stare right up at it. No fear.

There is no whisky bottle on the coffee table when I let myself back in. No ashtray waiting to disturb my peace of mind.

Instead, there's Serena, huddled asleep in the armchair, her long hair trailing over the arm. Her knees are held to her chest, her chin resting on top. She looks precariously peaceful, one tiny move and she'd topple.

I forget how small she is, my little sister. I forget how Jake and I used to be so fucking protective over the little girl with big dark eyes, even if she was full enough of spit and fury to ward off demons herself.

171

If only she could ward off mine. Hell, she's tried – trapped between two bulls baying for each other's blood, even though it's the same fucking blood in their veins.

I prop myself in the doorway, just to be there awhile. I collect my thoughts until she stirs.

She starts as she sees me there. "I was waiting up for you. What time is it?"

"Late," I tell her. "Why aren't you upstairs? You do still have a bed."

She looks away. "We can't go on just pretending everything is normal, Leo."

She's right about that.

Her eyes meet mine. "We need to talk… about Jake…"

"Fuck Jake," I say.

"I said some awful things, Leo. Awful. But I said the truth… we don't know…"

I shoot her a glare. "You think I'm too chicken shit to let him see my son? You think this is some shitty excuse for denial because I'm too scared to face the truth?"

She shrugs. "I don't know. Is it?"

I shake my head and smile at the ridiculousness of all this. "Jake's a fucking mess, Serena. He's a drunk who can't keep his shit together." I glare at her. "He hates me too fucking much to keep a lid on his crap. His bitterness is toxic to everyone, not least himself. Cam sure as hell doesn't need Jake's fucking baggage, he's got enough of his own."

"But you can't do this…" she whispers. "He'll never cope if you stop him seeing Cam."

"I never fucking *started* letting him see Cam."

She shrugs again. "He's my brother, yours too."

"I know who he is, and I don't like it one bit."

I see her clock the mud on my clothes. "Where did you go tonight?"

I wave her question aside. "Doesn't matter."

And she loses her shit, just like that. "And *this* is where the problem is. So many secrets. So many lies. We're sinking, all of us. Jake looks like death, you're so tightly wound, I don't even know you anymore."

"You know me," I tell her. "You know Cam, too."

"And Jake… I know Jake… I know how much he loved her…"

I knock my head back against the doorframe. "Jesus Christ, Serena."

And we're there again. Arguing over the fucking L word. Arguing over a woman who's long in the fucking ground, lost to us all.

"He'll never let it go," she carries on. "If you stop him seeing Cam, it'll send him over the edge… it's the last he's got… the last piece of…"

"*Her*," I finish. "And I don't give a fuck, Serena, I swear. He's my boy. I'm the one who tucks him into bed at night. I'm the one who picks him up when he scrapes his knees. I'm the one who'd kill to keep him safe." My eyes are wild but I don't care. "And I *will* kill to keep him safe. *Whoever* he needs keeping safe from."

It's her turn to slam her head backwards. "Fucking hell, Leo. Where will this ever end?"

I don't have an answer, so I don't give her one.

"I love you," she continues. "Enough to give you the truth, even though it feels like shit, and I'm telling you now, this is a bad road. We're *all* on a bad road." She sighs, then gets up from the chair. "I can't choose you or him, but I can choose Cam. Please let me come back home for him."

"You want to move back in here? With us? Abandon poor, sad Jake?"

She bites her thumbnail. "You haven't really left me a choice, have you?"

She's got a point. "And you'll stop the secret fucking visits?"

She shrugs. "If that's what it takes. You and Jake will have to sort the rest out for yourselves. I'm done."

"He's not Jake's boy," I say again. "I know it."

"We're talking about Mariana, Leo. None of us know anything."

That makes me smile. "Ain't that the fucking truth of it."

She closes the distance between us. I'm tense as she wraps her arms around my waist. "I'm sorry I hurt you. I'm sorry the truth was so brutal."

"I'm sorry you felt you had to."

She nods.

I kiss the top of her head.

I watch her head upstairs to bed, back where she belongs.

And then I message my fucking brother.

a b i g a i l

Something has lifted inside. Even as I wince, walking wounded, through my Sunday, I feel it.

My pain is all external, my outlook sunnier than I've known it in months.

I feel… good.

Excited.

Hopeful.

Even a little optimistic.

Optimistic enough to log into my social media accounts for the first time in months and not feel a crippling sense of loss.

I browse my newsfeed, smiling at posts by my friends back home. I even comment.

I laugh. I smile.

I'm human again.

Human enough to realise that the new contacts I've been making at work, the people I've been spending my time with, are becoming more than just empty connections.

I add them, one by one. I add Lauren and Kayleigh and even pink-shirted Jack.

I catch sight of a glorious sunset over the cathedral from my living window and capture it on camera.

I save it as my phone backdrop.

I smile at life – at the life a stranger in the night gave me back.

A stranger who watches me.

Who wants me.

Who'll be lurking around some shadowy corner when I least expect it. The thought gives me shivers.

I walk to work on Monday with a smile on my face and my head held high. I walk with a thrum of excitement in my belly, as if his eyes are on me. Always on me.

I make a round of coffees first up, as though I really belong in the office.

Maybe I do.

Lauren seeks me out at my desk. She fans her face and leans in close, and my heart does a little burst at the thought of juicy gossip.

Sandra and Frank from the Worcester accounts team. Both at Diva's, hitting up the dancefloor and snogging each other's faces off at 2 a.m.

I haven't met them, so I pull a face.

"Summer barbeque, you'll meet them all there," she tells me, and I grin. Summer barbeque is bigger than Christmas here, so they tell me. "You missed a great night," she continues, and I actually believe her. "Say you're coming along to George's leaving party on Thursday! You *have* to be there, it wouldn't be the same if you weren't. We're all dressing up as vicars and tarts. Wear your sluttiest."

"I think I'm washing my hair," I reply, and she rolls her eyes. I laugh. "I'll be there. Sounds too entertaining to miss."

And it does.

Sarah from next door is struggling to open the communal door on Tuesday evening when I arrive back home. She's loaded up with enough shopping to feed the five thousand for a week.

I pull the door open for her and she grins.

"Lifesaver. Got a bit carried away with the special offers."

I take a couple of bags from the floor. "No shit. Those buy one get one frees are fatal, right?"

I help her upstairs with her haul, and when she invites me in for coffee, I accept with a smile.

Her place is so different to mine. The mirror image in layout, but so much warmer. So much more lived in.

She tells me she only moved in a few months earlier than I did. I find that hard to believe as I look around.

"It gets lonely sometimes," she says as she sits down at her kitchen table. "My family are all up north, I got relocated down here for work. New branch. They're all old where I work. I haven't made it out once yet." She takes a breath. "So, what's your story?"

"I had a break up," I tell her with surprisingly little hesitation. "I left everything behind. Even my nail varnish."

It makes her laugh. "Must have been pretty dire to leave without beauty essentials."

I look at my chewed-up nails and find myself laughing back. "It was pretty dire, yeah."

Was.

I said *was.*

"Where are you from?" she asks.

"Hampshire. Fleet."

She nods. "Was he worth it? All the shit? Worth running across the country for?"

I've never been asked that question before. Never even contemplated it.

The answer comes easily. "No. Had a nice dick, though."

She splutters her coffee. "Did he know how to use it? That's the clincher."

The memory of Stephen is hazy. Distant.

Sore feet and soil and barbells are the only things that feel real.

My definition of *knowing how to use it* has changed somewhat in my frame of reference.

"He was okay."

She tips her head. "He was okay? Just okay?"

I nod. Giggle. Sip my coffee. "Just okay, yeah. I thought he was the best ever at the time."

"But not now?"

I think of my monster. The dark soul in his dark eyes. The way he pushes me, pins me, stretches me and makes me love it.

"No. Not now."

"Intriguing." She laughs, but I don't elaborate.

I look at the woman opposite me, her kind eyes and her easy smile. I see a loneliness in her that's gone from me, floating just under the surface.

"I'm going out to Diva's on Thursday with the crowd from work," I tell her. "Vicars and tarts. You could come, if you wanted to check out the Hereford nightlife."

"I could?"

"You sure could. Just wear your sluttiest – I'm under strict orders. No suspenders, no tequila."

Her eyes twinkle. "I'll see what I can cobble together."

I'm strangely pleased by her acceptance.

"I've got plenty of nail varnish," she says. "Just tell me what colour you're wearing. I'll pick some out."

bait

"Red," I say, even though I have no idea. "Scarlet harlot."

"Red," she repeats. "I'll bring a shortlist over. Give you a knock."

"Thanks." I finish up my coffee and put my mug on the drainer.

And then I head back home for some late-night online shopping.

twenty

It's not the size of the dog in the fight, it's the size of the fight in the dog.
—MARK TWAIN

phoenix

My message to Jake was simple.

Stay away from my house. Stay away from my son.

The barrage of abuse I received in response was even more vehement than I anticipated.

I barely gave it any credence whatsoever until his sign-off message on Sunday evening.

I want a fucking paternity test.

He can fucking want.

I'm busy at work on Monday – a shitload of fresh shipments arriving in from Germany. I've barely got a spare minute to think, and yet she's always there, a flashing circle on my GPS software.

It's easy to take a second to find out where she works – a place called *Office*

Express on the edge of the city centre. I look up their website and find a standard, generic-looking office supplies company. I click on their *meet our staff* page and find her staring back at me.

Abigail Summers, administration clerk.

It strikes me as odd, that job title. Whichever way I look at it, it feels like a major career back step. I guess that's what happens when you get as chewed up as she did – you run, fast. Take whatever you can find.

We lost our office manager here after the fire. Just one of many who drifted away when the business was on the ground. Gillian had been good, at the heart of operations, equally positioned between the pair of us – me and Jake. Close to Marianna, too. Her resignation had been just another unfortunate piece of shit in the aftermath. Tears and apologies and a 'see you around'.

I haven't replaced her.

I don't even know why Gillian presents herself in my consciousness. I wouldn't even consider having Abigail here. Not for a single sensible second. Not for a fraction of one.

Never.

But my cock is throbbing like a motherfucker under my desk. My heart a pounding fucking mess at the thought of chasing her around the warehouse after hours.

My Germany shipment can wait a few more minutes. I click on the Office Express company blog and scroll through, searching for snippets, photos, anything that will give me more insight into my pretty black swan. That's when I notice their updated events schedule listed loud and clear.

Office Express summer barbecue. Castle Green. In aid of Herefordshire Air Ambulance.

Summer ball theme, dress to impress.

Staff, suppliers, and clients – all welcome.

Clients welcome. My cock twitches.

Interesting.

It's on the twenty-eighth of the month. A Saturday three-weeks away.

I flick back to their company brochure. Most of our furniture at this new depot is odds and sods from clearance sales – the best I could do under the circumstances at the time.

I need a new filing cabinet and a fresh batch of printer cartridges. That's what I tell myself when I fill in the online form and click submit.

Order confirmed. A representative will contact you shortly. Thank you for your business.

And just like that I'm an Office Express client.

I check my calendar. The twenty-eighth is clear. I'm sure Serena won't mind taking over duck pond duties for the day.

I key in the date and smile as my calendar turns to busy.

The circle is still firmly in her office location when I check my phone again. I'm sure she'll be there, at the barbeque. I'm sure she'll be dressed to impress amongst her co-workers chowing down on a burger in the sunshine.

I'm sure I'll be there watching her, too.

I turn my attention back to my shipment logs, busying myself before the last of the trucks arrive back for reloading. I'm finally knuckling down with paperwork when the office door squeals on its hinges and slams against the wall. I've barely turned my head when my piece of shit brother comes flying in with his fists in the air. I can smell the drink on him before he's halfway across the room.

"You gonna fucking message me back then, or what?" he grunts. "Gotta use our fucking sister as your fucking guard dog now when you're not around?"

He's easy to out manoeuvre as he swings a clumsy fist across the desk at me, and he's easy to spin on his haunches and disorientate enough to slam to the ground.

The guy's like an angry fucking bear as he scrabbles to his feet. He tears my paperwork to the floor with his efforts, and I resist the urge to kick him right in the gut while he's on his knees.

"Back the fuck off, Jake," I bark, but he's too gone. Too fucking drunk.

His lip twists into a sneer as he glares up at me. "It's *Ash*," he spits. "*Ash*, because there's no rising from the flames for me, *Phoenix*. I'm still fucking dead inside." He pauses. There's enough hate in his eyes to make my neck prickle. "He's *my* fucking boy!" he yells and I curse his loud fucking mouth. I'm aware of people gathering in the corridor outside, aware that news of brothers at war is spreading like the pox through this building.

"Fuck you, Jake," I hiss. "She was mine. Cameron's *mine*."

"You're a fucking fool," he snarls. "She was *mine*. I saw her first. I loved her first."

I grab him by his filthy t-shirt and haul him to his feet, and I'm as bad as he is, all restraint lost to me now the beast's boiling in my blood. "Tell me what fucking happened that night. Tell me what started that fucking fire."

His eyes are full of hate. "*You* did. *You* sent her running."

My fist tightens against his throat. "Why were you there? What were the two of you fucking doing?"

His hate turns into a sneer. "What do you fucking think?"

I throw him over my desk. He hits the floor hard, but still he's flailing, grappling. "You were fucking her the whole fucking time?" My eyes fill as full of hate as his. "That's really what you're saying? The whole motherfucking time, Jake?"

"More than *you* fucking were," he snarls, and he's back on his feet. "The boy's mine, Leo. You know it. I know it. Ain't no fucking way he's yours and you know it."

But I don't.

He's drunk. Full of fucking shit.

"Get out!" I bark and point to the exit. "You're a fucking wreck. Go sort your fucking life out."

"I *have* no fucking life," he growls. "You stole it from me then let it fucking burn. You should have left me there to fucking burn with it."

"I'm beginning to wish I fucking had," I tell him.

His eyes flash with pain. "Maybe you should. She could've been still breathing."

But no.

That's fucking bullshit.

For the first time I don't feel the gut punch of guilt. Or self-loathing. Or failure.

I feel nothing but disgust at what he's become. What *we've* become.

"I'd never have gotten to her in time," I tell him, and I'm so calm it takes me aback. "The explosion loosened the racking, that door was barricaded tight."

"Keep telling yourself that," he rasps. "You didn't even fucking try."

My scars are burning all over again. I can smell them. Taste the seared meat in the air.

"You have no idea how hard I fucking tried," I tell him. "You're a fucking disgrace, Jake. A loser drunk on his knees. You're not Cam's fucking father and you never will be. You're just the sad excuse for an uncle that everyone feels pity for. Maybe that's why she chose me and not you, ever think about that? You always were a fucking loser."

"Shut your fucking mouth, Leo."

"Straight up choice, *Ash*. She chose me. Meeting you first made fuck all difference, it was always me."

"Is that fucking so?"

I nod. Don't take my eyes off his. "Yeah, that's fucking so."

"She called you a cunt that night," he snarls. "Said she hated you. Said she was sorry she ever fucking met you. Wanted us to take the boy and get away from here. Away from *you*."

I smile a terrible smile. "Glad that little gem managed to make it through the amnesia. Care to enlighten me with any others while you're at it?"

"You took everything from me!" he booms. "Let me see my boy, or I swear to fucking God, I'll take everything away from you too. Don't make me tear you down, *Phoenix*. I'd hate something to happen to this sweet little place you got set up here. Be bad luck for lightning to strike twice now, wouldn't it?"

He pauses. I stare, unwavering as he continues with his shit.

"Be a fucking shame if you were the one who didn't make it out next time, Leo. Poor little Cam would need good old *Uncle* Ash around to make it better."

"You're a piece of work, and you're fucking leaving."

"Paternity test!" he snarls. "I want a fucking paternity test!"

"And I'm telling you, Cam's my boy."

We glare.

Simmer.

Fester with fists clenched and ready to go.

And then my phone vibrates on the desktop. I see Serena's name flashing.

He does too.

"I'm gonna fucking answer that," I tell him, "and you're gonna fucking leave."

He kicks my desk chair flying. Stamps on the calculator he's knocked from the tray. "You've got until the end of the fucking month," he says. "Plenty of time to organise a fucking test."

"Fuck you," I sneer. "Close the door on your way out."

"End of the month," he repeats, "or I'm fucking coming for you."

He barges my scarred shoulder with his as he passes. I fight the urge to tear his skull from his neck.

I wait until I hear his truck tyres skidding on the gravel, and then I listen to my sister's voicemail.

It tells me Jake might be on his way down here. That he might be drunk, too.

Better late than fucking never, I suppose.

twentyone

Resolve to be thyself: and know that he who finds himself, loses his misery.
—MATTHEW ARNOLD

abigail

Tarts and vicars is a whole lotta fun. I open my parcels with glee as Sarah looks on.

I hold the tiny red slip dress up to my chest as she watches from my sofa. It's ridiculously short, ridiculously split, ridiculously everything.

I'm laughing as I do a twirl. "It looks like a nightdress. I'd feel like a slut even in bed alone in this thing."

"You'd *look* like a slut in bed alone in that thing." She pours another wine for both of us.

I pull out the stockings and suspenders from the parcel.

"Yes!" she says. "Yes, yes, yes!"

I've got a black feather boa and black elbow-length velvet gloves, and some actual hooker heels that I'm likely going to break my ankles in. "In for a penny, in for a pound," I say and take another swig from my glass.

In fairness, Sarah doesn't look any more demure than I'm going to look. She's wearing a leopard print boob tube and satin micro-mini. Her shoes are red PVC with a heel that could be classified as a lethal weapon.

I wonder where she's dug all this stuff out from, since she hardly struck me as being some kind of vixen behind closed doors. Still, I guess you never really know someone until you've seen their bedroom wear.

I feel like I'm getting to know Sarah. I feel like I'm getting to like her too. A lot.

She digs a bottle of nail varnish from her handbag. "Should match like a dream," she says, and she's right.

I'm glad we're doing this. Really glad.

I've been excited for days, giggling over outfit choices with the girls at the office, checking out websites during quiet minutes. Sarah was over last night to help me confirm my orders for real, and was straight back round this evening for the great unboxing.

"Any hot guys I should keep an eye out for?" she asks, and straight up I tell her about pink-shirted Jack and his oh-so-conventionally attractive cheekbones. She tips her head. "So, how come you aren't out to hook up with Mr Cheekbones?"

I flash her a smile. "Too clean cut for me. I prefer my guys a little more… rugged."

"Rugged?" She sips her drink. "Rugged like hairy and sweaty and built like a bear?"

I shake my head. Smile to myself. "Partially. Maybe." The wine has gone to my head, clearly. "I like them wild. Dark. Dangerous." I glance at my phone, knowing full well he's out there somewhere, watching me. *Maybe.*

Maybe tonight. "Unpredictable," I add.

She nods, waves a finger. "I got it. You like the excitement. The chase."

She's more right than she realises. I can't hold back from expanding. "I like tattoos on the neck, and arms that could crush me to death. I like pierced cocks and sharp teeth and a guy who's rough enough that I'll know about it next day." I laugh. "Or next week."

"You're a dark horse," she tells me. "I had you down for a fey little thing. Fragile and floaty."

Her observation takes me aback. "You did?"

She nods. A lot. As though it's stating the obvious. "Yeah. Sure thing. Very floaty. Didn't think you'd say boo to a goose."

I ponder her statement. *Fragile and floaty.* I think of how my old friends back home would collapse in hysterics at that description.

Or they would have... before...

I don't feel so fragile and floaty right now. I feel sharp and daring. Bold and brave and... tipsy.

"What did you think of me?" she asks. "When you first saw me, I mean?"

I try to think back, but there's nothing there, just a vague memory of some blonde woman next door. I didn't even notice, didn't care.

Didn't care about anything.

Not even myself.

Especially not myself.

Shit.

I think of all the people I've neglected in my own misery. All the obligations I've ignored. All the life I've missed out on.

And it's there, in my barren living room, with a red hooker dress hanging from my shoulders, that I realise I'm myself again. Or at least some convincing semblance thereof.

I've been gone a long time. Too long.

I tapped out of life for a whole season and then some.

I take a breath and slide my feet into my new heels. I'm back in the life game.

Back for a whole new season in a whole new team.

I like it. I like all of it.

I like him best of all.

"We'd better get ready," Sarah says. "Plenty of hot vicars ready to hear our confession."

"That's priests," I say.

She shrugs. "I don't give a shit, I'll confess to any hot guy who'll listen."

I don't doubt that. I laugh aloud at how wrong I was about Sarah. About this town. About everything.

And then I bring out my inner tart. It's about time she got an airing.

phoenix

I've been watching her. Keeping an eye on her location through the app on my phone with compulsive frequency as soon as Cam is snug in bed at night.

It's almost become an addiction. Borderline unhealthy.

As of yet she's been home every evening. It's been a struggle to hold back from joining her there, but a fine wine needs time to mature.

I don't want her to be expecting me when I use that key for the first time. I don't want her to be waiting expectantly when I use her sweet little body however I want with the luxury of time on her own turf. So I hold back, even though my cock hates me for it.

It's when I see that circle move on my handset that my heart speeds into life on Thursday evening. By eight o'clock she's out at some club in the centre of Hereford. I look it up online.

And then I check her social media. The social media she's only just been using again these past few days.

Really, I'm amazed at what a stalker I'm turning into.

I'm taken aback by the picture she's uploaded to her timeline. She's with some pretty blonde woman with bobbed hair, and I don't need to see any more than the selfie shot to know she's dressed to impress.

To impress *or* get laid. Or both.

The thought is a lead weight in my gut.

She's wearing gloves, and a feathery wrap around her neck. Her tits are high over red satin. Her lips are glossy red.

I'm downstairs in a heartbeat, holding up my keys to Serena in the living room as I ask if I'm okay to head out for a few hours.

"Where are you going?" she asks.

"Just out," I say as I grab my jacket.

She puts her TV show on pause. "Just out with *someone*?"

I feel acutely uncomfortable with the implication, but she had a point the other night. Too many secrets, too many lies. "Maybe someone," I admit.

She smiles. "And what is this *someone's* name?"

"Abigail."

Her face is a picture. "*Abigail*," she repeats. "And does Abigail enjoy mud wrestling by any chance?"

"We may have taken a stroll in the countryside."

"A stroll, sure."

I hold up my phone. "Call me if Cam wakes or you need me. I'll head straight back."

She rolls her eyes. "I'm sure we'll be fine. You just worry about strolling with Abigail."

I smirk. "I'll do that."

I experience an additional sense of reality for having spoken her name out loud. My mind is as wired as my body as I take the drive over to Hereford.

Her selfie is firmly on my mind as I drum my fingers on the steering wheel. My balls are tight and aching. My cock fucking desperate to feel that sweet pink cunt squeezing tight.

I wonder what I'm walking into. I wonder who else she's out with, if anyone.

I wonder how easy it'll be to grab her with no spectators. I wonder how easy it will be to wait for the right moment.

My composure feels stretched pretty thin already.

I park down the street from this place. *Diva's* the glowing sign reads. The place is busy but not heaving. I'm careful as I make my way through the throng inside, skirting the edges to ensure I see her before she sees me. She's nowhere inside. I watch the entrance to the women's toilets long enough to make sure she's not in there either.

The beer garden out the back is surprisingly big compared to the interior. Picnic benches and outdoor heaters are dotted around the terrace. The gardens stretch right back into the darkness and curl around the pub to the left. Drinkers congregate in groups. I see hers immediately – a huddle of girls wearing virtually nothing. Leopard print and lace and feather boas. Abigail looks different tonight.

It's more than the clothes she's wearing or the slutty lipstick. It's the way she stands so confidently. The way her eyes sparkle. The sound of her laughter.

The blonde woman is on one side of her and a guy is on the other. I clock his black outfit. I don't need to see him from the front to know he's dressed as a vicar. *Tarts and vicars.* Of course.

I edge closer, making sure I'm always a wall of bodies from her eyeline. I'll never make it beyond her to the shadows at the back of the garden without her seeing, so I opt to venture around to the side instead.

It's a good call. Edgy, and arguably borderline insane, but good. There's an emergency exit onto the street from here, but it's closed and latched. There's a big wheeled recycling bin and a load of trolleys for general waste. The vents from the pub kitchen come out this way and the lights are off inside.

The sound of voices is loud enough to be invasive. I'm close enough to her group to make out almost every word.

They're talking work. Innocuous chatter laced with drunken laughter. Abigail's laugh is loud and free. I step closer to watch her body language.

Her legs are tense and tight on those stupid heels, and her skirt is short enough that you can see her suspenders.

It makes me prickly.

Agitated.

The guy on her right likes her. His face is turned to hers, smiling. He laughs at every fucking word she says.

His arm hovers at her back. He presses his hand to her as she regales everyone with a tale about a client at her old company. She's either too drunk or engrossed to notice, but I do.

My gut twists. My hands are clammy.

My jaw clenches as his hand slides lower. He's a heartbeat from her ass when I disregard every one of my sensibilities and pull my phone from my pocket.

She's laughing as the ringtone sounds from her handbag. She looks confused at the unknown number.

I hate the way handy boy looks at her screen along with her.

I listen as she excuses herself. "Maybe it's my mum," she says, and presses it to her ear.

"I'm not your fucking mother," I whisper, loving the way she stiffens.

I wait. Watch as she looks around her.

"Hi," she says. "I, um…"

"You will say this is a family call. You will keep your phone to your ear and you will excuse yourself. You will walk to your right, down towards the emergency exit. If you've any sense, you'll make sure nobody follows you."

The prick is staring at her. Puppy dog eyes.

I almost hope he can fucking hear me.

She flicks her gaze in my direction. "Okay," she says, but I've already hung up.

twentytwo

Jealousy is the tie that binds, and binds, and binds.

—HELEN ROWLAND

abigail

The thrill pulses right through me – that incredible mix of excitement and fear all at once.

I'm an addict, always craving that next fix. My body is a puppet on his strings. My clit throbbing the very moment I hear his voice.

I daren't look too hard for him, just chancing a quick glance in the direction of the emergency exit. It's dark over there. Dark but close.

Really close – just a stone's throw away.

I can almost feel him on me already. My legs tremble on my ridiculous heels.

I take the handset from my ear and address the now quiet group around me. "It's my mum," I lie. "I need to take the call. Don't wait for me, just keep on drinking. I'll catch you up."

I could die inside as Jack leans in close, his mouth to my cheek. "Hurry back."

I've barely noticed his ever-narrowing proximity this evening. Laughter and alcohol and a huddled group make it so easy for hints to go unnoticed.

I wonder if they've gone unnoticed by the stranger around the corner.

I wonder if he cares.

I hope he cares.

His call is disconnected but I press the handset right back to my ear as I walk away. "Hey, Mum," I say. "I've been meaning to call you."

Every step is dithery as I head into the shadows. My eyes haven't even adjusted to the darkness when his hand clamps tight across my mouth.

"You wanna be real fucking quiet," he growls. "Unless you want your friends to hear you squeal, that is."

I shake my head.

His breath is so hot on my ear. "How about lover boy? Do you want him to hear what I'm making you take? Would that make you wet, you dirty little slut?"

Warm fingers trail up my thighs to press against my pussy. I buckle against him, breath already ragged.

My dress is short enough that he barely has to hitch it. He slips his hand down my knickers and I'm well aware I'm already soaking.

"Is this for me or him?" he whispers, but doesn't let me speak. "It matters little, you'll be too fucking sore to take him when I'm done with you."

There's an edge to his voice. A harshness.

Jealousy.

My whole body sings.

He's jealous.

He's really jealous.

I'm glad I'm a tart tonight. I'm glad I'm wearing slutty suspenders with my tits out on display. I'm glad my skin feels so chilled all of a sudden in the night air.

I'm glad he's seeing me like this.

I'm glad he came for me.

The angel on my shoulder is freaking out. I feel sparks of panic underneath the thrill.

I'm with work colleagues on a night out. Actual work colleagues who gossip and laugh and pry, and would want to know who the fuck this crazy hot guy is.

I'll never ever live it down if they catch me with his hand down my knickers. It'll be all over the office before I even step foot in there tomorrow.

"You'll do exactly what I say or I'll parade you out there with your cunt on display and fuck you in front of everyone, loverboy included. Understand?"

I nod.

I take a deep breath when he pulls his hand away. I spin to face him before he can grab me.

"He's not my *loverboy*," I whisper. "He's just a friend. A co-worker."

"A friend who's got designs on that tight little cunt of yours."

"He can have all the designs he wants," I say. "He won't be getting any." Even in the shadows I see the darkness in his expression. Drink makes me brave. Brave enough to press my body tight to his. "Are you jealous?"

He laughs a low laugh. It doesn't convince me any. "Do I seem like the jealous type?"

"You do right now," I tell him.

"You're a drunk little tart on a night out. I'd just rather it was me who pounded that hot little slit of yours."

"You don't need to be jealous," I whisper. "You're all I think about. I hope you're waiting around every corner. I fall asleep with my fingers between my legs, pretending they're yours."

I gasp as he grabs my arms. I stifle a whimper as he slams me hard into the wall.

"No pretending necessary tonight." His voice is raspy. Dangerous. He lifts my dress up around my waist, tugs my knickers to the side.

He's going to fuck me here, just a few paces away from people who know me. Close enough that they'll probably hear the wetness.

He can't do this here. *We* can't do this here.

"We should move," I whisper, but his weight presses tight on my back.

"We'll do what I fucking say we're going to do," he growls. "I might even take that pretty asshole of yours while I'm here."

"Please don't." I shiver. "Not here. I won't be able to stay quiet…"

"What makes you think I fucking care?"

And oh fuck how I want it. Holy fuck, how I want *him*. His brutal touch, his painful cock. I want it all.

I can't help but whimper as he pushes a finger in my ass. I squirm against the weight of him as he circles it deep. "Tight," he grunts. "You'll scream when I take you. You'll be a gaping fucking wreck when I'm done."

"Please…" I hiss, and I'm not even sure what I'm asking for.

"I'm gonna fuck your ass until you scream for me," he says. I take a gulp of breath. "But not tonight."

The disappointment hits easily as hard as the relief.

I flinch as he tears my knickers off. I cringe at how loud the ripping fabric sounds.

"Let's make this easier for you," he whispers. I struggle against him as he shoves the wet lace into my open mouth, but there's nowhere to go. I taste myself, and I taste fucking dirty. Wanton. A slut in a tiny red dress.

He edges me closer to the corner, I screw my eyes closed tight as my friends come into view.

"Look at them," he orders, and I do. I burn with humiliation. Scorching with embarrassment at the prospect of them finding me with my knickers in my mouth and his monster dick inside me.

He tugs my dress from my tits so sharply I hear the fabric tear. I just hope it stays functional enough to hide my modesty later.

He flattens me to the brickwork. The wall is like sandpaper against tender skin. My nipples graze and spark. My legs threaten to buckle.

"Loverboy won't fuck you like I can, I promise you," he says, and thrusts four fucking fingers at my pussy. I spread my legs to take them, sucking in air through my nose. His other hand wraps around to strum my clit. I'm writhing against his touch even as his fingers force me open. "He'll never give you what you need."

He's preaching to the converted, but I fucking love it.

I buck against his fingers for more. I reach back for him, desperate.

I want so much to see him. To feel him. To taste his mouth on mine.

But it's not going to be tonight.

Tonight is going to be painful. Sharp. Beautiful.

I'm ready for it when it comes, even if my body isn't. His fingers are still on my clit as he fumbles with his jeans.

His rhythm is faultless, even as he frees his cock and guides it between my legs.

I suddenly love these hooker heels. I love the way they make the height difference so much more manageable. Love the way they make my ass stick out for him.

And I suddenly love the gag in my mouth, too. I need it as he shunts the head of his cock inside me.

Fuck.

I don't think I'll ever get used to the size of him. I don't think I ever want to.

I'm beginning to know his ridges. Beginning to predict the way they hurt as they push their way in.

I'm moving to the beat of him, using the wall as leverage when I hear the conversation change around the corner.

"Where's Abi? That call's taking a while." Lauren's voice.

It takes me aback that they call me Abi when I'm not around.

Nobody here calls me Abi. Here it's only been Abigail. I left Abi back in Hampshire.

"Maybe she's gone to the bar on the way back?" Sarah suggests.

"How long have you known her?" Lauren's voice.

"A few months. As actual friends only a few days, though."

Actual friends. The description makes me smile around my gag.

I buck back at my monster a little harder. A little braver.

I wince as he makes me take another metal rung. My pussy clenches as hard around his dick as I dare, just because I love to hear him moan.

If I'm going to struggle for silence, then so is he.

"She's great," Lauren's voice starts up again. *"Took us a while to get to know her, but we love her. She's amazing."*

"She's so funny," Sarah says. *"I just know we're gonna be friends a long time. I've had such fun these past few days."*

"She's a star," Jack's voice says, and the monster slams me hard enough to take my breath. *"She's so down to earth. Kind. Bubbly."* He pauses. *"Gorgeous."*

The crowd whoops and whistles and my monster fucks me so hard my eyes water. My poor makeup takes a pounding along with my pussy.

I'm grinning into my gag like a crazy. Slamming back at him with everything I have.

And then the conversation shifts. My stomach lurches.

"Hey, Sarah, do you know why she left Hampshire? Seems quite a drastic move." Lauren's always so nosey. Always.

"Guy trouble, I think," Sarah answers. *"Said she thought his dick was worth it until she got here and found better."*

More whooping, and I cringe. I know they all think it's Jack's dick I'm singing the praises of. All except Jack himself.

All except Jack and the monster behind me.

The monster's voice is rough in my ear. "Is that fucking so?"

My embarrassment thrums. My pussy eats him up.

"Where is she?" someone groans – Kelly from sales, I think.

The monster grunts against my neck. "They think you're fucking him, don't they? They think you and him have a thing?"

I nod and spread my legs for more. Harder.

"Let's put them right on that, then, shall we?" he growls. My nerves barely have time to prickle before his mouth clamps on my neck.

Teeth. Fuck, he's a biter.

He pinches. Hard. Sucks harder with his dick buried inside me.

I moan for him. I couldn't stop if the whole fucking world was watching.

I work myself back against that huge fucking dick and take everything he's giving. His fingers speed up on my throbbing clit and I'm so wet I feel myself trickling down my thighs.

One bite isn't enough. I'm on the edge at the second, and my ears ring as I crest at the third.

Oh fuck. Fuck.

It's beautiful agony. My whole body screams in silence.

And so does his.

His body is wired muscle against my back, his grunts pained as he comes inside me.

He pants against my shoulder and I press my cheek to his.

Our breathing matches.

I feel his heartbeat against my back.

"I'll go look for her," Jack says finally, and the horror zings through me like lightning.

bait

I tear the gag from my mouth and toss it to the floor, scrabbling to push the monster away enough to tug my slutty dress back down.

I've barely covered my tits as the footsteps round the corner. The monster is still zipping up his jeans as Jack comes into view.

And oh the fucking horror.

My smile is zany and awkward, my cheeks burning as the two parts of my world collide.

Jack starts when he sees me. His eyes widen as he sees the guy at my back.

My heart pains for him as he shifts into professional gear. There's only a flash of disappointment before he's all smiles.

"We were worried about you," he tells me. "Wondering where you got to."

I don't even know where my phone is. I gesture to nothing as I tell him I just got back from my call with Mum, but Jack's already stepping to my side, his hand outstretched to introduce himself to the monster.

I wish the ground would swallow me up.

I don't even know his fucking name.

"Jack," Jack says. "I work with Abi."

There it is. Abi again.

I can't look behind me. I can't face the awkwardness as his eyes meet mine.

I figure he'll bail with a grunt and a *see you later*, but he doesn't. His hand is big and warm against my back. The bulk of him so reassuring as he steps to my side.

"Leo," he says, and my jaw hits the floor. He takes Jack's outstretched hand. "Good to meet you."

"Same," Jack says, even though he's lying. He gestures back to the garden. "Do you wanna join us? Excuse the stupid outfits, it's tarts and vicars."

I hold my breath. *Please. Please, please, please.*

"I'm driving," he says, and my heart drops. "But introductions would be nice."

I've lost the power of basic bodily functions when my monster – *Leo* – steps out into the light after Jack.

I'd never be able to follow him if he didn't take my hand and pull me along after him.

The girls' faces are a picture. I can only imagine what mine looks like.

And I can only imagine the grilling I'm going to face when the monster leaves.

The thrill makes my heart sing.

But not as much as Leo does.

twentythree

Insanity is knowing that what you're doing is completely idiotic, but still, somehow, you just can't stop it.

—ELIZABETH WURTZEL

phoenix

I shouldn't be here. I don't know why I am.

I don't know why I'm shaking their hands and smiling so politely and using my real name.

Abigail can't stop staring at me. Her eyes are big, blatant, the alcohol stealing any coyness. Though she might be a little more self-conscious if she could see the love bites darkening on her neck.

I'm glad everyone else can. I feel like a caveman with her at my side, my arm wrapped so possessively around her waist.

This is ridiculous. Crazy. Idiotic and most definitely fucking insane.

But I can't stop.

I can't bring myself to play this down as nothing and say my goodbyes.

"Where did you guys meet?" Lauren – I think – asks. She looks between us and

I look down at Abigail.

I love how my black swan flounders.

"I, uh, met *Leo* at, ummm…"

The sound of my name from her mouth makes me thoroughly uncomfortable, but weirdly excited at the same time.

She looks up at me, but I give her no help whatsoever.

And then she surprises me, which seems to be a running theme for this evening.

"We met online," she says. "On this like… introductions website…"

A circle of raised eyebrows give way to whoops and chatter. I'd usually hate this shit.

"Online?!" one of the other girls asks. She looks me up and down, and I think she's had more than her bandwidth of tequila already. "Wow, you'll have to give me the web address."

The Lauren girl points between us, one to the other. "So, is this a *thing*? Are you guys dating?"

"No," she says, straight off the cuff.

Her reaction makes me want to wrestle her to the floor in front of all of them and fuck her tight little asshole with an audience.

Her eyes meet mine and widen. "No, I mean, um…" she starts. I hold her stare. "I mean, I dunno… it's early days…"

Better.

Lauren laughs aloud. "Abigail Summers. You've been caught behind the bins with your knickers down. Proverbially if not literally. Have you even seen the state of your neck? I don't think the days are that *early* somehow, you little minx."

Oh the beautiful fucking horror on Abigail's face. It makes my dick harden all over again.

Her hand jumps to her throat, as though she has a hope in hell's chance of hiding them. It makes me smirk.

I love that I've marked her. I love that she'll be conscious of those for days.

She isn't the desperate lost soul I met online. She sparkles. Shines. She's lively and full of life.

Stunning.

Being at her side makes me feel all kinds of fucked up. My truck is calling, and so is familiar turf, but my feet stay rooted to the ground and my arm stays firm around her.

"Are you coming to the summer barbeque?" the guy asks, and it takes me a beat to remember I have to play ignorant.

"The what?"

It's Abigail who steps in to answer. "It's nothing really, just some work barbeque for charity."

I wonder if she's trying to head me off attending, if so it'll be so much more of a thrill to turn up unannounced.

She is trying to head me off, I see it in her eyes. In the way she sweeps the conversation around to her blonde neighbour and how she picked out her nail colour.

Even as she's angling the topic away from social engagements, her fingers come to rest against the small of my back. I like having them there.

I like it a lot less when her fingertips sweep upwards.

Slowly.

Steadily.

My scars itch.

Even as I want more, they itch and prickle under my clothes.

And unfortunately that's just about the moment I know this show has to come to an end.

"I'd better run," I announce. "It was nice meeting everyone."

I pull my arm back from her, hating the way she moves with me on instinct. Hating the way I have to force my body from hers.

She's confused. I see it in her eyes.

"Well, I, um…" she begins, as everyone watches on. "I'll be seeing you."

"You will," I say.

And then I leave.

Quickly enough that I don't change my mind.

abigail

For all the glitz and sparkle and optimism of having Leo at my side with his arm around my waist, there's a part of me that realises the futility of this crazy pairing.

People just don't meet like we did and manage to make an actual relationship out of it.

Even the thought is crazy.

Beyond crazy.

It should be a relief to dismiss it as an unfortunate case of social precedents forced upon us, but it isn't.

Knowing his name should have meant little more than a confirmation of the fact he's not a total psycho, but it means everything.

I can't stop thinking of him. Speaking his name in my mind. Hissing out his name as I come at night with my fingers inside me. Saying his name out loud as I stare in the mirror and touch the love bites on my neck.

The grilling I got from my friends was worth every second of awkwardness.

Having him at my side felt nicer than it ever should have.

And now he's gone.

No sign of him over the weekend. No ominous presence waiting in the darkness for me to venture outside. I know that, because I find myself outside a lot. Walking. Waiting. Lingering and hoping.

The next working week gets off to a perfectly regular start without any sign of him jumping out at me.

The guys ask if he's going to be joining us for the next night out at Diva's and it feels pretty disappointing to have to say it's unlikely. He doesn't join us. Not that week and not the next, either. His marks have all but gone from my neck and it feels like I've lost him.

Leo.

My pussy aches for him. *I* ache for him.

So I keep myself busy. I call people from back in Hampshire and keep on top of social media. I spend evenings at Sarah's place, or she at mine. I take walks for the hell of it and enjoy them.

I try not to be agitated at the radio silence. I try not to worry about the passing time and whether he's grown tired of me already.

In the main I do a good job of it, but by the time the second weekend comes and goes without hide nor hair of him I'm reaching the end of my tether.

I didn't want to use the phone number he called me from that evening in Diva's. I didn't want to have to ground this *thing* in something so ordinary as a telephone conversation.

I fear he's not going to leave me any choice, so midway through my next working week without him, I dig my phone from my handbag and try his number.

It rings and rings. My heart drops when I know he's not about to answer, but still I wait around for his voicemail.

It's generic. An automated voice reading out the number I dialled and asking me to record a message.

I record a simple one, as calmly as I can manage to pull off.

"Hey, it's me. I'm just… waiting…" I take a breath. "I hope you show up soon."

He doesn't. Not that night and not the night after, nor even the weekend after that.

I call again and it rings back through to the same voicemail.

This time I don't leave one.

I check online and reactivate my deleted profile. His is greyed out and unavailable.

I search for Leos in Malvern with tattoos and unsurprisingly find nothing at all worth anything.

Part of me worries something has happened to him. Part of me worries about the fact that something could happen to him and I'd never even know it.

Part of me wants to know where the hell he is and what's taking up so much of his time that he can't at least send me a message back in return.

A *see you soon*, or even a *thanks but no thanks*.

Anything would be better than being ignored.

I'm in deep with someone who I've never even kissed properly, even though I've taken his dick in all the way.

I feel invisible again, just like I did with Stephen in the aftermath of the great explosion. Questioning whether any of this ever meant anything at all.

Whether he was just a guy out for a good time and now he's done.

I don't want to believe it.

I don't want to believe my monster is gone.

But by the end of the next weekend I do.

twentyfour

*We shall not cease from exploration, and the end of all our exploring will be
to arrive where we started and know the place for the first time.*

—T.S. ELIOT

phoenix

Staying away from my black swan is harder than I ever anticipated. Ignoring her voicemail has been a far greater challenge than I ever expected to encounter as the result of a crazy online hook-up.

But it'll be worth it.

Using that front door key for the first time and have her genuinely not expecting it, will be worth it.

Worth the cravings for her sweet tight snatch that present themselves all day long.

Worth the pang in my gut that says I could be ruining something so much deeper than the fantasy we set out on in the first place.

But it can't be anything deeper.

As much as I may want to, I'm not about to drown the girl in my shit ton of baggage when she's only just getting clear of her own.

My scars itch for a reason.

Because they're raw.

Deep.

Ugly.

I've got a brother who wants my blood, and a boy who may not *be* my blood, who can speak but doesn't, and shows no sign of doing so for the foreseeable, and a sister trapped in the middle of it all.

All that and a business that may not survive the insurance verdict when it finally comes in.

No.

Abigail needs a monster in the darkness. A thrill to spike her adrenaline when real life proves too monotonous.

I'll give her both of those things and spare her the rest.

I'm beyond excited when the time comes. I've been aching for this for weeks.

A Monday night seems perfect timing. I'm barely able to function at the office as the time draws near.

The anticipation was supposed to be all for her benefit, but as my dick throbs with desperation enough to fucking pain through the afternoon, I realise it's been as much for mine.

Serena can't hold back a smile when I pick up my keys after Cameron's bedtime routine.

"Mud wrestling?" she quizzes. "I thought it must be about time."

"I've been busy," I lie.

"I hope you can make it up to her," she says with a quirked eyebrow.

"Make what up to her?"

She shakes her head like I'm a dumbfuck. "If she's happy to coast along for a couple of weeks without seeing even a piece of you, then she's a considerably more patient woman than I'd be."

It's my turn to quirk my brow. "We're not engaged, Serena."

She laughs. "Oh, Leo. You underestimate the savage seas of female emotion, I fear. Buy her flowers if you have any sense."

It makes me smirk as I leave. Flowers will be the very last thing on Abigail's mind this evening.

The drive over there is tense. The beast in my belly spreading its wings where there's no space for them.

I'll be all but breaking and entering. That itself is enough to spike my adrenaline. I feel strangely criminal, as though I'm being watched in the darkness. Followed as though I'm up to no good. Pairs of eyes feasting on my ill-intent and set to call the police out.

I could really do without that kind of attention.

I park up in the loading bay across from her place and watch the lights through the window. Two shadows move in the living room.

There's a sickening flash of jealousy until I realise the other shadow belongs to the blonde girl next door.

I guess they're watching something – I see the lights from the TV moving on her ceiling.

It feels like a lifetime before two shadows turn to one and those lights finally go out. I wait until long after midnight before I lock up the truck and head on over.

I've already considered the communal door lock. We had one similar on our old storeroom. These things aren't robust, just token gestures added to older buildings to deter opportunists.

I'm not an opportunist. My intentions are sinister and unbridled. It's easy enough to yank that thing loose from its catch with enough force behind it.

My footsteps are quick and light, the key to her apartment in my hand before

bait

I've even reached her landing. I slip by her neighbour's door and across, holding my breath as I ease that key home and turn it to the right.

The door swooshes as it opens, but doesn't creak. The catch makes the lightest click as I close it after me.

And then I'm in.

My heart pounds along with my fucking cock.

I feel like a fucking monster for real as I cross her darkened hallway and press my ear to her bedroom door. I hear nothing.

Perfect.

I'm careful as I retreat to the kitchen and take a glass from the drainer. I press myself into the corner next to her storage cupboard and count down from ten.

And then I slam dunk that pint glass straight into the sink.

Oh the fucking noise. It even makes me start, my pulse in my temples as my mouth waters.

I count up from one. At five her bedroom door opens. I feel every second of the tension as she pauses in the hallway. At ten the kitchen light flicks on and I see her face reflected in the window. No makeup, tired eyes, her long hair piled up in a messy bun.

She's wearing a simple white cami and knickers.

She looks fucking delicious.

She's jumpy, even through her sleepy disorientation. Her eyes widen as she steps forward enough to see the smashed glass in the sink.

I wait. Hold my breath.

She moves the other items on the drainer back from the edge, even though they don't stand a chance of falling.

She curses under her breath as she wraps the bulk of the broken shards in one of those crappy free ad papers. She's yawning even as she tackles the rest and turns on the tap to swill the remnants down the drain.

My sweet little black swan doesn't even suspect I'm waiting. Lurking.

My demons take control, every muscle poised for action.

And then I make my move.

She jumps clear in the air as I step out into the light. There's no recognition in her eyes as they fly wide. She spins on her heel in a flash, letting out the kind of scream that comes from pure instinct and nothing else. I take her breath when I snake my arm around her ribs and pull tight. My hand is brutal as all fuck as it clasps over her open mouth.

And today she struggles.

Today she's a flapping bird in the mouth of a cat. Her heels lash at my shins. Her nails dig into my arms even through the denim of my jacket.

She thrashes against me hard enough that I question if she's done with this game for real.

And then I speak.

It's my voice that cuts through her panic enough that she stills in a beat.

"I'll hurt you if you fight me," I whisper. "If you're a good girl, I may even let you enjoy this."

Her breaths even out just a little. Her head presses back against my shoulder. Her feet hitch against my shins as I carry her through to her bedroom.

When I drop her it's with some force, straight onto her bed. I open the curtains to the road outside, just for the glow of the streetlights. She looks beautiful in the orange glare.

Scared. Wanting.

She flips onto her back and scurries back toward the headboard.

Her nipples are hard through her cami top. Her eyes are wide.

Fuck, how I *need* this.

How I need her.

"What the–" she begins, but I bark at her to shut her fucking mouth.

She squeaks as I lunge for her, swiping out at me with dainty fingers as I stalk up the bed.

They land surprisingly hard on my cheek.

Land again before I can pin her.

When I do she squirms and bucks underneath me, hissing as her thighs open wide.

I'm waiting for a *yes* or a *no*, or even a *don't hurt me.*

I'm waiting for her to play this fucking game like she really believes in it.

I'm waiting to give her the monster she claims she wants, and this time take it all the way.

But when she opens her mouth I get none of it. None of the playacting and none of the fear, either.

"You're an asshole," she hisses as I pin her wrists above her head.

My eyes widen on hers, and hers are angry.

"What the–" I begin, but it's her who cuts me off this time.

I'm not prepared for the way she fights to be out from under me. I take her struggle easily, holding her down with nothing more than a hiss of breath in exertion. My eyes are fierce on hers, even through the shock.

And then, just as though I didn't hear her well enough the first time, she speaks again.

"You're an absolute motherfucking asshole, *Leo.*"

twentyfive

To put meaning in one's life may end in madness, but life without meaning is the torture of restlessness and vague desire. It is a boat longing for the sea and yet afraid.
—EDGAR LEE MASTERS

abigail

Relief and lust and anger. A whirlwind of emotion that lashes out at him just as soon as it rises in me.

He pins me without even flinching, his weight crushing me to the bed so hard I can't move an inch.

His voice is low and dangerous. "What the fuck are you talking about?"

"I called you," I tell him, like he doesn't know already. "I've been waiting weeks to hear even a fucking peep from you."

"And you're hearing it now." His breath is hot against my mouth. My soul screams to feel his lips on mine, but I'm too scared to taste him. "You wanted a monster in the darkness. You wanted a stranger. You wanted *this*."

But I want so much more…

I'm so painfully aware of how much more.

My tummy flutters as he continues. "You thought I was gonna rock up here with bunch of flowers and knock on the door? You thought I was gonna call with advance warning so I could find you ready for me? That's not how this game works."

I stare right into his eyes. I want to hate this, how I feel about him, but I can't.

I don't know how I fell so deep so quickly. I don't know why I'm so afraid of losing something I should never have even wanted in the first place.

"I didn't think you were coming back," I whisper.

"I was always coming back."

I keep on rolling. "I thought something could've happened to you."

"I left enough time to make the hunt feel fucking real, Abigail, *that's* what happened to me."

And it did feel real when he slammed me in my kitchen. My fear was all real.

It still is.

I feel nervous under him. Unsteady.

"Don't disappear like that again. Not unless you mean it."

"Point taken," he says. "Are you done with fighting? Or do I have to tie you to the fucking bedposts?"

His hips grind against mine and my thighs loll wide. My body is his.

I suspect my soul might be too.

"That's more like it," he whispers as I uncoil underneath him.

I can feel how hard he is for this. His cock is tight against me through his jeans.

I want him too much to fight. Too much to hate the hold he has over me.

"Be my monster," I breathe as he hitches hard against my pussy. "I want it all…"

"That's just as fucking well," he says. I groan as he thrusts between my legs, denim rough against my bare thighs. "Since you're gonna fucking get it all."

He rises enough to wrestle my cami off over my head. My tits feel so bare under the glow from outside. They rise and fall with my breath as he watches.

He takes one in his hand. "Bad girls have to earn their fucking pleasure, Abigail. They take what they're fucking given. This is something you'll have to learn the hard way."

I hold in a groan as he squeezes tight. His fingers are brutal on tender skin, my eyes closed as he crushes my flesh.

I whimper. Squirm.

He squeezes tighter.

"Scare me," I whisper. "Scare me enough to think I don't want this."

His eyes are so dark. "You'll be scared, don't fucking worry."

I'm not prepared for his mouth to clamp around my nipple. I'm not ready for the pain as his teeth grip hard. His jaw is scratchy against my ribs, and I love it.

I fucking love it.

I moan as he pulls away, my teeth gritting as my nipple stretches. I love the way it burns as he lets go.

"They're so fucking beautiful," he grunts. "It's such a shame I need to punish them."

He sucks so hard on the other nipple I can't keep still.

I thread my fingers through his hair and hold him tight. My feet hook around his legs and grip him close.

I watch his mouth in fascination as his tongue circles the bruise he just put on me. I'm in love with the shape of his mouth. The heat of his breath. The way his scalp feels under my fingers.

With him

With a stranger.

A monster.

A man who could be anyone. Have done anything.

I've never had love bites on my tits before. I've never felt the beautiful pain of a cruel mouth on tender flesh.

I've never been so afraid of someone's mouth moving down my body.

Never gasped so loudly at having my knickers tugged down my thighs.

"I've been aching to taste your pretty fucking cunt for weeks," he tells me, and I believe him.

I prop myself on my elbows so I can watch his inked fingers spread me open. He runs his tongue along my parted slit. His dark eyes are beautiful as he stares up at me.

I feel like a dirty whore as I roll my sore nipples between my fingers. I'm already too far gone for self-restraint as I roll my hips back for more.

"Suck me," I whimper. "Please. Suck my clit."

He hooks two fingers inside me.

"Beg for it."

"Please." My voice sounds pathetic. Desperate. "Please suck my clit. *Please.*"

His eyes flash with something truly terrifying as he pushes a third finger inside me. "Use my fucking name," he growls.

Oh fuck.

I guess we're done at playing strangers after all.

I burn up at the memory of grunting his name into my pillow at night. I'm so fucking embarrassed as I summon the words.

"Please, Leo. Please, suck my clit. Please suck me."

His breath is torture. His fingers rough. "More. Louder."

My voice sounds so loud in the room. "Leo, please. Please suck my clit. Please."

"Louder. I want them to fucking hear you outside. I want them to hear you scream my fucking name."

Fuck.

I daren't even think of the outside. I daren't think of the view from the side street and the apartments opposite. I assure myself it's dark in here, that they won't be able to see me, but I still feel so fucking exposed.

"Beg for me like you fucking mean it," he growls, and I do. I just fucking do it.

"PLEASE, LEO! PLEASE SUCK MY CLIT! PLEASE!"

He smirks. "Good girl." He circles his thumb against me before he lowers his face. "You won't come," he tells me. "If you come before I say so, I'll pound your asshole so hard you'll bleed."

My clit throbs like a horny little bitch as he sucks it between his lips.

The rush from shouting out loud makes me strangely uninhibited.

"I thought you were gone," I whimper. "Please don't go, Leo. I need this... I need this worse than I ever knew..."

He sucks harder. Curls his fingers deeper.

My face must be a grimace as I fight the urge to come.

His tongue darts and laps at me. I whimper as I resist my own pleasure.

And then he stops.

My pussy aches.

"One of these nights I really am gonna tie you to the bedposts," he says. "I'm gonna tie you up so fucking tight you can't even squirm, and then I'm gonna suck on that fucking clit until you scream the whole fucking building down."

He shrugs his jacket off as I watch. He's wearing short sleeves underneath.

Oh my God.

Fuck.

My heart pounds as I strain to see his tattoos in the meagre light. So many tattoos. More than I ever dreamed.

My fingers reach out of their own volition to flick the bedside lamp on. He blinks against the light.

"You really do want the fucking street to see you, then?" he asks, but I don't care. The window is big and the curtains are open wide and my own naked body greets me boldly in the reflection, but I don't give a shit.

"I want to see you," I tell him, and I'm reaching out, tracing the lines on his forearm.

He strikes like a snake as he forces me back down onto the mattress.

"I don't care what you want," he grunts. "You'll see whatever I want you to see. Feel whatever I want you to feel. Do whatever I want you to do." His fingers clamp around my throat. "I'm gonna take your asshole, and it's gonna fucking hurt." He pauses. "The light will stay on because *I* want to see *you*."

I take a breath as he lets go of me. I don't move an inch as he loosens his jeans.

There's a whole other layer of harshness in his tone when he speaks again. "You'll see as much as I want you to see and nothing more."

I don't protest as he lifts my legs up high and hooks them over his shoulders. I don't try to hide the fear as his cock thumps hard against my pussy. My head is as high as I can lift it, my eyes greedy for the sight of his cock in decent lighting, and it's every bit as terrifying as it looked on that photograph.

"Make me nice and fucking wet," he grunts, and forces the head inside.

I hold my breath as the first ridge pushes in. I breathe it out at the second. I whimper at the third. Screw my eyes shut at the forth.

"Good girl," he says. "Fucking take it."

Five and six make me groan like a slut. My cheeks scorch at the sounds my pussy makes around his dick.

He comes to rest with his mouth just an inch from mine, his eyes open wide as he fucks me deep and slow.

"Harder," I hiss, even though I'm fucking crazy.

I cry out as he slams in, feeling so fucking small underneath him. The ridges are painfully fucking perfect at this angle. I'm grunting for more even as it hurts.

"You'd better pray to God I find some lube in your bedside cabinet," he says, and my embarrassment blooms.

Lube, sure… and a monster dildo…

Oh fuck.

"We'll both be a bloody fucking mess without lube, Abigail. You won't be able to walk for a fucking week," he threatens. I point at the cabinet and he smiles. "Sensible girl."

He reaches to the side of us and tugs open the top drawer. I close my eyes as he roots in there. I don't want to see his face as he finds my secret preparation weapon. I hear it thump against the side as he takes it out.

"Or maybe not such a mess…" he whispers. "Maybe you can already take it, however it comes." He pulls out of my pussy in one and every ridge feels like I'm burning in heaven. "Shall I find out? Is your asshole a good liar, Abigail? It was like a vice in the pub garden…"

I'm struggling against him even as he slides his cock towards my asshole. "No," I say. "That thing… it's never been in my ass… I can barely take it at all in my pussy… I've never even tried it back there…"

There's such dark amusement in his eyes. "Hold this," he says and forces the dildo between my teeth. My jaw stretches and holds while he digs around in the drawer for the lube. He finds the bottle easily enough.

He takes the dildo back from me and slicks it up.

I'm trembling as he works the thickness of it in his hand. Trembling at the thought of his dick ploughing on in there after it.

"Was this practice?" he asks, and I hate myself for nodding. "And did it work?"

"Not really," I admit.

"Better luck this time then." He smirks as he shifts away from me. I cry out as he forces two slippery fingers into my ass.

I've barely adjusted to them when I feel the silicon monster pushing its way through my poor tight little asshole. I feel so exposed as he repositions himself, wide open as he stares at every private part of me.

His strength pushes that dildo in deep in one short burst. My ass sucks that monster in like a donkey punch.

"Ow, fuck," I grunt, but he keeps on going. "Fuck..."

"Take it."

"Make me," I say, even though my heart is in my throat.

And he does.

He does make me take it.

He works that big veiny dildo all the way inside me, even as I whimper, even as tears spring to my eyes.

It's slimy and slippery and sounds it. I could cry from that alone.

"Your holes are crying out to be destroyed," he grunts. "But you know that, don't you? That's why you let the monster in."

"Please stop," I whimper, even though I'm already rocking back at the pain.

"That's it, slut," he says. "Beg me." He twists the dildo inside me until I curse. "Beg me to fucking stop."

I hitch my legs higher to my chest even as I say it. "Please stop. Please, Leo, stop. It hurts. Oh fuck, it hurts so bad."

I blink tears down my cheeks. I'm smiling even as I cry for him.

"Please stop, Leo. *Please.*"

The burn changes to something else. Something primal and fucked up and raw.

His mouth clamps over my swollen pussy even as he keeps on fucking me.

"No," I breathe. "Please don't."

But he does. Oh he does.

His teeth feel like life and death on my clit all at once. My asshole makes noises that curl my toes.

My feet rest against his back, muscles tight. My fingers are vicious on his scalp as he makes me take it.

"You really are my monster," I breathe. "You make it hurt better than I ever dreamed."

I cry out as he tugs my clit between his teeth. His breath is ragged as he pulls away.

"I'm only just getting fucking started," he says.

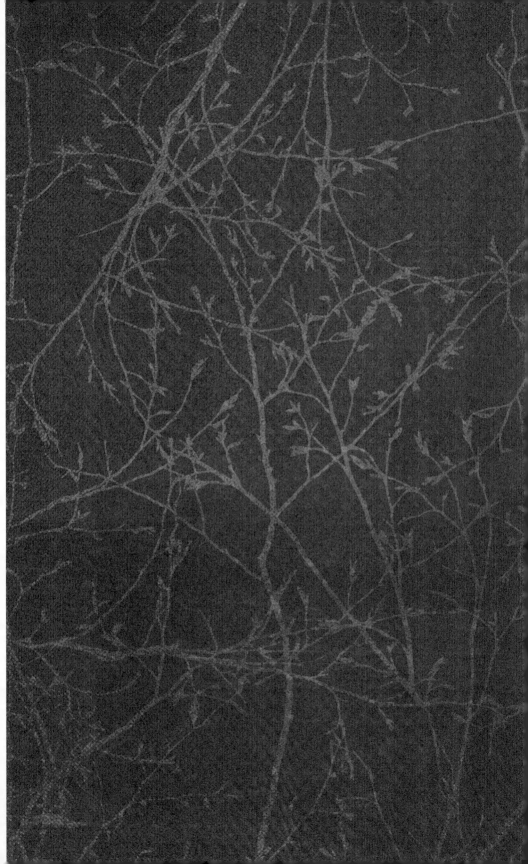

twentysix

He who hesitates is lost.

—MARCUS PORCIUS CATO

phoenix

I want the whole fucking world to see us. I hope the whole neighbourhood is staring from behind their twitchy curtains as I stretch Abigail's pretty asshole raw.

Her desperation has knitted itself to mine under the surface. I feel it there, both of us bobbing along with the current of a tsunami.

I wouldn't know how to stop this if I tried, but what I do know – against every fucking sensibility I've ever had – is that I'll never be able to leave her alone again. Not even for a couple of weeks.

Her eyes are watery even as she smiles. She's spreading her legs for more even as she begs me to stop.

I toss the dildo to the floor and squirt a fresh load of lube onto my fingers. I work it right the way over my dick, and then squirt another glob straight onto her battered asshole. She flinches at the chill, but it's the least of her worries.

"Look at me," I tell her as I position myself against her ass and ease down on top of her.

She nods. Smiles. Threads her dainty little fingers in my hair.

She's so naked under me, so pretty in the lamplight. I'm well aware that I'm still clothed, well aware of how badly I'm craving the softness of her poor bruised tits against my skin.

But I can't.

Not until she knows my secrets.

If she ever knows my secrets.

It would be so easy to kiss her. So easy to throw the shirt off my back and dive all the way in.

I do neither.

Her eyes widen like pretty white saucers as I force the head of my cock into her puckered hole.

Steady.

So fucking steady.

My jaw is tight as I ease my way in. My weight is on my elbows and my face is right in hers.

The first barbell tugs as it pushes through, even slicked up with lube. She flinches as it sinks deeper.

"I'm scared," she whispers. "This is really gonna hurt."

She closes her eyes as I push forward. Her ass is like a vice as the second and third piercings push inside.

Her breath is ragged against my lips.

"Bad?" I ask.

She whimpers and nods.

I'm careful with the fourth, barely moving at all.

It feels like fucking heaven when the fifth slides in and her ass opens up to take me.

"I feel so full," she whispers.

"Not full enough." I ease in the final inch or so and she groans. My balls are tight against her bare ass, I'm in deep enough that the thought nearly sends me over the edge.

Her eyes are still right on mine as I rock my hips. Her breath is jagged against my lips as I sink into rhythm.

Steady, so fucking steady. The lube is slick but her ass is tight.

"Ow, fuck," she hisses as I pick it up a gear.

"Don't fight," I tell her again and press my forehead to hers.

"Kiss me," she whispers.

"You don't want to kiss a monster. Believe me," I tell her.

I shunt hard in her ass to take the idea away.

"I don't understand you," she whispers. "I don't understand any of this."

"Don't try."

"You have secrets, don't you?" she continues, and I contemplate ramming my filthy cock down her throat just to shut her pretty mouth up. "They're bad, aren't they?"

"We all have secrets, Abigail. If you want to tell me yours while my dick stretches your ass open, then go ahead."

She tips her head to the side, and that suits me just fine. I nip her ear until she shivers. Kiss her neck until she's forgotten how to speak.

"Hurting?" I ask again, and she moans.

I slide out all the way and she whimpers at the ridges. She braces herself as I push back in.

She's as open as she'll ever be, as ready as I can make her.

"Gonna fuck you, hard," I tell her, and the way she tenses is divine.

She cries out as I slam in, shivers as her ass squelches on my way out.

"You wanted a monster," I breathe and shunt so hard the bed rattles. "You'll feel me for fucking days."

Three deep slams and she's spluttering. Three more and I'm wound too tight to stop.

Her nails dig into my back. They graze my scars through my shirt and I turn wild, pounding her ass like I'm punishing her.

Maybe I am.

It sends her as feral as me.

Her hands find my bare ass and grip for dear fucking life. Her forehead presses tight to my shoulder.

And then she bites me, latching on to my shoulder through fabric.

I spit curses into her ear as she whimpers. Change angle until she lets go enough to scream my name.

And then I pin her. Hard. My fingers grip her chin and hold her steady, big scared eyes so close to mine.

"Beg me to stop."

She shakes her head.

The girl is fucking insane, but so am I.

Insane enough that I tumble across another fucking line.

My mouth is already open as it fixes on hers. My tongue is fierce as it hunts hers down.

She moans as she kisses me back, grips my ass harder as she urges me on.

She tastes like pain and fear and oblivion. She tastes like a disaster waiting to happen.

She tastes like devil's blood and quicksand. Like the broken fucking parts of me.

Like I'm burning all over again.

Like she's life itself.

"Don't stop," she hisses into my open mouth. "Fuck me."

She comes as I do, her pussy pressed tight to hard flesh. Grinding. Bucking and hissing and spluttering and fucking begging.

My cock is all the way in when I blow.

I unload deep. Really fucking deep.

My tongue is in her mouth as the world spins. My pulse is in my ears as her hands slip under my shirt and up my back.

I've moved before she can feel; pulled away before she can touch.

Her eyes widen as I recoil from her, limbs flailing to cover her exposed body, like she needs to. Like I want that.

"What?" she asks. "What did I do?"

"Nothing," I lie, but I'm an ocean away. She grapples with the bedcovers, trying to pull them over herself.

"Did I do something wrong?"

"No," I insist, but she's buying none of it.

"You didn't have to kiss me if you didn't want to," she says, and I feel like a cunt.

"Oh, I wanted to," I tell her, even though she doesn't believe me.

I shove my dick back in my jeans and zip myself up. She looks horrified.

I feel horrified myself.

The words are a jumble in my throat. I don't even know where to begin the terrible fucking tale of woe.

So I don't.

"You were perfect," I tell her. "This is all on me."

"So, what happens now? You just disappear again?"

I sigh. "Maybe I'll turn up with flowers and knock next time. Would that be better?"

She doesn't smile like I'd hoped.

She's tense as I lean forward enough to plant a kiss on her forehead.

"I have secrets," I tell her. "But they're not for now."

"When?" she asks as I get up from the bed.

I grab my jacket from the floor. "Soon."

"Soon?"

"Yes, Abigail. Soon."

She pulls her knees to her chest really fucking slowly. Leans on her arm as she stares. "You don't have a wife, do you? Please tell me you don't."

I raise an eyebrow. "You think I've got a fucking wife? Please."

"Wouldn't be the first fucking time," she hisses, and shifts her gaze to the ceiling.

"Is that what happened to you? He had a wife?"

She laughs a hollow laugh. "Lots of things happened to me, Leo. He wasn't exactly forthcoming with the whole truth, it seems."

"I haven't got a wife," I tell her. "I'm not with anyone. I'm not lying about anything."

Her eyes meet mine. "Good."

I check the time on my phone. Late. Really fucking late.

I gesture to the wide open curtains. "You probably want to close those before you get up."

She flashes a smile, at least for a moment. "Anyone out there will have seen enough already, don't you think?"

"Better than pay-per-view. Maybe we should give them a regular time slot." I dig my keys from my pocket.

"Don't leave it weeks next time. A couple of days should see me walking vaguely normally again."

"I wouldn't count on that." I smirk.

And then I go.

twentyseven

I do not deal with threats and ultimatums.

—YAIR LAPID

phoenix

I'll tell her everything. The whole sorry tale.

I'll show her everything.

Soon.

And maybe, just maybe, our broken parts will fit together enough to fix us both.

It's a longshot, but isn't it always.

I'm still on high alert as I slip back out the way I came in. I make sure the entrance door is locked just as I found it, and then I cross the street to my truck with one last glance up at her living room window.

I don't know what it is that first sends a shiver up my spine. Some early cognition of being watched, or maybe the familiar hulk of a vehicle parked just down the street from mine.

I've only just ventured close enough to read the license plate when I hear his footsteps behind me. I'd recognise that gait anywhere.

Any-fucking-where.

His voice is slurred and spitting rage when it comes.

"Barely a fucking year and you've moved on like she was fucking nothing."

He's not expecting the full force of my weight as I shunt him backwards. Not prepared for the venom with which I lift him clean off the ground and slam him up against his truck.

"What the fuck are you doing here, Jake?"

He swings for me but misses. "I fucking followed you, you stupid cunt. Wanted to see where you fucking went."

"That's bullshit," I snarl. "I'd have clocked your fucking truck a mile away."

His eyes are like coals. "You've got a fucking tracker, asshole."

"Great. Congratulations, you found me on GPS. And now you can go on your fucking way."

"What's her name?"

My pulse is frantic. Icy. "She's none of your fucking business."

He sneers. "She's everyone's fucking business tonight. The building opposite has fucking scaffolding. I've seen the dirty little slut's pounded fucking asshole already, what's in a fucking name?"

"Shut your fucking mouth."

But he doesn't. He never does. "No wonder Mariana wanted out. No wonder she begged me to take her. You're a filthy fucking animal. Always fucking have been."

"Watch it," I snarl. "Just fucking watch what you're fucking saying."

He manages to slip his hand under mine, twists hard enough to shake me off. I watch him stumble a few paces, cursing the fact that I ever fucking dragged him out of that fire.

He gestures up at the window. "Like her, do you? Wanna play happy families with her? You, her and my boy?"

"For the thousandth fucking time, Jake. He's not your fucking boy."

He jabs a finger at me. "That's for the fucking paternity test to decide."

I close the distance between us, ignoring the fact his fists are raised. "There's not gonna be a fucking paternity test. You're a fucking drunk, Jake. A bitter fucking drunk who wants to torch the whole fucking world with your misery. Do us all a fucking favour and either go fucking join her, or sort your fucking life out."

He points at Abigail's window. "Like you have, you mean? Got yourself a pretty new thing to make yourself feel better? This one gonna end up in her grave in a few years too?"

I take a breath before I tear his fucking limbs off. "Get a fucking cab and go home. I'll get one of the guys to pick your fucking truck up in the morning."

"PATERNITY TEST!" he yells. "I WANT THAT FUCKING TEST!"

I stare him out. Wonder for the thousandth fucking time what happened to the brother I grew up with.

I feel as poisoned as he is. Just being around him makes me feel fucking cursed.

He struggles to light a cigarette. I struggle to bear fucking watching him. "I want to see the boy."

I shake my head at his fucking audacity. "I want an island in the Caribbean, Jake. Not gonna fucking happen."

"That boy is mine and you know it. You've always known it."

I tip my head. "So Cameron is yours, and Mariana was yours. What about the business? Is that yours too? How about my fucking living room carpet? My fucking cutlery? All fucking yours or what, Jake? Because from what I'm fucking seeing, the only things you've ever really been interested in are mine."

"Bullshit."

"You want my fucking jacket? My truck?" I take a step forward. "How about my fucking scars too, Jake? Fancy having those? You'd be fucking welcome to them."

"You got off lightly."

"Sure I fucking did," I sneer. "It's a walk in the fucking park. My life's a bed of fucking roses."

He takes a drag. "You may have scars outside." He taps his head. "But I've got scars inside."

"We've *all* got scars in here, Jake." I tap my own head. "Cameron still wets the fucking bed half of the fucking week. Serena's brain's fucking addled with all this shit."

He gestures back to Abigail's building. "Does she know?"

"About what?"

"About the fucking fire, Leo. Does she know what you did to Mariana?" I don't even grace him with an answer. He grins a sour fucking grin at me. "Oh, she doesn't. Fucking surprise."

"Mariana was off the rails."

"Because of *you*."

I shake my head. "Because of *her*, Jake. She was off the rails long before I came along. Long before we ever had Cam. And you fucking know it."

"You don't deserve another shot," he snarls. "You don't deserve anything."

"So you keep fucking telling me. Why don't you look at yourself instead, Jake? You might fucking learn something."

"Give me that paternity test, Leo, or I swear you'll rue the fucking day you turned me down."

I shoulder him on my way past. "Hold your fucking breath until I call."

"Next week," he snarls as he tosses his cigarette away. "You've got until next fucking week, Leo, and then I'm coming for what's mine."

My voice is low and deadly. I mean every word I say. "If you come anywhere near my son, or my house, or the business, or Abigail, I'll fucking kill you."

He fishes his keys from his pocket. I should call the police and have him arrested for his own fucking good, but he'd just do it again tomorrow.

"*Abigail*," he says, and I curse my mouth. He hauls himself into his truck and turns the ignition. I find myself hoping he drives into a fucking quarry on his way home. "Next week," he repeats. "Or you'll fucking regret it."

"Sleep it off," I tell him. "Have a fucking shower. Get your sad life sorted, Jake."

I stand in the road to watch him away. His truck swerves a little before he speeds out of view.

I call up his tracker on my mobile and assign it to favourites. Even having him in that list is fucking sickening. I wait until he's long back on the Worcester road before I head back to my own truck.

And I resolve to call my fucking lawyer first thing in the morning.

twentyeight

*clouds come floating into my life, no longer to carry
rain or usher storm, but to add colour to my sunset sky.*

—RABINDRANATH TAGORE

a b i g a i l

"**H**e turned up again, then?" Lauren's eyes sparkle as she props herself against my desk. I play dumb, my face as impassive as I can make it until she tuts at me. *"Leo,"* she says. "He turned up, right?"

I can't stop the grin. "What makes you say that?"

She gestures to the open office. "Uh, hello. You're beaming across the whole building this morning. Only one thing that gets a girl limping like that on a coffee round."

She really has no idea how much effort it's taking to walk at all. I put down my paperwork. "He may have turned up again."

My very expressive friend raises her hands to the sky. "Halleluiah. I knew he'd be back. The guy looked at you like I look at greasy fries after a night clubbing. Praise be for online dating and the slim odds," she raises a finger, "and I do mean *slim*, of finding an actual hottie in the ether."

"I guess fate threw me a break." My cheeks are burning up. The urge to laugh at life's craziness fizzes in my throat.

"Lucky bitch," Kelly calls in my direction as she heads to the meeting room. "I'd ride that stallion all night long. Yeehaw."

I doubt that very much. Not if she wanted to be vaguely mobile anytime the week following.

"Did he bring you flowers?" Lauren asks. "Chocolates to soften the blow of radio silence?"

I shake my head. "Somehow I don't think he's much of a flowers and chocolates kinda guy."

She sighs. "He doesn't need to be. He's all darkness and brawn and pure, hot man flesh."

"He's definitely all of those things, yeah," I agree. *And secrets, and pain, and kisses that taste like thunder.*

"Will he be with you at Diva's on Thursday?"

I shrug. "Your guess is as good as mine."

She rolls her eyes. "Maybe you guys should try a little communication alongside your more physical activities. Guy has a phone, right?"

My skin prickles. "Yes. He does."

"So call him. *Ask* him. *Demand* him to get his bloody dancing shoes on and come out for a good time."

If only. I stumble over a lacklustre excuse. "We, um... prefer things to be spontaneous..."

I'm relieved when her phone extension summons her back to her own desk. "Call him!" are her parting words.

I think I'll give that advice a miss. I'll just be glad if he shows up at all. Diva's or no.

There are some distinct downsides to his random appearances. Not least that I've been wearing some pretty awesome outfits for his benefit, only to have him show up when I'm in my plain Jane nightwear with my hair piled on my head.

I'd invite him along to our summer barbeque if I could face it. The gaudy affair is billed to be the event of the century. Dress to impress and all that jazz.

It only feels like yesterday I was dreading the whole sorry affair and everything that went along with it. Now I'm pretty much as hyped about it as everyone else in this place.

Lauren is wearing her old prom dress with a fascinator she bought for a wedding and never went to. Kelly is wearing a ballgown she bought for her ex's Christmas ball last winter. Kathleen from the management team has gone all out designer couture by all accounts. Won't even show anyone a sneak preview.

I'm wearing something new.

Figures, since I don't really have anything old.

The dress I've picked out is sexy in that demure kind of way. Ankle-length plum satin with a diamante trim, fitted like a dream, and delicate enough that I feel like I'm wearing negligee.

It's a fucking travesty that Leo won't see me in it.

Not unless I wear it to bed every evening on the off chance he's going to break in.

I smile to myself. Maybe I should start jogging in it at midnight along the river path. Could be my cool new hobby.

I check my phone is still on in my drawer, wondering if he really is keeping close tabs on me.

Maybe I could use it to hunt *him* one of these days. Use it as a decoy to coax him into a dark alley somewhere. The idea gives me a strange chill.

The bait using a decoy to snare the hunter. I do love a good twist.

bait

I could jump him. Use the element of surprise to get the bastard half naked for once.

My smile widens.

Yes. I'd like that.

I'd like that a lot.

I picture the bulk of him. The weight of him against my chest. The way he feels inside me with his forehead pressed to mine.

And then I giggle because life is good.

Life is really good.

Even if I don't stand a hope in hell of jumping the monster in a million years, it matters not.

I'm perfectly fine with him jumping me.

phoenix

My lawyer says a paternity battle will be both lengthy and expensive. She gives me her most professional stare over the top of her fine-rimmed glasses and assures me I should call Jake's bluff and count on him running out of both energy and cash. But she doesn't know Jake like I know him.

She hasn't seen the desperation in his eyes.

I'd have trusted Jake with anything on this planet before Mariana came along. Back when it was just the three of us – Jake, Serena, and me – I'd have sworn on everything I had that we'd be tight for all time.

We're blood, after all.

I'm amazed it's come to seeking legal advice about a non-molestation order to keep him away from the house and Cameron. But it has.

I feel grim as she lays out my options and what evidence I'd need to gather to support my case.

It needs more than my testimony. It needs dates, times, witnesses. It needs police involvement.

I feel weighed down by the process before it's even started.

"Off the record," she says. "Wouldn't it be better to throw the dog a bone for the time being? Is there any way you can negotiate some access rights? You said he's demanding you sell the old business premises, is that not something you could entertain for the sake of compromise? It might at least buy you some favour and some time to gather the evidence you need, no?"

I lean back in the chair opposite her, realising all over again how different she is from us – Jake and me. She's got a wall full of qualifications and professionally highlighted hair. She flinches whenever I reach over for a handshake, even though she doesn't know she's doing it.

In short, the woman has no idea what I'm dealing with here.

"Jake isn't the kind of dog you want to throw a bone to," I tell her.

She shrugs. "In that case, I'd say just keep on doing what you're doing. Start keeping records of your interaction. Refuse to take the paternity test. It's your name on Cameron's birth certificate, and you were Mariana's common law partner when she passed away. Legally, at this time, Cameron is undeniably your son. The onus will very much be on your brother to prove otherwise."

I thank her for her time, even though I'll pay through the nose for every second of it.

The sun is shining bright when I step outside and head back to my truck. I check the time. Early enough that I should head back for the last of the daily shipments. Late enough that I don't want to.

I can't remember the last time I've taken an afternoon for myself during work time. The combination of the warmth of the sun on my back and the need to take my sunglasses from the glovebox makes my decision for me.

Instead of taking a left back onto the industrial estate, I take a right.

I cruise back up the hillside with my window down low and music up high, feeling ten years younger and a whole lot wiser than I did this time yesterday.

Happier, too.

And it's not just from the sun.

Serena nearly falls over herself as I pull onto the driveway. I see her through the window, pointing me out to Cam. And how my boy smiles. He smiles and waves, and I forget in that one moment that he's anything other than a normal kid enjoying the summer.

Maybe treating him like he's anything else has been the problem all along.

It's the perfect day to finish up my refurbishments on the swimming pool. It's also one of the only bastard times we'll get to use it, given the fact it's raining at least eighty percent of the time up here.

The pool was Mariana's whim, definitely not mine, and far enough back that I indulged her.

I only scoop Cameron up for a minute on the way through before I'm straight out there working out what still needs doing.

And then I remember why I agreed to this stupid installation in the first place.

Our house is positioned right on the slope of the Malverns. The ground drops sharply away and rolls down to the town below. The pool is down three flights of steps from the back porch. It had to be that way to clear enough ground space to house the thing.

It's heated, but barely. It's shallow enough at the deep end that my toes still touch the floor and barely long enough to get a decent swim out of.

Its saving grace is that it's an infinity design. Another one of Mariana's whims.

In that pool you feel like you're on the edge of the world. No barriers. No manmade protrusions. Just a ledge and the whole fucking vista down below.

Mariana used to say she was sitting amongst the stars. My breath catches in my throat as I picture her there, propped on the ledge to nowhere with wet hair and a champagne flute in her hand.

It's like we're flying, Leo. Can you feel it?

I pull the tarp back and wind it in. The water sparkles like gold in the sun.

It's been a long time since I've seen it in its glory. Aside from the maintenance I've been working on over long nights recently, the cover hasn't been off once since she died.

Not for me, and not for Cam, either.

I look back up at the house and find him there, staring at me over the railings. I wave and he waves back.

He points at the water and I give him a thumbs-up.

I'd forgotten how much he loved this pool. I'd forgotten all the afternoons we spent splashing about in here when the weather held. Even when it didn't.

It's been easier to forget than to feel.

I check the filter is working just fine, and run a final water check. My maintenance has paid off. The pool is perfectly usable.

Cam is jumping around the living room as I dig the old inflatables out of the pool cupboard. He's reaching up for his inflatable turtle and his armbands before I can even finish blowing them up.

"Alright, champ." I laugh. "Give your dad a minute, will you?" I tip my head towards the kitchen. "Go ask Serena to grab your shorts."

I hear Serena trying to decipher his message as I head upstairs to sort my own pool wear.

bait

I dig out a pair of shorts and a towel from the airer. Change quickly before the weather decides to change on me.

Cam is frustrated when I get back down, Serena shaking her head as he tries to communicate.

"He needs shorts," I tell her. "For swimming." And then the tiniest intuition hits home. Hard. I keep my voice easy. Calm. Steady enough that even I barely notice the tension. "You could have just asked her, champ. We'd have been down there already by now."

Serena hands him a pair from the laundry basket. I resist the urge to jump in and help him change.

I hold back from congratulating him for doing it himself, playing the whole thing down as we head outside.

It's been a long time since I've felt the sun on my bare back. A long time since my scars have seen the light of day. For the first time in a while they barely bother me. I'm all smiles as I get Cameron kitted up in his armbands and throw the turtle in the water.

"Let's go, bud," I say and drop myself in the shallow end. I'm lazing on my back quite happily as Cameron tackles the steps on his own. He launches himself into the water with a grin and bobs about for just a second until he finds his feet.

He can swim. He's been in this pool since before he could walk, even if it's been a while.

That knowledge makes it easier for me to play it cool as he splashes over to the deep end. He chases the turtle but the turtle keeps on moving, always just that little way out of reach.

I hold back. Hold firm. Reining myself in tight from grabbing it for him.

He's laughing his silent laugh as he paddles the length of the pool after it. I keep out of his way to give him a clear path, and something happens in that water.

Something quite extraordinary.

Maybe it's the familiarity of happier times. Maybe it's the challenge of the chase that distracts him enough to forget his usual inhibitions.

Maybe it's just all in good time, like they said it would be.

But my nerves prickle as I hear him grunt and grab for that big green turtle. My feet are firmly on the floor as he reaches out for its inflated fin and holds on tight.

And my heart is in my throat as he squeals in triumph when it's his.

Like father, like son.

"Good work, bud!" I call, and he grins. I try my best to keep my voice light. "Now let him go and chase him again. See if you can catch him a second time."

He looks so proud of himself, my boy. He lets go happily and watches that turtle go bobbing back across the pool. I'm watching too, pretending I'm in the race to grab him myself, and Cam picks up a gear, his feet kicking out like a trooper as he thinks I'm going to steal the glory.

I hang back, pretend I'm straining. "Go, champ! You got this!"

Kicking and sploshing and concentration – that grin still firm on his face as he swims.

And then he catches him.

He catches him at the corner of the pool and slams his hands around that turtle's goofy head. And he laughs.

My boy laughs.

My heart soars so high it's fucking painful. I've got a lump in my throat I can't swallow away, and a deadpan expression like it's no big fucking deal that he just made a sound.

"Great job!" I call. "Well done, Cam. You got him."

And he forgets himself.

I guess in that one happy moment he forgets it all. He points at the turtle's big green flippers and looks me right in the face, and then he speaks.

Two simple words that change my whole fucking world. "He's fast."

I splash myself with water so he can't see the tears. I pretend I'm coughing water and laughing as I make my way over.

"Yeah, bud. He sure is. But you're faster. You swim like a fish." I pause. "Remember this game, Cam?"

I don't know if he does, but I sure do. He's not expecting it as I slam my hands flat on the surface. Not expecting to get splashed as the water spurts.

I'm not sure it really is the memory that has him giggling his head off, but I don't give a shit either way.

He splashes me back, kicking and slapping water all over me, and I'm laughing too.

And then I see Serena at the railings. I point and wave and Cam does too.

"Shall we shout her, Cam? See if we can get her to hear us? Maybe she'll come down too if we're loud enough."

I don't really expect him to join in as I shout her name.

She clasps her hand over her mouth as he does.

I spin him around so he can't see her surprise.

And I thank my lucky fucking stars that Mariana got her way with this stupid bloody swimming pool.

twentynine

Summer has filled her veins with light and her heart is washed with noon.

—C. DAY LEWIS

abigail

My monster doesn't come for me all week. I'm having fun all the same, planning the barbeque and dancing until my feet ache at Diva's on Thursday night.

I only check my phone once when I get home, but when I do, there's a single message waiting for me.

It makes my heart soar.

Soon.

That's all it says.

I get ready on Saturday morning with high spirits and a smile on my face. I style my hair in curls with Sarah's help and slip on my beautiful new dress, only sighing once in the mirror at the pity he won't get to see me like this.

And then I go.

Lauren and the girls are already on Castle Green when I get there. The wine is flowing freely, the smell of charcoal is in the air and the weather is holding.

Everything is great.

Jack takes great pleasure in introducing me to all the people I've yet to meet from the other office. I shake hands and smile and struggle to assign names to faces, scouting the crowds for any clients I should be recognising but haven't yet met.

"Stop bloody working," Lauren giggles in my ear as I've introduced myself to the fifth person at the salad table in a row. "Kick back, get drunk, have fun."

"You're such a slacker," I tell her, and stick my tongue out.

"No," she says. "*You're* such a bloody *professional*. You're giving the rest of us a bad name." She nudges me in good humour.

She has got a point. For all the enjoyment I've come to find in the position I grabbed hold of during my crazy relocation effort, I'm beginning to think it's time for more of a challenge.

It amazes me that I feel ready. Hell, it amazes me that I'm back up from my knees with my head held high.

Because of him.

I crush that thought.

Not just because of him.

Because of Lauren, and Kelly, and Jack. Because of Sarah. Because of stupid nights at Divas and learning to enjoy phone calls home again.

Because of *me*, too.

I'm chowing down on a burger when my skin prickles, happily tipsy enough on two large glasses of white that I brush the sensation off as nothing.

I convince myself I'm imagining things when I catch a glimpse of a familiar silhouette weaving through the crowd at the raffle table.

No.

It can't be.

But it is.

Kelly's voice shrieks in my ear before Lauren's. "You didn't say you were bringing him!"

I turn to stare blankly, even though my heart is thumping.

She points to a huddle of clients by the bandstand. "There. Look."

I don't see a thing, until I do.

And there he is. Large as life at my work barbeque. Looking thoroughly at odds with everyone else here, even though he's wearing a tux.

He's wearing a fucking tux.

Fuck.

He looks fucking magnificent.

Better than magnificent.

He looks like a perfect nightmare. Darker than I've ever seen him, even in the glaring sun.

"You could knock me over with a feather," Kelly says. "That man is fucking delicious."

"He really is," I tell her, and then I grin. "Hung like a donkey, too."

I leave them with open mouths as I abandon my burger on a trestle table and head straight for the beast himself.

He meets me halfway, as though this is the most natural thing in the world.

"What are you doing here?" I whisper-hiss, before he can even speak.

"I said soon," he tells me. "This is soon."

"And *this* is my work barbeque." I can't hide the smile. "Technically for employees, suppliers and clients only."

My tummy flutters as he leans over and presses his lips to my ear. I love the sound of his breath.

"And technically I'm a client. I ordered some filing cabinets, you can check the records."

My eyes widen and his are laughing.

"You're a client?! Of Office Express?!"

"Like I said, you can check the records."

He lets out a low laugh as I grab my phone from my handbag. My fingers are shaking with a strange jittery excitement as I call up my work login.

Filing cabinets... Malvern... past ninety days...

I get a few hits. Names I recognise. A few clients I've seen today already.

And then him.

I know it.

Scott Brothers Logistics. Enigma business park, Malvern. I call up the order details. *Leo Scott. Managing Director.*

No. Fucking. Way.

My mouth drops open.

"That night..." I begin and he smirks.

"I told you I found one of your shoes under a truck. I omitted the fact that it was my truck. I thought I'd keep that little detail to myself."

"I came looking..."

"And you found me. You just didn't know it. I was right there, I drove past you on your way back to the car park."

"And you followed me," I finish.

"Yes," he says. "And how the pieces fit so snugly together when they all come into view."

"That was your building..." I whisper. "You grabbed me by your own building."

"And deleted the security footage after. I enjoyed watching that back, I can tell you."

The wine makes me heady. My legs feel like jelly. "Leo Scott."

"Pleased to meet you," he says and holds out his hand. It feels so ridiculous to take it, but I do. I stare at his inked fingers in mine. The rose I recognised on the fuel station counter. "So now you know some of my secrets." He smirks. "How does it feel to know the monster for real?"

"It's a good start." I smile. "I'm kinda digging the unfolding mystery thing."

"See if you still feel like that when you get more of the picture. You look incredible by the way," he says, and my cheeks burn. "It'll be a shame to tear that dress off you later."

My clit tingles so hard I clench my thighs.

"You're looking pretty incredible yourself."

"I can polish up," he says, and then he lowers his voice. His eyes are dark and dangerous, his brows heavy. "When the band finishes this evening, you will leave. You won't look for me. You'll say your goodbyes to your friends and you'll make your excuses. You'll leave via the Cathedral Walk and head down to the old bridge."

I'm too horny to hide it. Even my voice is dripping as I speak. "And until then?"

My heart jumps as his hand slips into mine. "And until then you introduce me to everyone. Until then we have regular fun like regular people at a summer barbeque."

"And what shall I introduce you as?" I ask, hardly daring to meet his eyes. "As a client, or..."

My voice trails off when he snakes his hand around my waist and pulls me tight. His palm is hot through the satin.

Hot enough to make me tingle.

So many eyes on me. On *us*.

So much whispering and gossip and chatter about the sinister looking businessman at my side.

And I love it.

I've never been so happy to be on display as I am next to him.

"I think we go with the *or*, don't you?" he says.

phoenix

I love seeing her like this.

She's in her element and she doesn't even know it. She's a natural as she works the event. Gracious and vivacious as she makes introductions with my hand tight in hers.

I've never been so happy to be on public display as I am next to her.

Her dress is a perfect drape of satin. Her hair smells of coconut and hours of styling. Her makeup is flawless even after a greasy burger.

And she's mine.

Even though there's a whole fucking jigsaw of secrets still to dust off between us, she's mine.

I intend to keep it that way.

It's the first Saturday daytime I've spent away from both Cam and work in over a year. Under normal circumstances I wouldn't be here, not with the business still precariously trading and Cam's speech intermittent at best.

But these aren't normal circumstances.

I had to see her like this.

I had to be here to watch her sparkle on her own turf.

I can't wait to show her the sparkles on mine later.

She gets jittery as the band starts up and evening draws in. She's pressed tight to my side as we gather at the bandstand. My hand is on her hip and hers is on top, her fingers threaded through mine as she bops her head to the beat.

I should be watching them but I'm watching her.

The set list takes an age. My cock is throbbing for her long before the band are done.

I pull her in front of me between songs and hitch up against her ass as the crowd applauds the musicians on stage.

I feel her breath quicken as she reaches back for me.

"*Soon,*" I remind her and she nods. She rests her head back against my shoulder and rocks her hips to the beat.

It takes all of my restraint not to drag her behind a trestle table and fuck her until they hear her screams over the music.

I wince at the ache in my balls when I pull away from her and make my exit.

I feel her eyes on me all the way as I retreat into the last of the evening sun.

My truck is waiting in the car park. I take the route I've already mapped out, pulling into a short stay space down by the old bridge.

I get out and position myself between two buildings, out of view of the road and invisible until the last minute from the direction she'll be travelling in.

She'll walk right past me without a clue, that's what I count on.

And she does.

I've only been waiting twenty minutes when I hear her heels heading in my direction. I'm ready for her as she turns the corner and carries on down the street none the wiser.

She doesn't even have time to squeak when I snatch her. Her legs barely flail before I bundle her straight up and into my backseat.

"No questions," I snap, before I close the door. "You ask me where we're going and I'll hurt you, understand?"

Her eyes are wide as she nods at me.

I slam the door and jump up into the driver's seat. I'm pushing the speed limit as

bait

I head out onto the Worcester road with my pretty little piece of bait on the backseat.

"Don't fucking look at me," I snarl as I catch her gaze in the rearview. She drops back down onto the seat. "Don't look outside, either. You'll go wherever I say we're fucking going and you'll keep your mouth fucking closed."

I wonder if she's still scared of me. I wonder if I'm still bad enough to be her monster in the night.

I'll make it so.

I take a scenic route until the sunlight starts to fade. It's well into dusk by the time I pull up outside my house.

I give her no indication that I live here, just drag her from the backseat and keep a solid grip on her.

She's shaky as we cross the road and take the track up toward the beacon. Her breath is raspy as we reach the top and still I keep on shunting her ahead.

My black swan stares in wonder at the vista down below just as soon as she can see it. She edges closer to the bank to admire the sparkling lights of a sleepy town.

I'd let her admire them a while longer if the beast wasn't burning in my belly.

She flinches as my voice cuts out loud. Her eyes are wild and wide as she glances back over her shoulder.

"Run," I bark. "Now."

She sucks in breath and takes off on her heels without so much as a question.

She's frantic but slow, her skirt in her hands as she dashes across the uneven ground to clear some distance.

I wait.

Watch until she's got a decent head start. Until she's far away on the path ahead and the sun is finally thinking about dipping under the horizon.

And then I let out the beast.

thirty

Great things are done when men and mountains meet.

—WILLIAM BLAKE

abigail

That crazy wild thrill. The fear thrumming right through me. The flutters and the jitters and the beautiful rush of adrenaline.

I feel it all.

It's windy up here. So dark I can barely see my hands in front of me, scrabbling in the darkness.

There's nothing ahead. Just open ground. Scrubby grass under my heels and the whole world twinkling down below, so stunning it would take my breath if I had any to spare.

I can't run. A stumbling walk is all I can manage. I have no idea where I'm headed or how far he is behind me.

I listen out for his footfalls but all I can hear is the wind.

The wine is still in my blood. I'm not cold, even though my hair is whipping

255

and my nipples are stinging under my dress.

My heels suddenly hit solid ground. A path of some kind. Grainy and gravelly. I spin to check it out, tapping my foot around me, but in a beat I've lost my bearings. I'm on top of the world with no idea whatsoever how I arrived here. I take a stab on a direction, but it leads me into a thicket. Wiry branches scratch at my legs through my dress. I back up, try another route, but end up in more of it.

My heart picks up another gear, knowing he must be closing. I'm listening hard, hearing nothing.

Maybe I've lost him.

I don't know which is more terrifying – the thought of him slamming into me in the darkness or the thought of being lost for the night.

I curse as bracken spikes my outstretched hand, curse again as my heel sinks into soft ground.

Fuck.

And even in my terror, I'm laughing. Even as the adrenaline pulses, my soul soars free.

I dig deeper, push myself on, stumbling out of the undergrowth and back onto open grass. I fix my gaze on a set of lights in the distance and use them to keep my focus. Slow steady steps. Moving with purpose. On and on.

And then I see the stars.

They're easily as brilliant as the lights down below.

A whole panorama of brilliance. All for me.

I stop.

Breathe.

Stare up at the universe.

I don't feel the monster at my back until he's close enough to bite me.

His mouth is the first thing I feel, hot lips and vicious teeth on my bare shoulder.

I'm smiling as it hurts. My fingers in his hair as he tears my dress open at the neckline. My tits prickle at the chill as he unclasps my bra and tosses it aside.

A brush of his fingers and my dress falls to the floor. Ruined.

I don't care.

I whimper as he pulls my head back. Squeal as he nips at my jaw. His grip is rough on cold skin. His kisses are fierce on my open mouth.

I love him for all of it.

I know he's going to tear my knickers before he does it. I spread my legs as his hands slide down my stomach.

I'm open wide as he spreads me and ploughs his fingers in in one. My clit throbs against the chill before his thumb presses hard and circles.

I hook my arm around his neck for balance. I rock on his hand for more.

"Come for me," he growls. "Scream my fucking name to the stars."

"More," I grunt. "Give me more."

"Your cunt is a greedy little slut," he says and kisses me again.

I'm a greedy little slut. My fingers on his tell him so.

More.

I want more.

A stretch.

A burn.

"Fuck me," I whimper. "Please."

I'm naked and windswept with goose-pimpled skin, grinning at the sky as my monster plunges his inked fingers knuckle-deep.

I know I can take him. My body cries out for the pain.

My thighs are warm with my own wetness as he pulls his fingers free. They're wet as they land on my stomach and hitch me into his arms.

I barely keep my heels as he carries me. I have no idea where we're heading in the darkness but I hold on tight and enjoy every ragged breath.

"You're gonna scream my fucking name," he whispers, and I know it.

He takes a step up. His feet thump on solid ground.

There's a cold ledge waiting for my ass as he drops me.

"This is the highest point on the hills," he tells me as my hands reach back to explore. A circular plinth.

Makes sense, this is some kind of monument.

My feet dangle over the edge. His crotch shunts forward and I feel him through his suit.

Perfect height.

His breath on my lips. His fingers on his belt.

My soul in his hands.

My legs wrap around his waist on instinct. I lift myself up on my arms as my hair blows wild.

He rubs his cock against my slit and tugs me onto him.

It's my own weight that impales me.

Fuck.

"Steady," he grunts, but there's no steady about it, not with my arms straining behind me and my legs struggling for grip.

I don't care.

Three barbells shunt inside in one. I groan and so does he.

My back is arching even as it pains. My pussy swallows him whole even as he's cursing.

"*Fuck,*" he grunts. "You're gonna fucking tear."

"Slow," I hiss and buck my hips.

His arms slide under mine. He pulls me onto him and takes my weight.

My ass is precarious on the edge of the monument. His ridges feel divine behind my clit as he bounces me like a ragdoll.

It's not slow. Not steady.

There is only my slick pussy and the steel-studded monster slamming inside me.

There's only his open mouth on mine and the wind in my ears.

"Scream my fucking name," he grunts.

I barely remember my own.

He shunts harder. Bends me backwards until I cry out.

There.

Oh, fuck. *There.*

"Fuck me!" I groan. "Fuck me, Leo!"

His teeth nip my cheek in protest. "Louder."

"FUCK ME!"

"Scream my fucking name!" he hisses, and I smile.

"OH FUCK, LEO! FUCK ME!"

"Good girl," he hisses.

"DO IT! FUCK ME UP, LEO! MAKE ME TAKE IT!"

And oh fuck, I'm on the fucking edge, writhing and squirming and gulping for breath.

My pussy feels battered enough to cry for a week. My clit is swollen hard as it grinds his belly through his shirt.

"Gonna destroy your cunt, Abigail," he tells me. "Your body's gonna learn to take me. Gonna fucking beg for my dick in raw."

I smile at the hope.

Yes.

It's enough to send me over. I ride him right the way back as his thrusts become frantic. I'm whimpering into his suit jacket as he fills me up, coming all over him as he comes inside me.

I feel the bite of the wind so much harder against my skin once I'm done. I feel how hard his breaths are against mine as he drops me back on my ass.

He shoves his dick away and he's still immaculate, a tux to my stark bollock nakedness.

I can't even imagine where the remnants of my dress are. I know full well my bra will be someone's lucky find when they go out walking tomorrow.

"You're so beautiful," he breathes. "I love how beautiful you are when you hurt."

Thanks sounds stupid even in my head, so I don't say a word.

He shrugs his suit jacket from his shoulders and drapes it over mine. I tug it tight around me and loosen my grip on his waist.

I drop to my feet, and he buttons me up. "This will have to do," he says, and I nod. I don't care.

I like being in his jacket.

The white of his shirt is easier to see in the moonlight. It's easy to follow him with my hand in his.

He carries me down once we reach the steepness of the hill track, holding me tight as my pussy leaks all over him.

I feel it dribbling.

He doesn't seem to care.

The streetlights are a welcome sight as we arrive back on the road. I can do it alone from here, wobbly legs perfectly able to carry me across the street to the truck.

I look around me. The houses are big here, perched right on the edge of the hill.

No sign of life. Nobody asking what we're doing here, parked up so randomly in the middle of the night next to someone's front garden.

His fingers graze my tit as he retrieves his keys from his jacket pocket. We're right in front of a Neighbourhood Watch sign, but there's nobody watching us. Not even a twitching curtain as his truck alarm flashes and bleeps.

Sure-footed. He was so sure-footed.

Knew just where to find me.

And just where to fuck me.

He knows this place.

Just like he knew the last one.

The tiniest shimmer of intuition, nothing more. It's wild, but I go with it anyway.

"You live here…"

His eyes lock on mine. "Sorry?"

I gesture to the road. "You live here. This is your street."

He pauses. Waits.

"I'm right, aren't I? This is your street?" I spin on the spot. "We must be close. Are we close?"

I fix my eyes on a tall old place a few down. Maybe that one. Or maybe the redbrick place opposite, I think. Just far enough away to keep me off the scent.

But no.

He smiles a dirty smile. Gestures beyond the truck to the house right alongside us.

"We're more than fucking close, Abigail. You're standing on my driveway."

thirtyone

*Out of suffering have emerged the strongest souls; the
most massive characters are seared with scars.*

—KHALIL GIBRAN

abigail

I stare dumbfounded at the property before us.

"This is yours?"

He nods. "Home sweet home."

The place is gorgeous – period brickwork with big windows and an arched front door. Shrubs line the path to the doorway. The pane looks like stained glass, but I can't be entirely sure in this light.

"It's beautiful."

"It is," he agrees. He hovers by the truck, his eyes as dark as ever, his jaw tight.

He's emanating tension. It makes my nerves spike.

"We should go," I offer, but he takes a step forward.

"I want to show you something." He takes my hand. Grips tight.

I follow in silence, terrified of breaking whatever moment this is we're having. The revelations are rolling and I don't want them to stop. I want to know the man behind the monster, stare into the shadows behind his eyes and uncover the secrets there.

He leads the way around the side of the house, unlatches a gate and steps on through. I'm excited. Nervous. My heart fluttering with every step. He flicks a switch on the wall and the whole place comes alive in front of me.

I can't even breathe.

We're on a balcony ledge staring over wrought iron railings. The view is breathtaking, just as it was up on the hills. Only this time there's a tiered level down below, and that level has a swimming pool. It's dotted with gold mood lighting. The water shimmers like it's breathing.

"Wow," I say. "Just... wow..."

He doesn't say a word.

"Is this all yours?"

"I had it put in a few years back."

"It's incredible." I can't hold back a smile, can't help wanting a swim in the darkness.

He knows it. "Be my guest," he says and gestures down the steps.

I grip the railing tight on my way down. "Skinny dipping? You want me to skinny dip?"

I know he's smirking behind me. "Unless you want to swim in my jacket."

"Maybe you should stop tearing my clothes off me." I laugh.

"Not gonna happen."

Oh, how I smile.

I look around before I take the plunge. There's a light on in a neighbouring house far above, but no other signs of life.

"You joining me?" I ask as he slips his jacket from my shoulders. He smirks as he drapes it over a railing.

"Not tonight."

My heart falls.

He has to.

The pool has no barrier on the far side, just a smooth ledge onto nothing. I imagine swimming up to the drop, staring down at the moonlit world.

"Come on," I protest, and he smirks again.

"Get your pretty ass in the water before I throw you in myself."

"Is that a threat?"

"A promise."

An electric moment, me bared to the whole world, naked in his back garden while he stares on from the shadows. And then he moves. Quickly.

He hoists me up before I can run. His hand clamps over my mouth, just as always, but this time I don't go easy. I kick my heels off in a beat, my arms snaking back around his shoulders to grab hold of him.

I pick the perfect moment as he reaches the edge of the pool. My feet hook his legs and hold. I don't let go as he drops me.

Don't let go as he fights for balance, teetering over the side.

Please, God.

It works.

My soul air-punches as I topple the monster. Surprise was my only real advantage. I doubt I'll have it on my side ever again.

But that's ok.

It's ok, because as I splash hard into that beautiful water, he's falling right behind me.

He recovers at the last second, manages to catch himself on the ledge before he goes under. He'd haul himself right back out if it wasn't for an impulsive moment of bravery that sees me throw my wet body at his and wrap my arms around his neck.

"Please," I whisper. "Be with me."

My tits flatten to his chest and soak his shirt clean through. He's ridiculously ripped, muscles taught as he supports my weight as well as his.

He lowers himself slowly. Carefully. My mouth is on his before he can protest.

He kisses me back as his feet touch the bottom.

This time I won't be thwarted. My bravery knows no limits. My fingers are lightning on his shirt buttons, hunting out his bare skin. I tug his bow tie loose and my hands slide up his bare chest in victory.

I break the kiss with a smile. Push away just enough to look at him.

He's inked from pecs to throat. A monochrome display of pure brilliance. My jaw drops.

I've never seen anyone so sculpted. Never seen ridges of hard flesh as perfect as they look on him.

"You are incredible…" I whisper, but his expression is grim.

He pushes himself across the pool to the ledge that leads to nowhere, and there's something very wrong here. Wrong enough to hitch my breath.

I'm staring at the most beautiful view I've ever seen. The most beautiful *man* I've ever seen, pale in the moonlight, in the most glorious state of undress as the water glitters. There's a whole universe of stars behind him as the world falls away.

But it all feels wrong.

He feels so wrong.

I stay back, dropping myself down into the water until my hair fans all around me. I wait for him to wrestle whatever demons he's up against, praying he'll come out the other side and still want to know me.

Right now I'm not so sure.

I'm not so sure of anything.

He looks tortured. Broken.

Haunted by demons worse than any I've seen in my nightmares.

I remember our initial conversation online. It feels so long ago.

I loved hard. I lost harder.

Him the same as me.

The question is in the air, just as it was back then. The same question that landed in my inbox amongst the idiots out for a cheap lay.

The one that I asked him right back.

The one he never really answered.

Secrets.

I can hear them twitching.

I take a breath, summoning every last scrap of bravery I have left.

And then I ask him, my breath barely more than a whisper in the moonlight.

"What happened to you?"

phoenix

"I loved hard. I lost harder."

My words are instant. My reply vague as shit.

I'm cranking open the trapdoor and staring the secrets right in their twisted faces, not knowing which one to pull out first.

I hate the way she feels so far away, her eyes so sad as she stares at me.

My breath feels tight. I feel like I'm on the edge of a confession, for sins I'm not sure are even mine.

"Me and Jake, my brother, we had a haulage company," I begin, then correct myself. "*Have* a haulage company. Mariana appeared out of nowhere. Backpacking through the countryside. Wild. Looking for something she wasn't sure she was searching for. She found us."

I meet her eyes.

"She found *me*."

Abigail nods. The water ripples as she kicks her way over. She rests against the ledge just a short way away. It feels like miles.

"She's the one you lost?" she asks.

"I lost her long before she left," I admit. "We were enemies sharing a bed as lovers. In the end, I wasn't sure whether she wanted to fuck me or kill me. Probably both."

She smiles. "Turbulent, then."

"It was like riding a tornado. A white-knuckle ride of fucking chaos."

"But you held on pretty tight?"

"Until the end," I say.

"She left you?"

"In a form." I take another breath. "She passed away just over a year ago."

"I'm so sorry," she says, and she is. She looks mortified.

"Passed away isn't the right term for it," I clarify. "Passing away is a gentle phrase. Soft. Like slipping underwater. Like falling asleep and never waking up. What happened to Mariana wasn't gentle." Her screams are ringing in my ears. My fists are clenched underwater. "There was a fire at the warehouse. We were storing chemicals for a client up in Huddersfield, a whole batch of them ready to truck down to Dover. The whole fucking lot went up. It was a fucking inferno. So fierce the sprinklers couldn't hold it."

Her eyes are wide as she intuits what I'm about to say.

"Mariana was in there. So was Jake." My breath strains. "The place was already burning when I got there. They say it was an explosion. It blew the roof out. It was like running into a tunnel of flames." I gesture above my head, seeing them right there, the heat on my skin. "They licked the ceiling, moved like they were alive, a blanket of flames. The heat…" I take a breath. "Jake must have been in the loading bay. The first explosion sent him flying. His head hit the concrete as he landed. He was barely conscious when I reached him. I dragged him out of there as his feet caught fire." I hold up my palms. "I put those flames out with my bare hands. His shoes were melting. He lost most of the skin on his heels."

She's shaking her head as I go on.

"He was screaming at me all the way. Begging me to get Mariana first." My voice catches. "But he's my brother… I couldn't…"

"You saved him," she whispers.

"If you can call it that." I shake my head. "When I got back in there the whole place was up. The explosion must have blocked the door through to the store. The other exits were on fire. She was in there…"

I hear her breath catch.

"She was right on the other side of that door, and she was so fucking scared." I close my eyes. "I told her I'd get to her. Promised I'd get to her. We had this racking, huge steel rigs to the ceiling. One of the bays fell when the drums blew and blocked the door. She couldn't move it. Couldn't even try. It was too hot to touch, she said. Everything was too hot to touch."

I gesture to my shoulder without even thinking. "The door was heavy, it burnt like a hotplate. I shunted it with everything I had. Even still, I couldn't open it more than an inch. I told her to get back, to run, but she had nowhere to go. The whole fucking world was burning around me and I couldn't get through that door, not for the fucking life of me. My skin…" I take a moment. A long fucking moment. "I can still smell it. Still hear her screaming." My gut churns. "You know the last thing she said to me?"

She shakes her head.

"She begged me not to let her die in there. Screamed that she didn't want to burn."

I have to look away as Abigail wipes tears from her eyes.

My heart fucking breaks all over again as the memory comes back. "She was so fucking scared. I was too. I promised I wouldn't leave her. Swore I'd get to her. Told her just to hang on, that I was coming."

I stare at the sky as I finish up the rest.

"The second explosion took the wall out. That's the last I remember. I didn't come around until I was already outside. The flashing sirens were hurting my eyes. My throat." I put my fingers against my windpipe. "It hurt so bad to even fucking breathe, and I was screaming for her, fighting to go back in there, even as they held me down."

"They didn't get her out," she says, and it's not a question.

I shake my head. "They say that would've been the last she felt of it. That explosion would have been the end." I rest back against the ledge. Fight to stay steady. "Jake says if I'd have got to that door earlier... if I hadn't taken him out first..."

"No."

"He says I'd have had more time... that I could have got to her... could've taken it off the hinges, driven a fucking truck through it..."

"No," she says again. "I don't believe that."

And I'm not sure I do either. Not anymore.

I look her straight in the face. "I have scars. On my shoulder, mainly. My back too. They're bad. Deep."

She fights back tears. Nods.

"I didn't want to..."

"You didn't want me to see," she finishes for me.

"I don't talk about it. It's not much of a conversation starter." I feel so fucking grim inside as I try to explain. "The scars aren't just out here." I gesture to my back. "They're inside, too. Guilt. Hate."

"What you went through…" she says. "I can't even imagine…"

"You don't want to imagine."

"Your brother," she asks. "Was he okay?"

"Physically."

She nods.

"We don't speak anymore. He hates me. Blames me for all of it. Blames me for her being there. Blames me for saving him first."

"How can he blame you for what happened?" she says. "It was an just accident. A horrible accident."

"That's just the thing," I say, and her eyes open wide. "I'm not so sure it was."

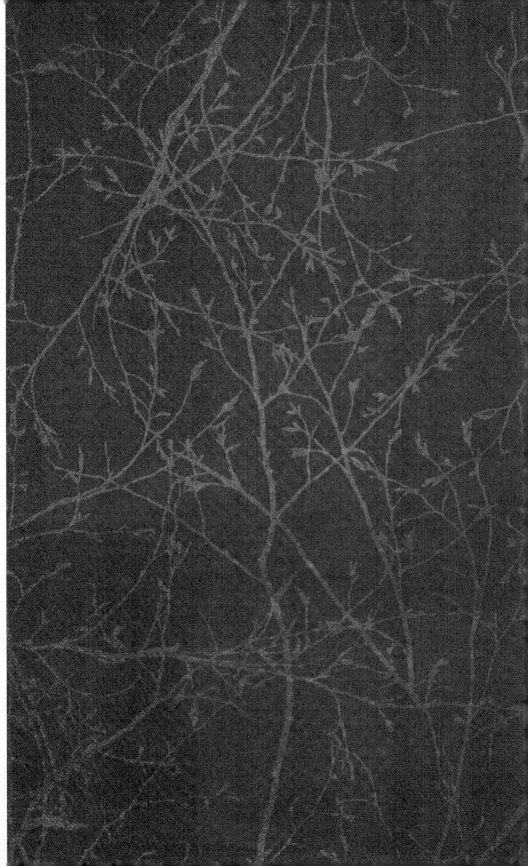

thirtytwo

My longing for truth was a single prayer.
—EDITH STEIN

abigail

The broken parts of my heart bleed, and it's all for him.

For the love he lost.

The scars he bears.

The sadness in his eyes as he relives this all for me.

"It wasn't an accident?" I ask, hating myself for even pushing.

"I don't know," he says. "They're still to deliver the absolute verdict. There are signs it was electrical. It may have been an unfortunate combination of a faulty chemical canister and a spark from one of the generators. It burnt so hot it's hard to call. So many factors to wade through, and a lot of the evidence was incinerated. They had to identify Mariana from her teeth. Officially, I mean."

I hate the way I flinch as he tells me.

"Sorry," he says.

I shake my head. "Don't be. It's amazing you're still alive." I inch a little closer. "If it was electrical, surely that's an accident?"

He smiles a terrible smile. "The fire happened at midnight. Two people in that building, Jake and Mariana."

"That's pretty late to be working," I comment.

"We'd had an argument," he says and my stomach tightens. "She spat at me, told me she was going. I'd have chased her... but..." He stops speaking. "I always chased her. We had a... dynamic..."

I nod. I know exactly what he's referring to.

"Anyway. I didn't chase her that night. I couldn't." He looks right at me, and there's more. I know there is. Whatever it is drifts away before he voices it. "I didn't chase her. I swore to myself I'd had enough of it."

"And she ended up at the warehouse? With Jake? Isn't that strange?"

"That bit doesn't surprise me. Not really. But the rest of it doesn't add up, not if it was an accident. You see, the chemical vats were stored down the other end of the warehouse. We're careful with fire regulations, always have been. When the place went up, they were at the top end by the loading bay. You could say maybe someone moved them earlier ready to load, but that doesn't make sense. It wasn't on the logs."

"Mariana moved them herself?"

He shrugs. "I don't know. Her or Jake. Or both of them."

"But why?"

"I have no idea," he tells me. "Not unless they were planning on burning the place down."

"You think they were?"

"That's the million-dollar question." He shrugs again. "Mariana was wild. Unpredictable. She hated the business, said it made me a workaholic, said she was a tiger in a cage, desperate to run free." He looks away, takes a breath. "I think sometimes that maybe she was trying to punish me, burn down what she thought I held dear."

"Seems drastic..." I offer.

"And unfortunate. A boiling pot of unfortunate coincidences. The chemicals being piled up in that one ridiculous location, for starters. Then there was the fact that another of our clients was a supplier of animal bedding. Tightly packed sawdust on high racking created a dust explosion of epic proportions." He sighs. "They know everything but how it started. According to our official documentation, the fire risk procedures were followed to the letter. Mariana wasn't even an official employee when that fire happened. They've struggled to assign any liability, but by the same token they can't seem to definitively rule out arson." He sighs again. "Then again, nobody seems to be willing to write this off as a freak accident, either. In truth, nobody knows."

I think it through. "What about your brother? What does he say?"

"Amnesia. I suspect it's selective."

His tone is bitter and I think better of prying too hard in that direction.

When he sighs again I hear just how strained his chest is. How much he's hurting.

I notice how his fists are clenched under the water.

My stomach flips as if I'm falling. My heart pains as I try to comprehend how he feels.

"How's that for secrets?" he asks. "Enough?"

Such pain. Such horrible fucking hurt.

I think of her, Mariana. Of her last moments. Of being trapped behind that door with the flames coming for her.

Of the desperation.

He's rigid as I go to him, every muscle tense as I press my body to his and hold

275

him tight. My body feels so soft against his firmness. My edges mould to his, skin on skin. My face in his neck as I breathe.

"I'm so sorry," I whisper and he flinches.

I grip a little tighter, flaying my soul alive against his jagged edges until they come to rest easy. He takes a breath. I hold mine.

My brokenness feels tender against his. I feel so small against him.

And then he holds me. Wraps me in arms so huge they could crush me alive but crush me just enough.

I press my forehead to his, stare into eyes that chase me in my dreams. I see his nightmares staring back at me.

"I was her monster," he whispers. "It destroyed her."

"You loved her," I say. "Right until the end."

"Just be careful the monster doesn't destroy you too."

"I don't want *careful*," I tell him. "I just want you."

"That's just as well," he says. "Because it's now you I'm chasing in the dark."

His lips press to mine so slowly. He squeezes the breath from me as he holds me tight.

And then he looks beyond me, up to the house above. There's a light on when I turn my head. A curtain moves.

He answers before I can ask.

"My sister," he says.

"I'm totally naked," I say, like it needs pointing out.

It makes him smile just a little. "That comes with the territory."

I smile back. "I'm not sure your sister will be all that impressed to find a naked stranger in your garden. It's hardly a great first impression."

He tips his head. "You may have a point. I guess we'll have to resume swimming pool nakedness another day."

I nod. "I think a rain check would be sensible, yes."

I smile against his mouth as his lips press to mine.

"Let's get you home," he says.

phoenix

I climb out of the water first. My jacket is waiting for her as she pulls herself out after me.

She picks up her shoes and opts to go barefoot.

I'm drenched right through to the bone, dripping water all the way. I hand her the keys to my truck and tell her I'll be back in a minute.

She nods and smiles.

I'm relieved she still has a smile for me after everything I've said tonight.

I ditch my clothes in the porch. Serena heads into the kitchen even as I'm tugging on a pair of fresh boxers from the laundry.

"Aren't you going to introduce us?" she says.

I smirk. "She doesn't think her nakedness will make the best first impression."

Serena rolls her eyes. "What happened to her clothes?"

"Don't ask."

She knows me well enough by now to take my word for it.

"Cam asked for a story tonight," she tells me.

I smile. "That's great news. He's getting better."

"Three full sentences today."

I nod. "All in good time. The lad's a champ. We won't be able to shut him up in a few months, you wait and see."

277

She gestures to the door. "When are you going to introduce them?"

"Abigail and Cameron?"

"Unless you have any other girlfriends you're not telling me about."

I pull my jeans on. "She doesn't know about Cameron yet."

Her jaw drops. "She doesn't know you've got a son?! That's a pretty major staple of an introduction, don't you think?"

"Our introduction wasn't particularly conventional," I admit. I meet her eyes. "I'll tell her. Soon."

"And then you'll introduce them?"

I tug on a shirt, then pull her close enough to kiss her head. "All in good time."

She slaps my arm. "Take the girl home, finish what you started in the swimming pool. Tell her to bring clothes next time."

She has no idea what we started in the swimming pool, but she's more right than she knows.

There is a lot more to finish.

A lot more to be said.

She's already heading back to bed when I pull the door closed behind me.

Abigail is waiting in the truck. Her hand slips straight into mine as I climb in.

"Thanks for the secrets."

"Thanks for the ear. It's been a while since someone cared enough to listen."

I pull away from the house and make a turn for Hereford. We drive in silence most of the way.

Her hand comes to rest on my thigh, and in spite of every harrowing word I've spoken this evening, I'm still hard for her.

Harder for her than ever, it seems.

I guess the sense of mortality does wonders for the urge to procreate.

There's an easiness between us that wasn't there before. A closeness in pain.

Her sadness holding hands with mine.

Now I've told her my secrets, I'm even more curious about hers.

I wonder if this could really be a thing, her and me. I wonder if her pieces will fit with mine in a way that Mariana's didn't.

I park up in my usual spot when we arrive at hers.

She covers her modesty as best she can as she climbs down from the truck. My jacket swamps her and she moves awkwardly.

"You don't have to come in," she says. "If it's too much, I mean."

"Am I invited?"

She smirks. "That doesn't usually hold you back. I hope you're not losing your bite."

"I was being polite," I tell her with a smile. "You could say no. I'd just climb in through the window and make you regret it."

"I guess I should save us both the trouble," she says, and slips her hand in mine.

She flicks on the lights in her hallway as I close her door behind me.

My jacket is off her shoulders before she's even dropped her handbag.

My mouth is fierce. Desperate.

Her body is needy as I hitch her legs up around my waist and pin her to the wall.

My thumb flicks at her tender nipples. Her skin is still clammy, even after the drive.

I walk her to the bedroom and nudge the door open.

I drop her straight onto the bed and drop down on top of her. I'm grinding hard against her pussy in a heartbeat.

"You summoned a monster from the darkness," I grunt. "Is it everything you were hoping for?"

"More than I was hoping for," she whispers. "But tonight I want to see the monster in the light."

She flicks on the lamp before I can protest. Her fingers are under my shirt before I can stop her.

I flinch as her fingertips graze across gnarled skin.

"Let me see you." Her eyes are open wide. "Please let me see."

"My scars are hideous," I tell her, but she shakes her head.

"You're the most beautiful thing I've ever seen," she whispers. "Even your scars will be beautiful."

Oh fuck, how I feel it in my gut.

This sweet little siren from the deep, opening my sores and kissing them better. Making me feel alive again.

Whole again.

It feels strange to undress for her. Strange to see her wonderment as she trails her fingers down my tattoos.

"So many," she whispers.

"A whole pile more secrets," I say. "Each one tells a story. Some of them happier than others."

"I want to hear them all." She smiles. "I want to know everything."

She wriggles out from under me even as her mouth is on mine. It's tempting to hold her firm and make her appease the throb in my fucking dick, but I don't. I let her up. She kneels before me, eye to eye, before she dips her head.

She's so careful as she kisses my collarbone and sweeps her fingers down my back. My skin itches, but I let it. Today, I don't fight it.

"May I?" she asks.

I love how she asks for permission.

I'm tempted to say no just to hear her beg.

But I don't.

Not tonight.

"You can have everything you want," I tell her. "Just know that I'll take your everything in return."

She smiles against my neck. Her fingers are soft in my hair.

"My everything is already yours," she says. "I just wasn't sure you wanted it."

Oh, how I fucking want it.

I close my eyes as she moves behind me.

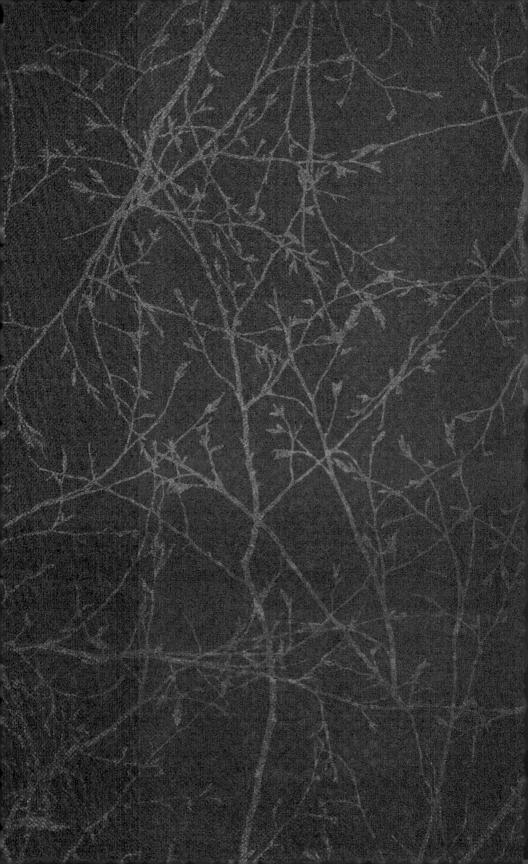

thirtythree

I've cried, and you'd think I'd be better for it,
but the sadness just sleeps, and it stays in my spine the rest of my life.

—CONOR OBERST

abigail

I tell myself I'm prepared for this. But I'm not.

I'm not prepared for the way his scars take my breath, or the way my heart bursts at the reality of his pain. I'm not prepared for the way I want to hold his wounds to my chest and never let go.

"I still feel it burning sometimes," he says. "I guess I always will."

My fingers dance down his spine, and my mouth follows them. He shivers as my lips kiss his ruined flesh.

I want to tell him how I get it. I want to tell him how I wake up some mornings convinced the blood is still running down my thighs faster than I can wipe it away. How I still feel the cramps as I bleed out on that hospital gurney.

How I still remember the moment the baby in my belly slopped out like offal onto the hospital floor as I tried to lift myself onto the commode.

But I don't say a word. Not as my fingers sweep across the taut skin on his shoulder and trail down his arm. Not as I kiss the marks the fire left on him, loving them just as much as the rest of him.

"It is as hideous as you thought?" he asks.

"I never thought it would be. Your scars are as beautiful as the rest of you."

He laughs. "That's quite a statement."

"Didn't really think you'd scare me off that easily, did you?"

He twists back to look at me. "No. I didn't."

I smile. "I'm kinda liking this lights-on thing. Maybe we can keep it running."

"Maybe I should start chasing you in the daylight."

I raise an eyebrow. "Maybe."

"Be careful what you wish for. You might end up naked in front of your friends at your next barbeque."

"You'd have to catch me first." I stick my tongue out.

I squeak as he pounces, flipping to pin me flat before I've moved an inch. "I haven't struggled to catch you so far."

"There's time," I whisper.

"All the time in the world," he says and my belly flutters so hard I could fly.

I squirm to get my hands free, and he gives me enough leeway to slide my fingers down the back of his jeans. "I want you naked," I say.

"I want your pretty mouth around my cock," he says back.

I'm on my knees and waiting even as he gets to his feet. My mouth is open as he drops his pants and presents the beast for my viewing.

His fingers are gripped tight around his shaft, just like on his photograph. The barbells glint in the lamplight as he works his fist up and down.

It's monstrously beautiful. My fingers look tiny as he wraps them around the base of him.

I love the way his piercings feel against my thumb. The bumps of metal under his skin feel alien. They clip my teeth as I suck him into my mouth.

"Good girl," he says and wraps his fingers in my hair.

I'm a slavering wreck in one thrust. My throat heaves at the pressure as he pushes deep.

But I take it.

I'll always take it.

There's a tenderness in the way his thumb brushes my cheek. A warmth in his eyes as he stares down at me, even as I choke and splutter.

He pulls away as I feel him tightening in my throat. The bumps tickle my tongue.

"Now I want to see everything," he says. "On your back, spread that hungry little cunt for me."

How I love his filthy fucking mouth.

I don't hesitate, spreading my legs as far as they'll go and splaying my pussy wide with my fingers. My clit is swollen, it sparks as he stares.

He drops to his knees and edges closer, pulling me forward until my ass hangs over the edge of the bed. Perfect height.

He wraps a hand around the back of my neck and holds me up. "I want you to see this," he says, and I do too.

I cry out at the glorious moment the head of him plunges inside me. It's divine to watch him shunting it in, inch by inch.

I watch every thrust. Grunting like a dirty little slut as he fucks me deep.

I keep my fingers splayed wide, my thumb brushing my clit enough to drive me crazy.

I come way before he does, and again before he's even broken a sweat.

I lose my shit as he circles his hips and his ridges press deep. I'm begging him for more even as it hurts.

His forehead is tight to mine as he curses and comes.

He stays deep as he comes inside me, his eyes right on mine as he catches his breath.

And I wish…

I shouldn't, but I do…

I wish that the baby had been his.

The revelation is enough to take my breath. My belly pains at the memory of losing half of me that night.

"What is it?" he asks, and I shake my head. He's not deterred. "What's wrong?"

I take a breath as he pulls out of me. My lips are on his as he shunts me further up the bed and climbs up to join me.

"It's nothing," I lie as he breaks the kiss and comes to lie by my side.

His hand is on my belly, his chin on my shoulder, and his seed is deep inside me.

But it doesn't matter.

It doesn't matter how many times he comes inside me.

How many times I get a flutter at the memory of having a new life growing inside me. Of talking to a little person who'll never be born. Of promising them we'll be just fine on our own, Stephen be damned.

It'll never happen.

Because my scars are deep.

Raw even though they are unseen.

Leo's heart is so strong against my ribs. His breath is steady.

"Are you thinking about him?" he asks, without even a hint of jealousy.

I shake my head. "Not him, no. He's a stupid prick. I wouldn't care if I never saw him again."

He takes a breath. "Tonight is a night for secrets, Abigail. Yours as well as mine."

I smile, but it's a sad smile. "I lost a baby," I tell him, even though he already knows.

His arms wrap me up and hold me tight. "You were ready to be a mum?"

"No," I say, wishing my laugh would sound more convincing. "I mean, yes, but no. I don't know if it works like that, if one day you wake up and know you're ready. The test was positive and I knew I wanted it. That's as ready as I felt."

"And what about him? Was he a class-A cocksucker from the word go?"

I sigh. "Pretty much."

"He was a fucking idiot," he says, and my heart thumps. "I'd never have left you."

And I know he wouldn't.

Not even if staying burnt him alive.

Stephen wouldn't risk his flat screen TV, let alone his personal safety.

Wouldn't risk a stable pay check to make sure I was still alive.

"Being a father is the greatest gift on earth," he continues. "He'll regret his mistakes every day of his life, even if you never know it. Even if he doesn't know it himself."

But he won't. I know he won't.

He doesn't need to.

Which makes it even more fucking painful.

My own secrets are right there, begging for confession.

Ones I've buried. Ones I've run from.

Ones that won't stay quiet now I've seen the beautiful strength in someone else's scars.

I just hope Leo can love my scars just as much as I love his.

Because he's right – being a father, a *parent*, is the greatest gift on earth.

One I may never know.

And loving me might well take it away from him.

Just as the universe took it away from me.

And handed it back to Stephen on a silver platter.

"Do you mean that?" I ask him, even as my words choke. "That being a father is the greatest gift on earth? You want kids?"

He smiles. Oh, how he smiles. "Yes, Abigail, I want kids."

I feel so exposed as he kisses my forehead.

"The miscarriage was bad. Bad enough that I nearly died," I tell him, then opt to spill the rest before I change my mind. "Stephen told me he didn't want to beg me to get rid of our baby, but he did it anyway. He didn't want the baby and he didn't want me. He told me his wife was estranged, that they were strangers in the same house, that he wasn't in love with her and had no idea how he'd ended up with a mortgage and a whole host of entwined families. He said she'd hurt herself if he left, that she was fragile, depressed, that she wouldn't handle it. He said that's why he stayed."

"Stephen is a fucking asshole," he says.

"I saw him every day for four years before anything happened between us. I knew his thoughts better than I knew my own, just by looking at him." I pause. "Or so I thought."

"Sometimes you can know someone for years and know nothing at all," he says.

He's got that right.

I meet his eyes. "I shouldn't have ever done it, not knowing he was under the same roof as someone else. I should've known better, but I loved him. I thought he loved me, too. I was stupid enough to think we'd end up together, that somehow he'd find a way to leave and make sure she was okay."

"He didn't want to leave her when it came to it?"

I smile a bitter smile. "I don't think he ever really wanted to leave her at all, no matter what he had to say about it. They had a nice little slice of suburbia. A Scandinavian pine kitchen and a big TV. A decent lease car on the driveway. Their own little corner of domestic bliss." I pause. "I didn't think it mattered to him. I didn't think he'd go running for cover as the fireworks started."

He takes my fingers in his. Squeezes tight. "Like I said, the guy's a fucking idiot. When it happens next time it'll be different, I swear."

I can hardly bear to look at him. "You really want kids?"

He smirks. "Right now? I'm sure we'd do just fine if the situation arose, Abigail."

"That's not what I mean," I say, and my voice is barely more than a rasp. "I mean, is that what you want, in your future? You're sure? Definitely sure?"

I know he's misunderstanding me. I know he thinks I'm looking for reassurances.

I know he thinks he's helping me when he rolls me to face him and presses his heart to mine.

"I'm sure," he says.

My cheek is on his shoulder. I'm glad he can't see my tears.

"And what if it never happens?"

He sighs. "These are supposed to be your secrets, Abigail, not mine."

I don't understand. He moves so quickly I have to swat the tears from my cheek.

"A miscarriage is awful," he says. "Believe me, I know. Serena, my sister, she had several when she was younger. They broke her apart." He digs his wallet from his jeans. My heart is in my throat as he opens it up. "But you can try again. We'll try again, if that's what you want. Maybe not now, but soon. We're gonna be good together, you and me. I think our pieces fit pretty well together, all things considered."

I stare dumbfounded as this horror unfolds.

"I'd love to have a baby," he says, and he's smiling. "Mariana didn't want one. I had to beg her to keep Cameron. I think that was what ended us ultimately."

He pulls out a picture. My stomach turns over itself as I see the little boy smiling at the camera.

"This is my boy," he says, "he's a real champ."

My voice is a ghost. "You have a son?"

"He's nearly four," he continues. "He'll love having a little brother or sister someday."

"Stephen is having a baby with his estranged wife," I say on autopilot. I've never spoken it aloud before, never allowed myself to think about it. "That's why I ran. Because I couldn't stand it. Because being around children makes me..." I stop.

Makes me feel empty.

Broken.

Makes me feel like my life is nothing.

That I'm not a woman.

That I'll never know the love of a mother for her child.

That my body killed my baby and nearly killed me too.

Leo's eyes are so kind as mine spill tears. I wipe them away but my lip is trembling. His hand is firm on my knee, his voice so strong.

"Hey," he says. "Abigail, listen to me. It's not over for you. We'll try again. You're gonna love Cam, he's got his issues, I mean, the kid's been through a lot, way more than any kid should ever go through. He was there that night, asleep in the back of my truck. Jake called and told me to get the hell up there and Serena wasn't with us at the time. I put him in his car seat and took him with me." He pauses. "And he saw the flames. He heard the sirens."

"My God," I cry, but he shakes his head.

"Cam's had his issues, but he's okay. Me and Serena, we do everything we can to make sure he's okay. He's elective mute, but he's getting better. Don't let that put you off him. He's a great kid. Really great. He just started speaking again, just a few days ago. It's early days, but he'll get there. He'll be a regular kid by the time he starts school, I just know it."

The picture is still between us. I stare at his son's big brown eyes as my heart breaks.

"He's beautiful," I say.

"He is. And ours will be too."

But it won't be.

"You don't understand," I say, and the desperation in my tone finally cuts through. He stops. Listens.

I guess he finally gets it.

I'm sobbing and I can't stop even as I say it.

"There were complications, at the hospital. The operation that saved my life went wrong. It left scars."

I close my eyes, just to find the strength to say it aloud.

"I can't have children, Leo, and I can't... I can't be around other people's children either."

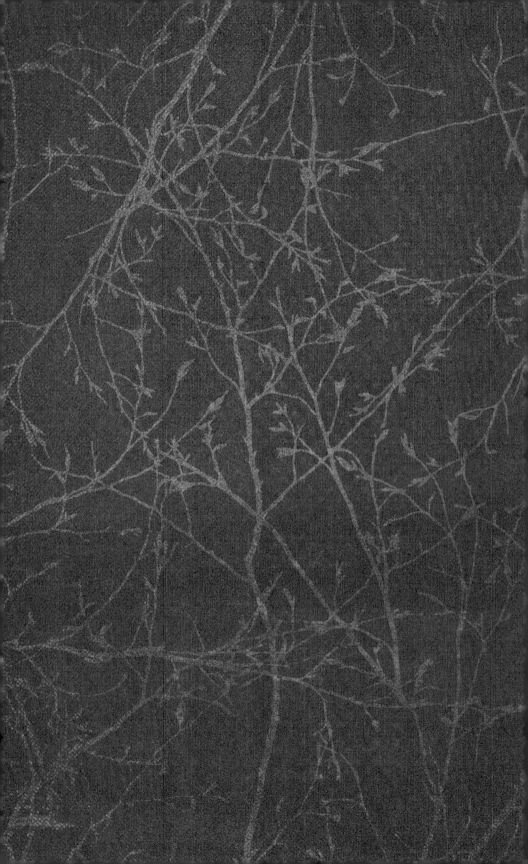

thirtyfour

The world breaks everyone, and afterward, some are strong at the broken places.

—ERNEST HIMINGWAY

phoenix

Oh fuck, how I've said the wrong fucking thing.

I feel like a fucking idiot as my black swan sobs in front of me. She crumples in my arms as I hold her tight.

I tell her it's okay, that she can take her time with Cameron. No pressure. No worries.

I tell her she doesn't need to worry about having kids now, that we'll sort it out, that there are ways. Options. So many things to consider.

I tell her everything I can think of to walk us both back from this shitty abyss, but I don't think I reach her.

"Fuck, Leo," she says. "Look at you, looking after me. Like you haven't been through more than enough of your own shit."

"We get stronger at the broken places," I tell her. "I did and you will too. Everything was in ashes when Mariana died, the business, Jake, Cameron. I knew I had to pick myself back up and keep on moving. We only lost one of the trucks in the fire, the one by the loading bay. The rest were intact. We had no insurance pay-out and our customers lost a fortune in the blaze, but I took those trucks and I set up again. I re-mortgaged the house and worked my ass off, even though it hurt, and slowly. *Slowly.*"

Her fingers are so soft against my cheek. "You're amazing," she says. "Truly. Cameron's lucky to have you."

"You'll be okay," I tell her. "You'll be strong at the broken places, just like I am."

"I hope so," she whispers.

And she will be. I know she will be.

I've seen the sparkle in her eyes, the fire in her belly. I've seen her work a crowd like she owns it. Owns *me*.

I squeeze her fingers tight in mine. "When I met you I was still running. Soulless. Her ghost was everywhere, and now it's not. I didn't even use my own name, couldn't face the man I'd been before."

She stares right at me. "Phoenix," she says.

I smile. "Something like that."

"It was your username online. Phoenix burning."

I nod. "And I was still burning, until I met you."

She takes a breath. "We'll take it slow?"

"As slow as you like, as long as we're moving."

"And what about the kids? What if I can never…"

"We'll worry about that when it comes up."

I hold my breath.

I'm so fucking relieved when she smiles.

Her voice evens out when she speaks again. "I ran here and found nothing. You brought me back to life, and I found everything. I love my life here. I love it all."

And I love you.

I don't say it. Not now.

I'm well aware that dawn is shining through the curtains. Well aware that Cam will be waking up for his breakfast in an hour or so back at home.

"I need to go," I tell her.

She nods. "You have a little boy to get back for."

I kiss her forehead. "I don't want to leave you."

"I can't come with you," she says. "Not yet, anyway. He doesn't even know who I am."

And she's right.

I know she's right.

"I'm not gonna say anything stupid, Abigail. Now isn't the time for grandiose declarations or mushy words, but I will tell you that monsters stay on your tail, always."

She laughs. "Is that a threat?"

I smirk. "It's a promise." I get to my feet and pull her with me. "Maybe I'll knock at the front door next time."

"Maybe you should bring chocolate." She wipes her eyes. "I'm clearly a hormonal wreck who needs it."

"Or a beautiful woman who lost something very dear to her."

Her eyes well up again. "Thanks. I'm grateful you can call me beautiful when I've been a snot monster for the past half hour. It must be the real deal."

She's joking, but I'm not.

I get dressed, even though it pains me. I'd give anything to fall asleep with her in my arms.

Maybe one day soon.

I take a look back up at her window as I leave. I watch the lights go out.

It's dawn as I cross the road to my truck. I barely even think to check my jacket pocket for my phone, but when I do it's there and flashing.

Five missed calls.

Serena.

Shit.

I call her back but there's no answer. I call the landline and she doesn't pick up.

On the third attempt, I leave a message on her mobile and tell her I'm on my way.

My foot is to the floor the entire way.

abigail

He has a son. A beautiful little boy.

My belly flutters at the thought, but there's no pain.

Not anymore.

I guess sometimes it's the confession itself that provides the most solace. It's by letting our demons free that we're able to see that they're not really demons at all, just scared children hoping to be loved.

I know I can love Leo's broken pieces. It's a welcome surprise to find that I believe he can love mine, too.

I roll onto my side to watch the sunrise through the window.

Fuck, this is all moving so fast. Crazy fucking fast.

But it doesn't feel crazy at all.

I wonder if he'll like me, Cameron. I wonder if in time he'll ever come to love me, if we even get that far. I hope so.

For the first time in forever, I wonder if there really is any hope in surgery. If maybe my scars can heal, just like Leo's have. Just enough to function.

For the first time in forever, I think maybe there's a chance.

I log into social media before I attempt sleep. It makes me smile to find the barbeque pictures have been uploaded.

I flick through the photos of my new friends, grinning at their laughter and their stupid drunk expressions once the party got wilder. I'm almost sad I missed it.

Almost.

I hitch my breath as I catch a picture from earlier in the afternoon. There we are, me and Leo, completely unaware of the camera, and smiling regardless. His hand is on my back, my cheek pressed to his collarbone, staring at each other, totally oblivious of the people standing by.

It's perfect.

It's us.

And damn, he looks damn fucking fine in a tux.

Goodbye cathedral backdrop.

A couple of clicks and I'm done. It's official. We're my phone lock screen.

I guess that means I'm going to be meeting Cameron for sure. I'm laughing even at the absurdity of my train of thought.

Too long a night, too many revelations. Too much cock.

No. Never too much cock.

My parents have always been early risers. I guess that's why my messenger pings when Mum shows online.

Are you up??

I type out a simple yes and hit send, and then I wait for it.

Who is the guy in the suit?

I take a breath. Ask myself if I'm really ready for this. Really, really ready.

I'm smiling as I call her number.

And I'm smiling even harder as I tell her about Leo Scott.

phoenix

My heart is thumping wild. My throat dry all the way home.

My tyres screech as I pull into the driveway. I don't even bother locking the truck.

I find Serena on the terrace. It takes me a moment to realise she's smoking a cigarette.

She hasn't smoked since she was a teenager.

"Was it–" I begin, but she doesn't need the question.

"Jake," she says. "I guess I wasn't the only person who caught you skinny dipping with Miss Pretty in the swimming pool."

The panic flares. "Cam, is he–"

"Cam's fine," she says. "Didn't even wake up."

I breathe. Allow my thumping heart to settle. And then I ask her what happened.

She stubs out her cigarette and takes out another. I realise it ended pretty badly if he left without his smokes.

"He was drunk," she says, as though he was likely to be anything other. I tell her as much but she shakes her head. "This was different, Leo. He's been drunk before, this was…"

"Really fucking drunk?"

She shoots me a glare. "*Desperate*. He's really desperate. I've never seen him like this."

"Desperate enough to do what exactly?"

She drops her eyes. "Fuck, I don't know, Leo. He was spouting on, about you, about Mariana, about the goddamn paternity test. He said he'd given you an ultimatum. That your time is up."

I shake my head. "There is no fucking time limit, Serena. I never agreed there would be. He's not getting a paternity test, and he never has been."

"He said you're too busy cavorting with the new girl to take care of your own family mess."

"He's not my fucking family." My voice is harsh. I regret it as soon as I've said it.

"We're *family*, Leo. All of us. Don't forget what he did for us. Don't forget what we did for each other."

"A long time ago," I say, like it needs pointing out. "The guy's off the rails. I'm calling my lawyer back on Monday morning. We'll get the police involved."

She stares into the distance as she takes a drag. "How the fuck did it come to all this?"

"Mariana," I say, because it's the truth.

That makes her smile. "I wonder if she'd be laughing, if she was still here."

"Probably." I lean over the railings with her. "I told Abigail about Cameron."

"And?"

"And I think she'll meet him. Not yet, but soon."

She nods. "That's good news. A step forward for some of us, at least."

She holds out her arm. "He grabbed me. Hard. I had to hit him with the ashtray." She points to the tray at her side. Chipped. I bet that fucking hurt.

"May have knocked some sense into him, you never know."

"We can hope." She sighs. "I think it'll bruise. I'll give a statement to the police if it'll help keep him away from Cam."

I raise an eyebrow. "You've changed your tune. What really went down here?"

"Nothing you need to worry about, trust me."

I do trust her, but not about this. Not about Jake.

She stares at me. "I mean it, Leo. Nothing. He barged in, spouted a load of shit, said he was going upstairs to see Cam and I told him I'd call the police if he did. I went for the phone, he grabbed me, I hit him with an ashtray."

"And then he left?"

"And then I called you and he went really ballistic. Charged upstairs before I could stop him." She's aged so much this past year, my sister. I notice fine lines around her eyes as she looks away. "I thought he was heading for Cam's room, but it was shut when I followed him. I stood outside to guard his door and I called you three or four times straight." She quirks her brow. "Guess you were busy, hey?"

"Talking," I say. "We were talking."

"Yeah, and the rest."

I change the subject. "If you were outside Cameron's door and Jake was upstairs, what the hell was he doing?"

She shrugs. "Your guess is as good as mine. You probably want to check your stuff, make sure nothing is missing."

"He was in my room?"

"You know how fucked up he is. *Mariana's* room."

I could strangle the sonofabitch quite happily. Choke his drunken throat for all his bleating on.

"You're sure he's definitely gone now?"

Serena nods. "Drove back toward Malvern. I'd hear his truck a mile off."

I kiss her cheek. "I'm sorry I wasn't here. It won't happen again."

She laughs. "What? You planning never to see her again? I don't think so, Leo."

"No. I'm planning never to leave my phone in another room again."

And planning to make sure that sack of shit doesn't come within a fifty mile radius again, but I don't point that out.

I head upstairs to check my boy. He's sleeping soundly with his mouth wide open, catching flies. His spaceman PJs are getting too small. He's turning into a proper grown up kid in front of my eyes.

I only have the chance to venture into my bedroom for a few minutes before Cam wakes up for the day. I check my things but nothing looks amiss, until I see it. The missing picture of Mariana from my dresser. *Piece of shit.* I take a deep breath and count to ten, assuring myself that things could be a lot worse.

I only notice my laptop is on when the screen switches to sleep mode in front of me. I lift it from the bed and log back in, wondering what the holy fuck he was looking for.

It's easy enough to figure it out. The browser screen is still on our banking homepage. I log in to find the sonofabitch has withdrawn five grand into his bank account.

I need that money to pay wages next week. I curse him under my fucking breath.

I'm still seething as Serena appears in the doorway, she shakes her head in horror when I show her the withdrawal listed.

"What the fuck does he want with five grand? You're still paying him?"

"Same as always," I tell her. "Plus his dividend payments."

"You think he's running away?"

No, I don't. It doesn't stop me hoping all the same.

"I don't like this," Serena whispers. "It doesn't feel right. It doesn't feel right at all."

But nothing about Jake ever does. Hasn't done since the fire. Maybe even before that.

"I'll sort it," I tell her. "I'll get right onto the lawyer and the police on Monday morning. We'll fix this. Try to get him the help he'll need, if he'll take it."

She looks so sad it breaks my heart. "You'll get him help?"

"I said I'd try."

She nods. "Thanks, Leo."

"Don't thank me yet," I say, but it makes no difference.

She's still hugging me tight as our little champ wakes up. It makes my heart smile when he joins in too.

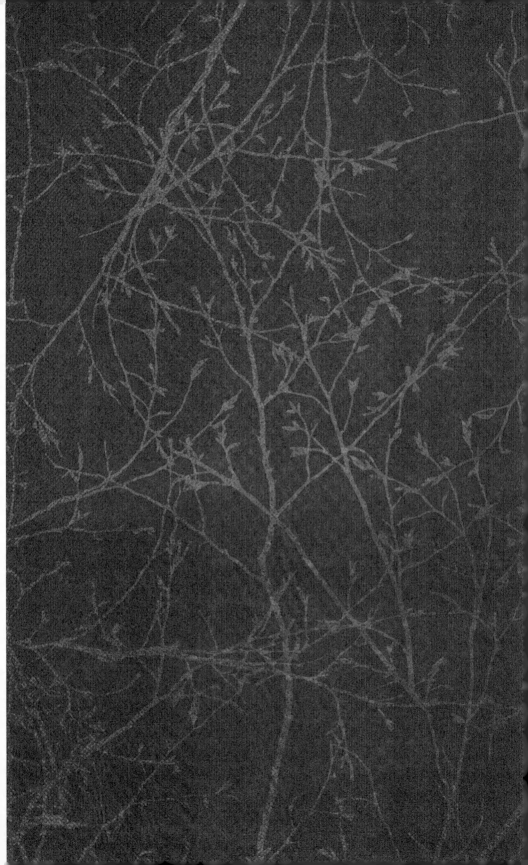

thirtyfive

Unforgiveness is like drinking poison yourself and waiting for the other person to die.
—MARIANNE WILLIAMSON

abigail

I sleep into the afternoon. There's a message waiting on my phone when I wake up.

Late dinner? I'll knock this time. Court a little traditionalism.

It's the best way to wake up.

Scrap that. Waking up next to him will be the best way to wake up. This is just a good runner up.

It feels weird to text back.

I'd like that. Bring chocolate. I'll cook.

I've already sent it by the time I realise I have no idea what he likes to eat. Crap.

Luckily, I have some resources close by these days to help me. Sarah is watching TV with her hand in a big bag of Doritos when I call round there. I fill her in on my crisis and she springs into action.

"Italian," she says. "Everyone likes Italian."

I hope she's right.

I'm pleased to have a companion as I venture out to the local shop. We pick the best ingredients we can muster and she talks me through the best way to prepare them.

"My grandma was married to an Italian," she says.

"You're part Italian?"

She shakes her head. "No, that was her first marriage. She had four."

I laugh. "Go Sarah's grandma."

"Sour old bitch." She giggles. "But she could cook."

I only hope Grandma's special recipe works a treat for me this evening.

I'm choosing what to wear when a familiar but unfamiliar ping sounds on my mobile. My fingers are shaking when I call it up.

Fuck.

My heart pounds even at the sight of his name. It's in email form, but it's there.

Phoenix Burning sent you a personal message. Reactivate your account?

How could I not?

A couple of clicks and I'm back in.

I'm grinning as I fire a message back to him.

So much for deleting my account. I played fair.

He replies in a beat.

Still want to meet the monster?

It makes me laugh out loud.

Always, I type back. *I hope he bites.*

I wait for another ping. It doesn't take long.

You will be ready for me later. You will make sure the bottom door is unlocked.

I reply in a flash.

Is this before or after dinner? I've got to time the vegetables.

I hope he knows I'm joking.

Eight. Be ready.

So much for humour, but that doesn't matter.

I'll be ready, I say.

And I will be.

p h o e n i x

I almost forget about the shit with Jake as I enjoy the afternoon. It's another glorious day with Cam in the pool, and even Serena joins us for a swim.

It would be perfect, if only Abigail was with us.

All in good time, so they say.

I'm strangely excited to see what she cooks. Thrilled at the prospect of a regular date like regular people.

Even if I do deviate from the chivalry to pound her dirty little asshole later.

I wear a black shirt over tight jeans. Make sure my hair is as just so as it ever gets. I'm no pink-shirted Jack, but I'll do.

I'm ready to go just as soon as Cam settles off to sleep, but this evening, typically, he wants every story in the book.

He's even willing to ask for it.

There's no way I'd ever be able to say no to that.

"You look great," Serena says as I finally get back downstairs. "Go get your girl."

"You'll like her," I tell her. "I can't wait to introduce you."

"Just as long as she makes you happy."

I love my little sister today as much as I've ever loved her in my life. She's a solid rock in our river. An anchor through whatever shitty storms life throws our way.

I'll never be able to thank her enough for what she's done for Cam and me. I just hope she knows it.

I feel a pang of regret for Jake as I step out to my truck.

It's so easy to forget these days that once upon a time it was the three of us against the world. It's easy to forget how he was the one who set us up in business in the first place and took care of me as well as Serena just as soon as he was old enough.

Easy to forget all the shit he shouldered when we were too young to deal with any of it.

I send him a text message before I pull away. One final olive branch before I get my ass down to the lawyer in the morning.

Sort your life out, Jake. We're still your fucking family. Put the money back, stop drinking and we'll talk properly when you're sober.

He can keep the picture of Mariana.

It's the least I can do, and deep down I know it.

Serena's question is a valid one.

How the fuck did it come to all this?

The answer is the same as it's always been. Just as I said it last night.

Mariana.

That's how the fuck it came to all this.

Serena could never see it, the appeal that one crazy woman held for two brothers. She didn't understand the magic in the madness, the way that woman's soul could shred you to pieces and keep you coming back for more.

I push all that aside for now.

I stop at the petrol station for a big bar of chocolate and grab some flowers while I'm at it.

And then I text my girlfriend, since that's really what she is now.

Soon.

abigail

Soon

That's what the message says.

I can't keep up with him. Pinging me here there and everywhere.

I laugh out loud when the knock comes at the door. His *soon* was quite a lot sooner than I expected.

More like *now*, in fact.

I'm grinning as I swing that door open, presenting my best chef smile in the heart-patterned apron I borrowed from Sarah.

But it's not him.

My grin fades.

I recognise the man in front of me, and yet I don't.

He's tall. Dark eyes. Gaunt and wiry.

Strong.

My eyes widen.

They widen a whole lot more when he shunts me inside and closes the door behind him.

I'm backing away on instinct, the lasagne still cooking in the oven as the panic takes my breath.

There's nowhere to run and I know it.

I try anyway.

I only make it as far as the kitchen doorway before he grabs me from behind. His bulk is familiar, but he stinks of whisky and something else. Diesel.

He reminds me of the seedy denim guy from the pub all those weeks ago.

And just like denim guy, his hand is straight between my legs, pressing his fingers so fucking hard against my clit that it aches.

I squeal when he clasps his hand over my mouth, but just like his brother, he's pretty damn good at muffling it.

I know this is Jake.

I know it with every single part of me.

"Good girl for leaving the door open. Are you always so fucking willing to do what he says? I guess it's him you're wet for, but don't worry. If you're a good girl I'll let you enjoy it."

I'm rigid in his grip, heart thumping in my ears.

"I don't know why you all go so fucking mad for my brother," he says. "He's a self-important, sour-faced fucking prick. The way he treated my Mariana…"

His voice trails off.

My chest is so tight it hurts to breathe.

His fingers keep rubbing me, but for the first time in memory, the monster at my back doesn't make my clit throb.

It makes me feel sick.

"I know how he likes to talk to you," he says. "I read it all online, the whole sorry fucking lot of it. You're a dirty little bitch, aren't you? Just like my Mariana was."

How I fucking cringe inside. The intrusion hurts far worse than his fingers on my body. It feels like he's been inside the darkest parts of my soul.

And he doesn't belong there.

That part's all for Leo.

"Let me talk in a language you'll understand," he grunts. "You will come with me to my fucking truck. You will do what I fucking say. If you don't, I'll hurt you. If you still don't, I'll hurt that sonofabitch boyfriend of yours. Understand?"

I manage a nod.

"I've got a whole fucking truck full of kerosene. I'll burn the fucker alive, and this time there won't be any fucking fire department to drag him out of there."

My breath is so shallow, so fast.

"Understand?"

I nod again.

He takes his hand away and I grab a breath.

"You don't have to do this," I say. "This is crazy."

"We're all a little fucking crazy, sweetheart. I think you're the craziest bitch of us all. Running straight into the path of some fucking stranger. Begging him to make it fucking hurt. You need help, girl."

I'm relieved when he drops me. My body feels filthy where he touched me.

Used.

Violated.

"Now get your fucking shoes on," he grunts. "Or I'll make you run fucking barefoot like he did."

I do as he says, stalling as much as I dare.

He doesn't let me get away with much.

I know Leo is heading here. I know he can't be that far out.

But he's far enough out that he misses us.

I'm petrified as I step out onto the landing and close the door behind me. I know Jake's batshit crazy and wired enough to follow through with whatever insane ideas are fizzing through that addled head of his, so when Sarah sticks her head out of her front door, all smiles as she expects to find Leo ready for Grandma's special recipe lasagne, I act like everything is totally normal.

"This is Jake," I tell her. "Leo's brother."

I pray she'll use her intuition, but if it's there she doesn't notice.

309

bait

"Oh, that's nice," she says. "I can see the resemblance. Really are meeting the family now, then?"

I nod.

She keeps on smiling.

Jake nudges me along the landing. I move as slowly as I can.

"Hope you enjoy the food!" she calls after us, and she's gone. Just like that.

My heart sinks, but I keep on walking, praying that my monster in the darkness will catch up with me as easily this time as he has every other time before.

thirtysix

A friend loveth at all times, and a brother is born for adversity.

—KING SOLOMON

phoenix

It's dusk when I arrive at Abigail's door.

It feels strange to be here while there's still enough light to see by, and stranger still to ring her buzzer like any regular visitor.

I wait for the click as she answers but it doesn't come. I look up at the window and the living room light is on. No sign of her.

I buzz again. Clear my throat as I wait for her voice.

Still nothing.

I call her number. It rings out.

I smile to myself, wondering if the cheeky little bitch is goading me to break in after all.

I'm tempted.

But no. I opt to press her neighbour's buzzer instead.

She answers in a beat.

"It's Leo," I tell her. "Abigail's boyfriend. She's not answering."

"Oh, sure," she says and buzzes me in.

She's waiting for me on the landing with a smile on her face.

"You can wait in here until they get back," she tells me. "If you're at a loose end, I mean."

I stare blankly.

"They?"

"Your brother and Abigail. I guess they were heading out for more supplies." She pauses. "Is he single?"

How my blood runs fucking cold.

"My brother?"

"Jake, right? He was right here."

Abigail's door key is in my fingers in a flash. I'm inside her place in a heartbeat.

It's boiling hot in the kitchen. I open the oven to find a burning lasagne. I turn off the oven and head through to the bedroom.

They can't have been gone long. The smoke alarm isn't even sounding.

I call her name as Sarah joins me in her hallway.

"They went about half hour ago," she says.

I spot her phone on the sofa. Her lock screen is us at the barbecue. I'd smile if I wasn't so terrified.

I call up her messages. Check her calls. Check everything.

And then I see it.

Her online fucking hook-up login. I call up the logs with shaky fingers.

My heart is in my throat as I realise how fucking stupid I've been.

My laptop. The sonofabitch was on my fucking laptop.

And he took more than five fucking grand from my bank account.

He took my black swan, too.

I call up his tracker on my phone but the sonofabitch has disabled it. They could be fucking anywhere.

I pace up and down as the fear seems to register for Sarah.

"Your brother… he's not gonna hurt her, is he? Come to think of it, she seemed pretty wired."

"She didn't say where they were going?"

She shakes her head. "I didn't ask. Didn't think."

I call Serena. I'm hissing fury as she picks up.

"It's Jake," I tell her. "The cunt's got Abigail."

She tells me she hasn't seen him, hasn't heard anything since last night.

Fuck.

My hands are in my hair. My scars itch worse than they've ever fucking itched since I've had them.

"Check my laptop," I tell Serena. "Look for anything. Any clue. Check the history."

I don't even want to think what he's using that five grand for. I don't want to think about how fucking crazy he must be.

"The bank," Serena tells me. "Some dating website…" She pauses. "Wellington's local depot." She clocks it as soon as I do. "Oh no, Leo. Oh my God, no."

And I don't need a tracker to tell me where the sonofabitch is heading. He knew I'd find him all along.

"Lock the doors," I tell my sister. "Lock the doors and stay inside."

"Don't go there!" she hisses. "Please, Leo! Don't fucking go there! Call the police!"

But I can't.

He's too fucking crazy for the police to turn up.

No.

There's only one person he wants, and that's me.

bait

Bait.

Of course.

How fucking ironic.

Tonight her username's more apt than it's ever fucking been.

"Don't call the police," I tell her. "I'll handle it."

"NO, LEO, DON'T!" she screams, but I'm already hanging up.

Wellington's will never mean anything but tragedy to me. They always told us their products were flammable, but they didn't tell us quite how much so.

Didn't tell us how they'd turn our warehouse into an inferno if one of their drums caught light.

Five grand.

I wonder how much fuel he can have bought for five fucking grand.

Enough.

"Is she gonna be okay?" Sarah asks as I leave.

"She'll be fine," I say, and I mean it. I'll make sure of it.

I call Jake's number knowing full well I won't get an answer.

It doesn't matter. He'll get my message and I know it.

"I'm coming," I tell his voicemail. "But you knew that, didn't you? You can let her go already, Jake, I'll be there regardless. Don't do anything fucking stupid until I get there. You don't need to hurt her. She's done fucking nothing to you. It's me you want." I pause. "And I'm on my fucking way."

For the second time today my foot is to the fucking floor as I pull away.

abigail

I thought I was scared in the back of Leo's truck, trussed up in the footwell in the middle of the night. But it's got nothing on how sick I feel in the back of Jake's.

I can smell the diesel from here. I can hear the liquid in the big vats behind the seats swishing around every time he takes a corner.

I don't need a memo to tell me that this stuff going up is what killed Mariana.

And I don't need a memo to tell me that Jake is planning on doing it all again.

Maybe he did it in the first place.

"Bait," Jake calls from the front.

I hate the way it sounds from his mouth.

"That's a fucked up username, you know? *Bait.*" He laughs. "But then again, if the cap fits."

I know I should do everything I can to avoid antagonising the drunken psychopath at the wheel, but I can't stop my mouth as it blurts out the obvious.

"You started that fire."

He laughs. "You think I fucking killed Mariana? LEO killed Mariana. She wouldn't have been there in the fucking first place if he wasn't such a cunt."

"You were in there when it started, not Leo."

"Yeah, trying to stop her losing her fucking mind!" he snaps, and I decide to keep my mouth shut from here on in.

I hope Leo's discovered my absence already. I hope he's called a thousand cops and they'll be descending on this truck any second in a helicopter. But no. The truck rumbles on.

I know we're climbing. I feel it.

"We were a good team once," Jack tells me. "Me, Leo, and Mariana. We ran the business together."

I don't say a word.

"I saw her first, you know? No matter what he fucking tells you, I saw her first." He pauses. I'm sure I hear him sniffle. "I fucking loved her. I loved her more than he ever did. He'd have kicked her to the fucking kerb long ago if she hadn't had Cam."

I wish he'd stop talking. I wish he'd shut the fuck up.

"Leo loved her," I argue. "She loved him, I'm sure."

"Like you know fuck all about it," he snarls. "She wanted to run from him."

"Good for her. Maybe she should have done it without taking a midnight detour to a warehouse packed to the rafters with highly-flammable chemicals."

I'm being a horrible bitch and I know it, but I can't stop. It's get angry or get scared, and I'm not ready to give up and go down without a fight. Not for this douche.

"She called me, you know," he says, but I sigh.

"I don't really care."

"You will."

Those two simple words make me shiver.

I close my eyes and pray for a miracle. Pray for a nightmare. Pray for a monster. Pray for anything.

For him.

I pray for another shot at having a baby. I pray for the chance to meet Cameron and see if we could grow to like each other. I pray for a chance to eat Sarah's grandma's special recipe lasagne with the man I love.

I pray to kiss his scars one more time.

I pray to see him in the moonlight and water one more time.

To hold him one more time.

To feel his ridges inside me one more time.

To tell him I love him.

To tell everyone back home I'm sorry for running and I love them, too.

The backseat is a lonely world. Tears stream easily as the sky turns dark through the back window. I try to hold them back, because these silent tears are the worst.

These silent tears mean defeat.

My heart drops into my stomach as the truck comes to a stop. I flinch as he opens up the back and tugs me out by my feet.

His breath is in my face as he wraps thick twine around my wrists. Fighting is no good as he crouches down and fastens it to my ankles.

I can hobble at best. I struggle to keep my balance, even against the truck.

His eyes are dark glass. Vile and angry.

And sad.

He's so sad.

It's that part of him I speak to.

"You don't have to do this," I say. "Not any of it."

"Run," he says, just like that. My eyes widen in realisation. "That's what you like, isn't it?"

I have no words as he takes my elbow and throws me into the darkness.

I stare around me at the high surround fencing. The spikes on top.

I stare into the darkness and see the toothy grimace of a burnt-out tower. And I know.

She died here.

"Run!" Jake shouts, and it's enough to bring me to my senses.

I hobble as fast as I can into the darkness with my heartbeat in my ears.

I trip and stumble but keep my footing.

Because I have to.

bait

I really have to.

Tonight, it's the monster's brother who's hunting me.

And if he catches me…

If he catches me, it may well be the end of all of us.

thirtyseven

From the deepest desires often come the deadliest hate.

—SOCRATES

abigail

There's nowhere to run in this place. It's completely enclosed. The only way out is back the way I came. Past Jake.

He knew it.

Of course he fucking knew it.

He's playing with me.

I drop to my knees and tear my fingernails loosening the twine from my ankles.

I can't get it from my wrists, but it's better than nothing.

At least it means I can move without hobbling.

There's barely any light to see by. I wonder if that will make it easier to hide instead of run, but I suspect Jake knows this place too well for that.

I can still hear him back there, lumping drums from his truck. The grind of wheels on tarmac.

I don't even want to imagine what he's doing. The guy's fucking insane.

It's so easy for my mind to play tricks on me out here. I'm prickled by nothing but the air, jumping as though Mariana's ghost is out here with me, as though she's calling me to join her.

I don't want to join her.

It's when the noises stop that I know I'm in trouble.

My breath quickens. The silence loud as I strain to hear him.

This game should be familiar but it's not.

It's anything but.

I back into the high fencing and stare at the warehouse. It's big. Much bigger than I pictured.

I can only imagine the pyre it made when it was burning.

When Jake's voice comes it chills me to the bone.

"Oh, Abigail... where are you, Abigail? You love this game, right? Give me a clue so this can get exciting."

I'd love to set fire to him my fucking self.

"I'll make it feel good if you let it happen..."

I'll never let it happen. He'd have to kill me first.

The most terrifying thing about that thought is that he might.

Leo, please. Where are you?

I scrap that train of thought as soon as it arises, and I guess it must be those silent tears getting the better of me.

I don't want him to come here.

I don't want him to walk into the path of this psychopath and his truck full of flammables.

The police is what I need.

A team of those elite snipers they use for overseas assassinations.

They could take Jake out from the fence before he even knew they were there.

I know I'm going insane when I laugh to myself.

I take a breath and force myself to get with the plot. I stare ahead at the warehouse and figure my best shot is the least expected one.

Straight through the building and out the other side.

I could be at his truck before he knows it. Maybe I'd head off Leo on the main road and send the fleet of police cars on up for Jake.

My plan is ridiculous and I know it, but it really is my best shot.

I don't know if I'll ever be ready for this. I summon my breath as I prepare.

And then I see him. Oh fuck, I see him.

He looks fucking petrifying in the darkness.

My heart is pounding so loud I swear he'll hear it if he comes any closer.

Which makes my decision for me.

Three, two, one and I run. Fast. Straight for the burnt-out building and whatever fucked up shit I find inside.

I have barely a headstart before he sees me, but I manage to make it inside before he slams into the back of me.

I'm screaming as he hoists me, lashing out with everything I've got as he holds me tight.

"Did you fight him like this?" he snarls. "I bet you fucking didn't. This is what you wanted, remember? This is the shit that gets you off."

My eyes are like saucers as he walks me on through an arch to a room beyond. The drums are stacked up everywhere. Liquid all over the floor.

Diesel.

No.

I realise how wet he is against my back. How much he stinks. Even worse than before.

bait

"Neither one of us should've made it out of this fucking place," Jake snarls. "If I'm gonna go and fucking join her, I'm taking him with me."

"You're insane!" I hiss and he laughs.

"And you're the fucking bait, sweetheart. You know what my last request is?"

I don't answer.

"Call it a last meal."

But I don't want to.

I don't want any of it as he slams me down over one of the barrels.

I'm crying as he hitches up my skirt. Sobbing with the bitter fucking irony as he tears my knickers off me.

"This is gonna fucking hurt," he says.

phoenix

I hope Serena hasn't called the police.

The signs are good as I speed up the lane with my headlights off, both for there being no sirens and no flames either.

Last time this place caught alight it lit up the whole sky.

It means I've still got time.

My tyres screech against broken tarmac as I brake hard next to Jake's truck.

I can smell the kerosene as soon as I step out.

Crazy sonofabitch.

I keep quiet as I take the same fateful fucking steps I took that night. My heart thumping just as it was back then.

The loading bay is empty, just as I expected. I step over the wreckage carefully. Quietly.

But he already knows I'm coming.

"So nice of you to fucking join us," he shouts, and it's game over.

"Let Abigail go now," I bark. "I'm here, aren't I?"

Oh how I fucking hate him as I approach the storeroom doorway.

My black swan is bound and trussed over a fucking barrel, her bare ass up in the air as my insane fucking cunt of a brother looks on.

"Don't worry," he laughs. "I didn't fucking touch her. Just let her think I fucking would." He waggles a finger in her face and she winces. "This will teach you to play with fucking monsters, won't it? I hope you've learned your fucking lesson."

"Let her go," I say, and he smiles, points to a container at my side. It's smaller than the others, already half empty.

"Show me you're serious," he says.

I can smell it everywhere already. The stench is already pooling under my feet.

"And you'll let her go?"

"Yeah, I'll let her go."

In for a fucking penny. Abigail screams as I tip that chemical shit all over myself. It stinks so bad it catches in my throat.

"Wow. You really love her, don't you?" Jake says, but I don't grace him with an answer.

I breathe in relief as he yanks her to her feet and sets her off in my direction. She runs at me with too much force to hold her off, even as I'm soaking through.

"No," I say. "Abigail, you've got to get out of here, don't get this shit on you. Get into the truck and drive away."

I tug the twine from her wrists as she shakes her head. Her eyes are streaming but open wide. "No."

"Yes. Right fucking now."

She's trying to tell me something, but we don't have time. She shrieks as I hoist her and dump her on the other side of the racking. She's climbing back over even as I curse.

And Jake laughs.

He fucking laughs.

"Why do they love you so much?" he asks. "They're all fucking crazy for you."

"Maybe because I'm not a total fucking head case," I tell him. "I don't know what the fuck's happened to you, Jake. What do you even fucking want from me?" I shrug. "Mariana's fucking gone. Dead. It's over."

"Not for me, it's not," he hisses. "*Phoenix.* Fucking *phoenix.* There's no fucking salvation for me, Leo, I'm still in the fucking ashes."

"So you keep telling me, Jake. Christ. Set us on fire or stop fucking wallowing already, will you?"

"NO!" Abigail screams. "DON'T!"

But it's alright.

Whatever happens, it's gonna be alright.

I'm tired of dreaming of flames. Tired of hating myself at the thought that Jake's right and I could've really saved her.

"Please go outside," I tell her. "I need to talk to my brother."

"I can't leave you," she sobs. "Please don't make me leave."

I sigh at the beautiful realisation that she'd burn for me, just as I'd burn for her.

If I ever get out of this fucking place, I'm gonna marry that girl tomorrow.

I tell her so and she smiles.

"Is that a threat?" she asks through the tears.

"It's a fucking promise."

And Jake slow claps. He slow claps and ruins the moment, just as he ruins fucking everything.

"This is how it should have been with Mariana and me," he snarls. "I was gonna fucking marry her. Not as if you ever fucking did. Never came close to putting a ring on her finger."

"She didn't want one," I tell him, and I'm not lying. "Said a ring was nothing more than an expensive shackle for the soul."

He smiles. "Sounds like her."

I lean in close to Abigail. My mouth is as close to her ear as I dare. "Did he hurt you?"

She shakes her head. "No. Kept threatening, but nothing."

I kiss her forehead. "Wait for me, just outside that door."

She looks back at it, at the warped metal all twisted and bitter. "That's the one, isn't it? The one you couldn't get through?"

I nod. "That's the one, but today it's wide open. I just want to keep you out of the flames."

My eyes are dark on hers, I hope she sees me inside. I hope she sees that I'm sure.

"Just there," she says and points. "I'll be just there."

"Good girl," I say, and she is. She's the very fucking best. Everything I ever wanted.

Oh, how fate is fucking laughing.

I breathe easy when she's a little way away from all this shit. And then I step up to my brother.

"Good use of five grand, Jake. A lot of guys will go without their wages next week so you can burn us alive. I hope that makes you proud."

He smiles. "You always were a funny fucker, Leo."

"And you were always my fucking brother," I tell him, and then I sigh. "If we're both gonna burn in here tonight then I guess we should at least clear the air before we do."

He stares at me with eyes like mine. So much like mine.

"You start," he says.

I start with a truth I should have told him a long time ago. It feels surprisingly good to get it off my chest.

"She should've been yours. You were right. It was on the cards, you and her – right from the moment she saw you. I remember how loved up you were when you found the girl outside and dragged her into our office for that poxy interview."

He smirks. "Had to drag her in, yeah. Claimed indoor work made her soul shrivel."

"I know you loved her," I tell him. "I know she loved you, too. What you had was more than I ever had with her. We were teeth and nails and crazy nights on the hills. You were steady. Kind. Exactly what she needed."

He grunts. "You're just fucking saying that to make me feel better."

But I'm not. I shake my head. "Think what you want, Jake. It's the truth."

"Why did you take her from me, then?" he asks. "Why you and not me?"

"Because she had a darkness behind her eyes," I admit. "She needed the chase. The hunt. The thrill. She needed it to feel alive, that's what she told me."

"*I'd* have given her a fucking thrill, Leo. *Me.*"

"Well, I guess I didn't give you the chance. I regret that, but she was right there, too. She made that call along with me. Probably earlier than I did. That girl didn't get swayed by anything other than the things she wanted, and you know it as well as I do." I sigh. "I regret ever ending up with Mariana. I regret being the one who took a wild young girl and turned her into a bitter crazy woman. I regret being the one who pushed her far enough to lose her mind." I pause. "But I don't regret Cameron, and I don't even care anymore whether he's yours or mine. It wouldn't make any difference. I'd love him all the same."

His eyes flash with pain. "I love that fucking boy, too. You took him from me!"

I shake my head. "You think this is really anything to do with a fucking paternity test, Jake? You think I don't know you were fucking her that whole fucking summer before she fell pregnant? I always knew there was a chance he might not be mine. I didn't care, I loved him anyway."

"Then why?!" he snarls. "Why fucking take him from me?!"

I gesture around me. "Because you're sick, Jake. You're a fucking drunk with a death wish. Cameron doesn't need your kind of fucking crazy in his life. His mother's dead and he wets the bed at night. He's barely spoken since she passed, and you know it. Why spring a load more shit on him? He's taken enough already."

I sigh again. "Seriously, Jake, if you want to burn this place, you'd better get on with it. Serena knows we're here, she'll call the police if she doesn't hear from me soon. She won't be able to stop herself."

"Shut up," he snarls.

"I'm ready," I say. "I said my piece. I swear to God I did everything I could to pull Mariana out of here. There's not a day that goes by where I don't curse myself for letting her go that night. There's not a single day I don't think about her and blame myself for what went wrong." I take a breath. "You want to kill us both for that, then go ahead. I'm done."

His voice is so low I barely hear him.

Just a grunt in the darkness as he drops himself to the floor.

"Go."

I step closer. "Sorry?"

"Go," he says again. "Go back to Cam. Tell Serena I love her."

My heart fucking pounds. "What?"

"You heard me," he says. "Get the fuck outta here."

I know I'm as crazy as he is when I don't move a muscle. "Wait," I say, and I'm sneering. "You just made me follow you up here and dowse myself in fucking kerosene, just to tell me to leave?" I gawp at him. "You said this was my fault, Jake. That I'm the one who's to blame."

"Leo, please!" Abigail calls. "Please, let's go!"

But I can't.

Call me fucking insane but I fucking can't.

Because my brother isn't out to fucking kill me, and I know it. It's not hate for me that's in his eyes as he stares up at me, but hate for himself.

"Something happened, didn't it? What happened, Jake? What triggered all this crazy? It wasn't just not being able to see Cam, was it? There's something else."

He shrugs. "Just go, Leo."

"Yes, Leo, please!" Abigail cries.

Jake smirks and gestures in her direction. "She's a lively one. I wasn't gonna fucking hurt her, Leo. You know that, right? Just wanted to shake her up. Wanted her to hate both of us."

"Why?" The question is so obvious. "Why did you want her to hate me?"

"Because I wanted you to know what it feels like to love someone with all your fucking soul and not have them love you back!"

I smile. "Wow, Jake. That's such bullshit. This thing with Mariana, it was you she wanted at the end, not me. She was seeing you the whole fucking time she was with me, you admitted it yourself! You think that's what happens when someone loves you?! Mariana never loved me. If I'm honest I don't think she ever really loved Cameron, either." I can't stop. Can't hold back. I'm stinking with kerosene and still I'm fucking talking. "Mariana loved *herself*," I say. "Herself more than anything else in the whole fucking world. Herself, and *you*."

When my brother laughs it's a terrible sound. It cuts right through my fucking soul.

"She never loved me," he says. "I lied."

My stomach falls through the floor.

It takes me a long fucking moment to fathom it.

"You what?"

"I lied," he admits. "I lied about fucking everything. I never fucked her, not even once. The boy is yours, undisputable."

I'm reeling. Floundering as he stares up at me. "But why?"

"Because I wanted it to be true. I wanted you to think she loved me better. I wanted to believe it myself, so I wouldn't have to face the fucking rest of it."

I've not seen my brother cry since her funeral. I've never seen his eyes crumple into redness as he tries to find his words.

I ask him again, because I have to. I have to understand this fucking insanity.

"What changed?" I ask. "Something fucking changed, Jake. This isn't right."

And then the tears fall. Oh how they fall for him. Big sniffling sobs that choke his breath.

I give him a moment, cursing myself for my idiocy. I'm still cursing myself as he speaks.

"You really wanna know what changed, Leo? Really?"

"Really," I say. "I have to fucking know what changed, Jake, or it'll be just another fucking mystery on top of all the others. I'm done with unanswered questions. I'm done with guessing."

He stares right at me, and the look in his eyes makes me question my decision. It's fucking horrible.

"I got my fucking memory back," he says.

My mouth drops open.

No. No fucking way.

I'm shaking my head even as he carries on, and in some deep part of me I already know what's coming.

"It was me," he says. "I'm to blame for that night. I started the fire."

I can't stop shaking my head. "No."

He nods. "It's true."

And it is. I see it in his eyes.

"I'm the one who killed Mariana, Leo. It was me."

thirtyeight

Truth is like the sun. You can shut it out for a time, but it ain't goin' away.

—ELVIS PRESLEY

abigail

I can't believe he's still in there.

I can't believe he won't run, fast, while he has the chance.

But then again I can.

I can't imagine Leo running from anything.

I'm close enough to hear their conversation. Close enough to get caught in the flames if this shit really does turn bad.

But I'm not running either.

"What are you talking about?" Leo asks. "You started the fire? Why?"

Jake shakes his head. He looks more broken than terrifying right now, but illusions like that can be deadly. "I got a call from her. Same old shit. Called you a cunt, said she was leaving. Said she needed my help, like always. I came running, like always." He slams his head back into a container behind him. I flinch at the clang. "She was already in here when I arrived, bringing up those containers on a trolley. You know what she was like. Her fury could move fucking mountains."

"She shifted the whole lot?" Leo asks.

Jake nods. "Most of it. I took one trolley load off her because she was straining. That's all. The rest was already done."

Leo sighs. "She wanted to burn the place down. I always thought she'd eventually lose control of the circus in her head."

Jake doesn't look at him. "I said she should just leave, stop the crazy shit and take off. I said I had money, that we could start over. I said we could leave you with the business and move somewhere new."

"And what about Cameron?" Leo asks.

Jake shrugs. "You know what she was like about Cameron. Hell, I don't know, Leo. She wasn't making all that much fucking sense. She said if she burnt the place you'd have nothing to stay for, that you'd go with her and explore the whole fucking world."

The woman sounds as crazy as sin, but I try my best not to judge her. I just take a deep breath of my own and keep my senses on high alert.

"Were you gonna help her?" Leo asks, and Jake shakes his head.

"Like I said, I suggested we leave together, me and her. I thought it was our chance. I was desperate for that chance."

He looks desperate too, sitting there. I try to put myself in his place, even though I think he's a psychopath. How I'd feel if Leo burned. How broken he must be after all those years loving her from afar.

My stomach churns as I imagine that terrible scenario playing out back then. Right here.

It all happened right here. It makes me feel queasy.

Jack carries on speaking. "She said no, of course. All those years of playing with me. Hinting there was something more. Giving me the *oh, Jake* and calling me up whenever there was any trouble. I thought she loved me. I thought we were victims of someone else's greedy emotions. Someone who didn't give a shit, but wouldn't move on and let other people have a shot."

"Me, you mean?" Leo says.

Jake nods. "I hated you for what you had. I hated you because you wouldn't let it go, even though you didn't want it. I thought you were the only thing standing in our way."

Leo shakes his head. Looks at the sky through the jagged roof. "She really was a special kind of crazy," he says.

"I was so fucking mad when I found out. So fucking mad that I was just a stupid part of her stupid fucking game. She had no fucking intention of burning this place down, not really. She just wanted to stack it all up for effect and make sure you'd be along to discover her at the last minute." He stops speaking to collect his voice. "You always ran after her."

"Not that day," Leo says.

"Not that day," Jake agrees. "So, that's the first fucking thing that killed her. You didn't come running."

"I'll take that," Leo says. "I should've stopped her. She was crying out for attention and I let her starve."

I love the way he can take responsibility for this shit so calmly, soaked to the skin in diesel in a room full of the stuff, with some crazy psychopath holding the reins.

He's got a shit-ton more composure than I'd have in his position.

"She was a fucking idiot," Jake says. "Playing with fucking fire so literally. She knew the stuff was unsteady. She knew there was too much of it up here."

"I guess the need for drama outweighed the risks," Leo says. "In her head."

"I dunno what the fuck was going on in her head, Leo, but as soon as she told me she didn't want me with her and never really had done, I lost my shit."

My breath catches. *What the fuck did he do?*

"It was a stupid fucking place to light up a cigarette, but you know me. I've smoked around a shit ton of explosive vats before when I'm out on the job. I shouldn't, but I do. *Did.*"

And I know the rest. Leo does too.

Jake doesn't need to say it, but he does.

"She must have disturbed some of the safety clamps in the trolley. That shit must've been leaking the whole time we were talking."

Leo nods. "You threw the butt."

Jake closes his eyes. "One split second of madness, because I was fucking angry. She was still in here, dicking about with shit she shouldn't be. I was already storming away, heading out toward the loading bay. It was quick. The explosion sent me fucking flying. I thought I was gonna fucking die myself when I hit the ground."

I know the rest and so does Leo. I've heard the rest.

I feel privy to secrets that don't belong to me. I shouldn't be listening but can't look away.

Can't leave him.

Jake's face crumples. "It was *me*. I'm the one who killed her." He blows this horrendous bubble of snot and pain from his nose, a wreck of misery as Leo looks down. "And now I have to go with her."

"Or you fucking don't," Leo says. "You threw a fucking cigarette like a dumb fucking asshole. She piled a whole fucking arsenal of flammables in this space to cause a scene." He pauses. "And me? I was a shit partner to Mariana. We didn't match. Didn't even come close. She was always pulling away as I was trying to rein her in. We were doomed from the minute Cam was born. I'm the one who didn't run after her. She was crying her fucking eyes out that night, hissing her usual stream of shit and accusations. I didn't care. I hoped she'd fucking go."

Oh what a sorry fucking mess this is.

A whole circle of hurt.

I dare to hope Leo's done now. That Jake will still let him leave.

"Go," Jake says and answers my question. "Take the girl and go."

But he doesn't.

Leo doesn't move an inch.

I cry out as he drops himself to the floor. Scream his name as he tips his head back and looks at the sky.

He's sitting in a cocktail of disaster while his brother pulls a cigarette lighter from his pocket.

"Go," Jake says again. "This ends here, Leo. I can't stand the pain anymore."

"I'm not going anywhere," Leo says and I could kill him myself.

"You gotta fuck off outta here!" Jake shouts, but Leo's still shaking his head.

I'd go in and drag him out myself if I'd be able to move him. My hands are in my hair as I curse this whole sorry situation.

Leo speaks again. "Remember when we were little kids, and Serena got picked on by those guys down on Harrow Road? Remember that?"

Jake's smile lights up. "I remember, yeah. We kicked the living shit outta them, you and me."

"You and me," Leo repeats. "Because we're brothers. That's what you said. *We're fucking brothers, Leo. We take care of our own, no matter what. No matter how fucking hard it gets.*"

"I said that, yeah," he agrees. "It was true, back then."

"Still is," Leo says. "You've just got to want to work at it."

"It's too fucking late for that," Jake cries. "I fucked up. I fucked up real fucking bad."

"And so did Mariana and so did I. We all fucked up, Jake. But we're still fucking brothers." He sighs. "If I was here again, with this place up in flames, I'd pull you out just like I did then."

"You should've saved her first," Jake blubs.

"I couldn't fucking save her *at all*, no matter how much I wanted to."

"Gotta set this place on fire," Jake threatens. My heart pounds. "Get out now, or you'll be coming with me."

"Well, I guess I'll be coming with you then," he says.

p h o e n i x

I'm deadly serious.

My ass is in kerosene. My clothes stink of it. My hair stinks of it.

It's all I can fucking taste, too.

My fucked up brother's got a lighter in his hand and he's on the verge of setting fire to us all.

But I can't leave him.

"*You've* got stuff to live for," Jake protests. "I fucking haven't."

"So *make* something to live for. Get sober. Help me build the business back up. Take up poker, or bowling and embroidery or any old fucking shit," I hiss. "Just to get you on your feet again." I chance brutal honesty. "And Jesus, Jake, stop fucking pitying yourself. You loved and lost, we all did. It's shit but it's life. Death is a part of life. No amount of guilt or hate is gonna change what fucking happened. Serena needs you. Hell, I fucking need you, when you're not a barrel of walking suck."

"I can't, Leo. I can't go on," he says and I'm at the end of my tether, make or fucking break.

I shoot Abigail a look as she stares on in horror. I can just make her out in the shadows. Waiting for me.

I mouth 'I love you' in case it's the only time I ever get to tell her, and then I bring this thing to an end.

He's not expecting it as I spring like a fucking snake and tear that lighter from his fingers. He's not expecting me to throw it as hard as I fucking can through the open roof and pray it lands innocuously on some piece of fucking dirt outside.

"You're fucking crazy!" Jake grunts. He's still on his knees, pained to all fuck with his insane red eyes streaming tears as mine threaten to fall too. "I want to fucking die!" he screams, but I don't care.

Not on my watch.

Never on my fucking watch.

It's then that I hear the sirens in the distance. I thank my fucking stars I moved in time, before the idiot sonofabitch flipped his lid in panic and set the lot on fire.

I kneel down at his side as they get nearer, loving and hating him and pitying and despising him all at fucking once.

"You can slit your fucking throat in bed at night, Jake, or take a fucking overdose, or drink yourself to death. Whatever. But it won't be now, and it won't be on my fucking watch."

He carries on wailing as my hand grips his shoulder.

I hear Abigail screaming at the oncoming vehicles. I'm still gripping Jake's shoulder as the torches shine in my eyes.

"We're alright," I say. "Be careful, it's flammable."

They're careful.

Careful as they pull us out of there and help us out of our clothes.

Careful as they scrub us of everything that could set us on fire and wrap us in fucking blankets.

They take Jake away in a cop car. I watch him all the way with the sirens blaring. It hits me in the gut, despite everything.

And then I feel Abigail's arms snake around my waist and hold me tight. "He'll be alright," she says, even though I know she's as unsure as I am.

"I didn't realise he was so fucked up," I admit. "I should've realised a long time ago."

I lift my arm and pull her under, hold her tight to my skin under the blanket. She snuggles in tight.

"That was crazy," she says. "The scariest thing in the world."

"At least we have all the pieces now. You can only start making sense of the picture if you have all the pieces."

She nods. "So, what do we do now?"

I shrug. "Answer some questions for the authorities. Put this fucking place on the market, finally." I smile. "Eat burnt lasagne in your kitchen."

"It was burnt?" she asks, and her eyes are twinkling.

Relief, it'll do that to you. I'm feeling it too.

"I'd say an eight out of ten on the burn factor, but that's still edible, right?"

She shrugs. "Worth finding out, no?"

I fill in the paperwork for the people who are asking, and I answer all the questions in the air.

She waits for me in the truck, her eyes on me all the time.

She never looks away, not once.

I sigh when I finally slip into the driver's seat. The dawn is breaking over the hills as we're finally ready to roll.

I've spoken to Serena on the phone, and she's already got Jake's whereabouts.

They'll keep us updated and all that jazz.

Which means it's time for Sarah's grandma's special recipe, as Abigail keeps telling me.

She takes my hand as I start up the ignition. I feel thoroughly ridiculous in a blanket with my clothes in a disposable bag on the backseat, but I don't give a fuck.

"You said we would get married tomorrow." She laughs. "I think it's technically tomorrow now."

I smile back at her in the shadows. "You really wanna get married today?"

She shakes her head, but her smile is bright. "Maybe six months? Give me time to get to know Cameron. See if he's okay with it."

"Six months sounds fair," I agree. "And you'll be okay?" I dare to ask. "With Cam, I mean..."

Her smile sets my world on fire. "I know I'm going to love him," she tells me. "Because he's a part of you. I can't think of anything better."

I pull her close and breathe in her hair, and despite everything she still smells like coconut, and fear on the wind, and the woman I'm going to marry.

"I'm fucking starving," I tell her, and she laughs.

"Me, too. Not gonna lie, I'm not feeling overly optimistic about that lasagne right now."

But I am.

I just know it's gonna be the best fucking meal in the world.

And if not, she'll just have to eat the chocolate I bought her, maybe the flowers, too.

And me?

Well...

I'm just happy to eat her.

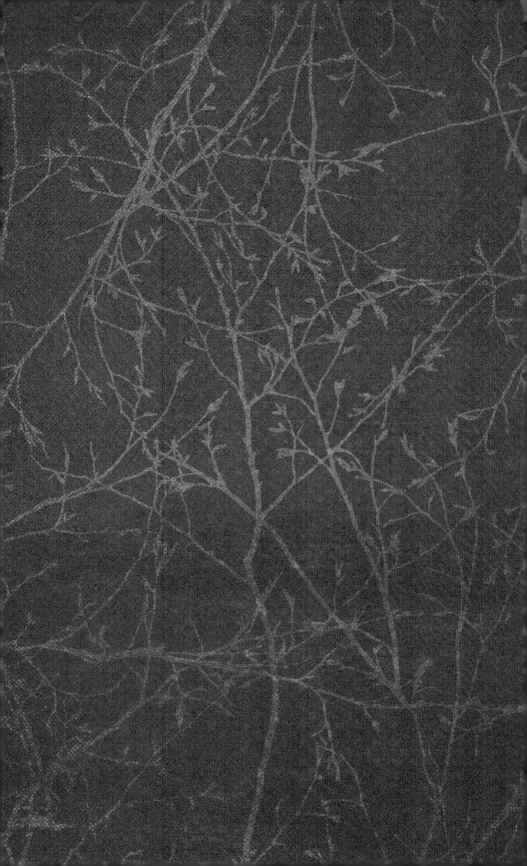

epilogue

Black as the devil, hot as hell, pure as an angel, sweet as love.

—CHARLES MAURICE DE TALLEYRAND

abigail

It takes three months for me to meet Cameron.

Three months of Leo dropping my name into conversations. Three months until *Abigail* becomes a normal word around the house.

I watch Cam often, snippets of videos here and there on Leo's phone. Getting to know him slowly, even though we've never been in the same room.

I almost feel like I know him already. *Almost.*

But my belly is still thick with nerves as I pull my coat a little bit tighter against the chill and walk up to the duck pond.

I see them in the distance. Leo crouching up ahead as Cameron points at something on the water.

Our eyes meet over the boy's head and Leo nods. So far so good. Everything going to plan.

Leo's smile makes my soul sing, more now than ever. More and more each day.

I just pray his son likes me half as much as he does.

"Hey, champ," he says as I get a little closer. "Look who it is, bud. This is Abigail."

I hope my smile is bright enough as I look down at the little guy with the biggest brown eyes in the universe. I hope he likes my silly wave as I say hello.

Oh God, I hope he fucking likes me.

Please, please fucking like me.

My prayer is a grimace inside, but outside I think I manage to keep on rocking it.

I've been planning this. Hoping for this. Dreading this at the same time.

But as Cameron waves up at me with his sweet little fingers, I know it'll all be worth it. Whatever the cost.

The kid is totally adorable, just like his daddy.

"Abigail," he says, and grins.

Leo smiles at him. "That's right, Cam. You've heard all about Abigail, right?" Cam nods. Looks so proud of himself. "We've seen her pictures too, haven't we?" Another nod.

I keep on smiling as Leo keeps on talking.

"And what did we bring for Abigail, just in case we got to see her today? Can you remember?"

Cam's eyes light up so bright. He's digging in his dad's pocket with glee as Daddy gives me a wink.

"That's it, you got it, champ!"

It takes my breath to see the folded piece of coloured card in Cameron's hand.

There's a stick picture of me. It's definitely me. I'd recognise myself even in wax crayon. Also, I recognise the colour of my dress from the summer barbecue. Plus, the stick figure at my side on the drawing is a real giveaway.

Leo even looks hot as a stick man. I flash him the eye as I point to the drawing.

He raises an eyebrow, and I know he's digging it, too.

"Did you do this?" I ask, and Cameron nods.

"Daddy," he says and points to the tall brooding stick man. "Abigail," he says after and points at the one of me.

My heart soars. Bursts.

My heart belongs to that little boy just as soon as he's uttered those words.

"Told you he was cute, didn't I?" Leo breathes, and I nod. Oh hell, he's cuter than cute.

I thank Cameron for my picture, and I guess I'm really doing okay at this introduction crap, because no sooner have I thanked him than he's holding his little hand up for mine and pulling me along to feed the ducks with him.

"He likes you," Leo whispers as Cameron tosses bird seed onto the grass. "I think he might even be as big a fan of you as his old man is, given a bit of time."

My smile is bright. "You think?"

"I know."

I clap as Cam tosses a handful of seed particularly high. I'm not sure what the etiquette on encouraging small kids with an air-punch really is, but I'm going for it.

"I'm pretty sure I'm going to be a big fan of his, too," I tell Leo.

He takes my hands in his. They're warm against the chill. "Yeah?"

I nod. "Yeah."

And it's just as well really, seeing as we're technically only three months away from our six-month wedding date.

We haven't booked it yet, it's all in theory.

But soon.

As soon as we can.

Serena is moving out at the end of the year, down into Jake's place to get it in order before his psychiatric hearing in the spring. I'm supposed to be moving in in her stead.

And it's stressful, and complicated, and intense, and wonderful, and fast, and scary and…

Everything.

It's everything.

"Breathe," Leo says on instinct. "It's going well."

And it *is* going well. Cameron waves again before he tosses another handful to the birds.

Leo moves in close, his lips a ghost on my ear. "Have you given it any thought yet?"

I play dumb. "Given what any thought?"

But he sees right through me. His fingers slip through mine and squeeze.

"Don't be a tease. You know you'll have it coming to you later if you don't watch it."

I'm counting on it.

"I need someone," he continues. "You know it's a good move, for both of us."

And I do know it's a good move. Even though it's a big one.

The guys at work have been so good to me for months. I'm going to miss the holy shit out of them when I leave.

Still, at least now Sarah's finally managed to sink her sexy minx claws into pink-shirted Jack, there should be some double dates on the cards.

And Diva's. We can still do Diva's.

"I mean it," Leo whispers. "We need someone. I'll have to recruit if you don't want it."

But I do.

I really do.

"I want thirty days holiday, minimum," I say and he rolls his eyes.

"You do, do you?"

I nod. "And lunch at my desk, courtesy of my hot new boss every lunchtime."

He smirks. "I'll see what he can rustle up."

"And I want him to wear a tux, every day. Every. Day. Except maybe Christmas Eve where he can dress up as Santa." I laugh to myself. "You'll have to get some of that silly white spray for your beard."

He tips his head. His eyes glint at me. "You wanna watch it with these requests, Abigail. If you're not careful, you'll end up naked in the middle of the office when you least expect it. Regularly."

I raise my eyebrows. "Is that a threat?"

"It's a promise."

I laugh as I hold out my hand. "Then you have yourself a deal, partner."

He grabs it in his, and as always the rose on his hand takes my breath. Just like it did that day in the petrol station. "Welcome to your new job, Miss Summers."

His breath is warm on my mouth, his forehead on mine as Cam waves to the ducks on the pond.

"Tonight," he says, and my skin prickles.

"The hills?"

He nods.

My cheeks burn.

And then Cam comes running back over to us. I'm grinning as Leo scoops him up high.

"Say, champ," he says, and his eyes are twinkling. "How about we invite Abigail along with us for dinner? You can show her your turtle, right? She likes turtles."

Please say yes. Please, please say yes.

I feel like I'm a gladiator in front of a tiny emperor, my fate balanced in his hand as he decides if he wants to see me fight again.

Cameron nods.

bait

I grin like a lunatic.

And as he tells me about his turtle, in the sweetest little voice I've ever heard, I know I'm going to love him forever.

Just like his dad.

Tonight's the first night I don't have to drive over from Hereford when Cam's long in bed.

The promise of the chase thrums in my belly right through dinner.

I see it reflected right back at me in Leo's eyes.

He's waiting outside once I've changed my shoes into more sensible heels. He takes my hand as he leads me through the darkness and all the way up to the top of the ridge.

I'm smiling into the darkness even as the wind whips my face.

I feel him at my back. Feel the swell of him against my ass.

This shit never gets old.

My monster is magnificent, hot as hell and as vicious as he's ever been.

His voice is liquid satin, dripping with nightmares and virgin tears.

My heart is thumping like crazy.

I *feel* crazy.

And I love him for it.

He presses his mouth to my ear.

I hold my breath.

Wait.

Every muscle holding tight for the moment.

Until it comes.

And in that moment I'm alive.

"Run," the monster says.

And, fuck, how I do.

the end

acknowledgements

Wow. This book was really something for me. One of those soul books that reached in deep and death-gripped my insides until I was done.

As always, there were so many people who helped me along the way.

Clears throat

John Hudspith, my amazing editor. I love you and you are awesome. I couldn't do this without you. This is all.

Letitia Hasser from RBA Designs, just WHAT THE HELL with this cover? How gorgeous can you possibly make something?! You have magic powers, and I LOVE them.

Wander Aguiar for the gorgeous photo, and Andrey for being so helpful in helping me acquire it so smoothly.

Jonny James for being the absolute hunk of pure gorgeousness that's actually *on* the cover. Thank you for the way you look so awesome half-submerged in a swimming pool in a tux. That rocks. It helped me write. For sure.

Also for being so polite and sweet and humble – these are a set of traits that are possibly even more gorgeous than the tux. It is close, though, not gonna lie. ☺

To Jon at Read Owl Book Trailer (who also happens to be my other half) – I'm very proud and super impressed by the Bait trailer. It is magnificent, and I apologise for being an epic pain in the ass during its creation.

Nadège, for the beautiful interior formatting. I love your work!

My PA Tracy, for always having my back when I'm in the middle of the craziness. I count on you and you always come through for me. Thank you.

Gel, for the amazing teasers – thank you so much for all your hard work.

My author buddies, who have been super amazing on this project – Isabella Starling, Leigh Shen, Willow Winters and Jo Raven. I love you all.

Isabella, yes, I'm mentioning you again. Having you in my life has made it a better place. You inspire me, you amaze me, and I'm so proud of you. I'm honoured to call you a friend. And you are ALWAYS welcome in my house. *Please come again soon… please…*

To all my other author buddies, who make me smile every day. You know who you are by now.

To my beta readers – your enthusiasm means everything. Of course, of note – as always – is the incredible Louise Ramsay, who I always count on so much for early feedback.

To my friends, who barely saw me throughout the creation of Bait, and who put up with my incessant book talk so patiently. Maria, Dom and Lisa, particularly – I love you all.

To the bloggers, reviewers, my book group members and all of you amazing people who support my work. I couldn't do this without any of you. I am, and will forever be grateful to all that you do for me.

And to my family – Mum, Dad, Brad and Nan – who it pains me so much to be away from when I'm buried deep in a project, your support always means the world. I count my blessings every day for the fact that I have you on my side.

about jade west

Jade has increasingly little to say about herself as time goes on, other than that she is an author, but she's plenty happy with that fact. Living in imaginary realities and having a legitimate excuse is really all she's ever wanted. Jade is as dirty as you'd expect from her novels, and talking smut makes her smile. She lives in the Welsh countryside with a couple of hounds and a guy who's able to cope with her inherent weirdness.

FIND JADE (OR STALK HER - SHE LOVES IT) AT:

Facebook: www.facebook.com/jadewestauthor

Twitter: www.twitter.com/jadewestauthor

Website: www.jadewestauthor.com

Sign up to her newsletter here, she won't spam you and you may win some goodies. :) http://forms.mpmailserv.co.uk/?fid=53281-73417-10227

Printed in Great Britain
by Amazon